Miss Frost Chills the Cheater

A Nocturne Falls Mystery
Jayne Frost, book six

KRISTEN PAINTER

MISS FROST CHILLS THE CHEATER
A Nocturne Falls Mystery
Jayne Frost, Book Six

Copyright © 2018 Kristen Painter

ISBN: 978-1-941695-41-8

Published in the United States of America.

Welcome to Nocturne Falls – the town that celebrates Halloween 365 days a year.

Jayne Frost is a lot of things. Winter elf, Jack Frost's daughter, Santa Claus's niece, heir to the Winter Throne and now…private investigator. Sort of.

Jayne takes Sinclair on a much needed visit to her winter wonderland home, the North Pole. She wants him to see what her royal life is truly like. She knows the protocol and regulations that define her existence as heir to the Winter Throne aren't for everyone and worries that it will be more than he wants to handle.

All seems well until a weird coincidence in a toy contest has some of the citizens of the North Pole giving Sinclair the side-eye. He's a necromancer, and not everyone is okay with that.

Jayne vows to prove his presence and the apparent cheating are unrelated, but digging deeper uncovers all kinds of strange occurrences that only complicate things and make another perfectly clear. Someone doesn't want Sinclair around.

When that someone cracks and takes action, Sinclair is in danger of losing more than his good name. Can Jayne chill the rumors that threaten the royal family *and* keep Sinclair from being permanently iced?

I had to be honest. A *lot* had happened since I've lived in Nocturne Falls. Some good, some great, some not so great, but most of it stuff I'd never expected in a million years.

For example, I'd never thought that, due to some magical circumstances, I'd have a talking cat for a pet. I'd never thought I'd end up solving a whole bunch of mysteries that I also, somehow, ended up getting right in the middle of. I'd never thought I'd be friends with vampires and werewolves and witches and all kinds of non-elf supernaturals.

And don't get me wrong—I loved all the friends I'd made and all the crazy things that had occurred in my life since I came to Nocturne Falls. I had just never imagined they'd happen to me, Princess Jayne Frost, heir to the Winter Throne.

I had always figured my life was going to be in

the North Pole with my family, prepping for the day I'd become queen.

Then my dad sent me to Nocturne Falls to figure out why employees were going missing at Santa's Workshop, the store where my uncle, Santa himself, tested out what worked and what didn't when it came to entertaining kids.

What wasn't a mystery was how I'd fallen in love with Nocturne Falls, the town that celebrated Halloween every day of the year. I mean, come on. Halloween? Yes, please.

And the way that celebration both attracted tourists and allowed the supernaturals to live undercover? Brilliant. No one here looked twice at my pointed ears or blue hair. Well, not twice in a bad way.

But more than any of those crazy-fun things that have happened to me since moving here, I really, really, really never thought Sinclair Crowe, necromancer, owner of Zombie Donuts and all-around amazing guy, would propose. To me.

That was sort of a heart-stopping moment. In a good way. But...it was also a little bittersweet.

Why?

Because no matter how much I wanted to, I knew I couldn't immediately say yes. Not until he'd been to the North Pole with me and experienced my life—my royal life—in a very real way. He had to know what he was getting into by marrying me and marrying into the whole chaotic royal scene.

And even though it would break my heart if he took me up on it, I had to give him the chance to bow out gracefully.

I loved him too much not to.

And that, dear reader, was why he and I were standing on the roof of the building that housed my apartment, the apartments of my employees, and Santa's Workshop, the store I now managed for my dad (Jack Frost) and my uncle (Santa Claus, as I mentioned).

Well, we were up there because the roof was one of the few places where my uncle's magical sleigh could land.

Granted, the roof wasn't all that inconspicuous a spot, but it was four in the morning, still dark, and most of the people who were up at this hour were vampires. Maybe a few shifters out for a run. Anyway, those awake right now were mostly all supernaturals who wouldn't freak out about seeing the sleigh the way humans would.

I was hoping that any humans who did see it would just think we were setting up for some kind of early Christmas promotion. Hey, the store was called Santa's Workshop. With a name like that, a giant red sleigh on the building's roof in October shouldn't be that odd.

Spider meowed at me from his carrier. Just a

meow, not actual words, which he was capable of, but then, he wasn't much on conversation in front of anyone besides me. He'd spoken a little in front of Birdie, but so far that was it.

I'd explained to Sin that Spider could talk, told him how an escaped imp had granted me a wish I didn't know I was making and all that, but Spider being Spider had decided he wasn't going to talk in front of Sin, even though I told him it was okay.

Stubborn cat. Sin probably thought I was a little bananapants for thinking Spider could talk.

Except, he could. When he wanted to.

I glanced down at the carrier, tipping it a little so I could peek through the metal gate. "It's okay, baby. I know you don't like being in there, but it's not a long trip, I promise. That's why we're taking the sleigh. To make it quick."

Spider sighed and sat down. I'd have to give him some extra Chicken Party to make up for this.

Sinclair lifted his carrier to check on Sugar, his pretty white cat. She had basically become Spider's girlfriend about two seconds after they'd met. "Sugar looks a little anxious too. She's usually a good traveler, but then, most of the trips I take her on end at your apartment for a play date."

We'd decided to bring our cats because we were going to be gone for a whole week, and my parents didn't mind. Had we been flying on a standard human airline, the cats would have stayed home.

But the trip by sleigh would be relatively short and sweet, so why not bring the fur babies?

This way they could hang out with each other and not be bored silly at home alone with the occasional visit from the pet sitter (aka Birdie Caruthers) to amuse them.

I wiggled my fingers at Sugar. "She'll be okay, won't you, girl?" I looked at him again. "I don't think most cats are good travelers."

He tipped his head, aiming an ear skyward. "Do you hear...bells?"

I smiled at the familiar sound. "Santa's coming to town."

He laughed. "You're pretty much the only one I know who can say that and really mean it."

The sleigh and the eight reindeer pulling it flew into sight. The bells on the reindeer's tack chimed with the light, crisp tinkling that was their signature sound. As the sleigh descended toward the roof, Sinclair and I backed up toward our luggage, cat carriers in hand.

My uncle was driving, which was standard operating procedure. He wasn't keen on anyone taking the sleigh out besides him, except occasionally for my father. Which I could understand. The sleigh was a pretty pivotal part of his job as Father Christmas.

Seated next to him was Archie Tingle, elf baker extraordinaire. He was here to help Sinclair by filling in at Zombie Donuts. Archie had helped out once before not long after Sin and I had first met and Sin had injured himself saving my life. That injury had resulted in Sin's arm being in a sling, which made doughnut production trickier than usual.

My dad had sent Archie then as a thank-you. Archie was coming now as a show of my parents' affection for the man who'd become such an important part of my life. They wanted Sin's visit to the North Pole to be as stress-free as possible. Knowing his shop was in good hands and not short-staffed would help a lot.

I think Archie really liked being at the shop too. He was a hard worker. He'd been one of the head bakers in my uncle's toy factory cafeteria for over thirty years. But of course, Archie wouldn't be here if my father hadn't asked him to come and given him the time off with pay.

My father's willingness to accommodate Sin and me on this trip home wasn't lost on me. I had a strong gut feeling that both of my parents were very much hoping I said yes to Sin's question.

He'd asked me to marry him, after all. With a stunner of a diamond and sapphire ring. But as much as I wanted to, I knew saying yes would be unfair to Sin until he got a chance to see what my life was really like.

My royal life. The life that would be the reason I someday left Nocturne Falls and returned permanently to the North Pole. As my husband, and the Queen's Consort, Sin would have to accompany me.

Being the Winter Princess wasn't all snowball fights and peppermint hot chocolate. There were meetings and appearances, balls and dinners, all kinds of things that required my attendance. Things I only got a pass on now because I was running the shop in Nocturne Falls. And when the day came that I took the throne, my responsibilities would increase tenfold. I would be in charge of the entire kingdom.

And, just like my father, I would have the power over winter.

Both important, but the North Pole took a special kind of guidance. As the headquarters for my uncle's work, Christmas essentially depended on things at the NP running smoothly.

Can you imagine if the tinkers decided they were no longer going to make toys? If the stable hands who took care of the flying reindeer went on strike? If the gift wrappers and the ribbon curlers got jealous of each other's jobs? If the candy makers went sugar free?

Chaos. Especially that last one. Riots, even.

Worse, no Christmas. And everyone would end up on the naughty list.

But besides my father's job of keeping things running smoothly, there were constant meetings for the various committees and organizations that my father was a member of or on the board of, charity functions, local business openings to attend, diplomatic trips, hosting other dignitaries, presenting awards, all kinds of official royal business engagements and events, weather patterns to schedule, etc., etc., etc.

So yeah, there was a lot of weight on my dad's shoulders. Weight I would have to bear someday.

I was mostly prepared for it. Some of the preparedness would develop on the job, I supposed. As for the rest, well, I'd grown up a princess, so I understood what was required of me, and what my life would be like the day I took over for my father. I'd had years of training, all focused on my future obligations.

But Sin hadn't had the benefit of growing up royal. I mean, who did, really? He was a necromancer and a doughnut shop owner. He was also the love of my life and one of the best men I knew. I thought he would adapt very well to life as the Queen's Consort, when that very-far-away day came, but it was his decision to make.

Once he did that, I could give him my answer.

Which I very much wanted to be yes. And let me just apologize for rambling and repeating myself. In case you haven't noticed, this whole thing has me a little shook.

But enough about that. The sleigh had landed. I

set Spider's carrier down and spread my arms wide, mostly ready for the adventure to begin. "Uncle Kris!"

My uncle climbed out of the sleigh and came toward me, gathering me in a hug that was warm and loving and perfect. Seriously, if you haven't been hugged by Santa, take my word that it's pretty awesome. He kissed my cheek, his beard tickling me. "How are you, my darling Jayne?"

"Really good. Glad to see you. You look well." He was in his green suit. He'd change to red on December first.

"I am very well. Too well, maybe. Your aunt Martha just made a new batch of eggnog fudge to have on hand for your arrival." He put his hands on his belly and laughed. "She might have had to make a second batch."

"Totally get it." I laughed. Aunt Martha's eggnog fudge was hard to resist.

Uncle Kris stuck his hand out to Sinclair. "Young man. Nice to see you again."

Sinclair shook his hand. "You too, Mr. Kringle. Thank you for coming to get us."

"No problem. It was a good chance to test the sled's new tachometer on a long-distance run." Uncle Kris glanced back at the sleigh. Archie was getting his things out of the back. "And the easiest way to get Head Baker Tingle here."

Sinclair greeted the baker as he came over.

"Really appreciate you giving me your time again, Archie."

"Happy to help, Sinclair." Archie slung his bag over his shoulder. "Truth be told, working at your shop is a vacation. And it's a real treat being able to make doughnuts. Pun intended, I guess." He chuckled. "Say, mind if I introduce something new while you're away?"

Sinclair squinted a little. "What did you have in mind?"

"I was thinking a limited-edition autumn flavor. A filled doughnut with pumpkin mousse and a spiced butterscotch glaze. Also, do you do an apple cider cake doughnut? Maybe with a little cream cheese frosting and a crumb topping? Just a thought."

Sinclair's brows shot up. "Sounds awesome. Both of them. Go for it. If they take off like I think they will, we can put them into the regular fall lineup." He dug into his pocket and pulled out the store key on a Nocturne Falls keychain. "This is for you too."

Archie grinned. "Thank you. I'll let you know how those new combinations are received."

Uncle Kris rubbed his hands together. "We should get going if we're going to minimize visibility."

"True," I said. I picked up Spider's carrier, then grabbed the handle of my rolling bag and headed for the sleigh, letting the handle go briefly to give Donner's nose a little scratch as I went by him. He nickered at me, snorting a little air in a happy way.

Uncle Kris helped me load my stuff while Sinclair put his bag in next to mine.

We kept the cats with us as we settled onto the front bench, tucking the carriers into the space in front of our feet where they'd be warm and secure. I sat in the middle between my uncle and Sinclair. It would give Sinclair a better view.

Uncle Kris climbed in and took up the reins. "Ready?"

"Yep."

Sinclair put his hands on the sleigh's front edge. "You bet I am."

Uncle Kris laughed and winked. "Here we go!"

The sleigh ride took a little longer than I'd expected it to, but I realized Uncle Kris had slowed down a bit for Sinclair's sake. Which I was totally okay with. Magical sleigh travel could be a little nausea-inducing for the inexperienced. Sleigh sickness was real.

And even though I wasn't experiencing it, I was still happy to be making our approach. Especially when the first wave of a different kind of malady hit me. Homesickness.

Seeing the vast stretches of deep green polar forests give way to the beautiful undulating plains of blue-white snow unfold below us made my breath catch. Then, when the twinkling lights of the city came into view, I almost shed a tear.

My home. My kingdom. My heart.

Well, part of my heart. The other part was

sitting next to me, holding my hand and leaning over the sleigh's edge to see better.

"It's beautiful," Sin whispered.

"Wait until you see it up close," my uncle said. He grinned, obviously pleased with Sin's reaction.

"I can't wait," Sin said.

Uncle Kris maneuvered the sleigh lower. "And you two are just in time for the annual Tinkers' Tourney."

"Oh, I'd forgotten that was this week. We picked a great time to visit," I said.

"What's the Tinkers' Tourney?" Sin asked.

My uncle answered. "It's where a select number of Master Tinkers, our toy creators and developers, show off their best ideas in hopes of being chosen to present their best idea for the toy of the year. There are three this year. Whichever toy wins, we'll put into production for Christmas. It's a very festive competition with lots of toy-themed edible goodies to go along with it."

"How are the tinkers chosen to compete?"

"They vote for each other all year long."

"It sounds like fun, but..." Sin frowned. "It's already October. Isn't that a little late for Christmas?"

Uncle Kris laughed. "Son, this is the North Pole. One of the most magical places on Earth. There's nothing we can't do."

He flicked the reins, and the sleigh descended again, skimming over rooftops. Below us, elves looked up and waved. I waved back. Sin did too.

Then he leaned toward me. "You might have to pinch me. I'm not sure I've processed that all of this is real."

"It's real, I promise."

He blinked as he pointed ahead of us. "Is that...a giant Christmas tree?"

"Yes. It's also the headquarters of Christmas Incorporated. Or, as we all call it, the factory. It's where all the toys are made." Grinning, I tried to see the NP through his eyes.

Everything was centered on my uncle's headquarters. From the enormous green Christmas-tree-shaped building (complete with ornaments, working lights, and garland) that occupied the heart of the city, the neighborhoods spiraled out like the arms of a galaxy. They each twinkled just as brightly too.

Most of the neighborhoods tended toward a distinct theme. In the bakers' and confectioners' neighborhood, many of the homes and businesses looked as if they were built from gingerbread and decorated with candy.

Where the builders lived, the structures sported visible rivets and clockwork cogs that were both operational and decorative. The lines were crisp and clean, all angles precise.

The tinkers' community was brightly colored and whimsical, with striped trims and curvy roofs that suggested the playful nature of those who lived there.

In one of my favorites, the decorators' quarter, shops and homes alike sported the crisp lines, bold patterns, and flawless bows of packages waiting to be opened. Here and there, colorful spiral accents of metal "ribbon" added some fun.

And then, just across the Meltwater River and north of town, was our destination, the Winter Palace.

It glowed with the soft blue-white light of ice and glittered with the diamond reflection of fresh snow. Both of those things were illusions. No ice or snow had been used in the construction of the edifice, but those accents, along with blue-veined white marble walls, blue slate roof tiles, silver accents, and an abundance of sparkling glass windows made it impossible to mistake the structure for anything *but* the Winter Palace and home of the Winter King, Jack Frost.

I took a breath as we touched down inside the palace walls. "It is impressive, isn't it?"

"I'll say." Sin climbed out, picked up Sugar's carrier, then offered me a hand, all the while taking in the scenery around him.

"Jayne!" My mother's voice carried to us as the towering double doors opened.

Behind her trailed several members of the household staff, coming to help with our luggage probably. I waved. "Hi, Mom! Hi, Gregory!"

Gregory waved back. "Hello, Princess. Welcome home."

"Thank you."

Gregory Brumal was the palace's steward. That meant he was the head of the staff, in charge of keeping the palace running, and without him, the palace didn't function. I was sure *he* wasn't about to carry luggage, but he would direct some footmen to handle it.

I hugged my mom and almost hugged Gregory, but I didn't want to embarrass him in front of the other staff. "It's so nice to be home." I got Spider's carrier out of the sleigh. He was quiet but busy sniffing the air. I wondered what he thought of all this. I was sure he'd tell me later.

I turned to introduce Sinclair to Gregory, but he was already directing which staff should take which bags and to what rooms. I let him be. The man liked things done a certain way. No reason for me to interrupt that. There would be plenty of time for him to meet Sinclair later.

My mom's smile was enormous. "It's so good to have you here." She put her arm around Sin and hugged him too. "Welcome to our home, Sinclair."

"Thank you, Lady Frost."

"Sinclair, I told you to call me Klara. Granted,

there are some occasions where Lady Frost would be more appropriate, but in private, Klara. Please."

He nodded. "I'll remember that. Thank you, Klara."

She smiled and gave him another hug. "You're welcome."

He glanced up at the palace's spires. "This is quite a place you have here."

"We like it." She laughed as she released him and turned to me again. "Your father's in meetings all day, but that will give you two a chance to get settled. You're in your own apartment, naturally, and Sinclair is in the Montebonne suite."

"Great." I kind of meant that sarcastically. The Montebonne suite was in a completely different wing from where my apartment was located. Not that Sin and I were planning on any secret midnight trysts, but it would have been nice to at least be in the same ZIP code. Just in case the need for a secret midnight tryst arose.

Kidding. Kind of.

But before I could say anything, my uncle put his hand on my shoulder. "Jaynie, I'll see you at dinner tomorrow night. I need to get going. Work to do. Lists to check. Meetings to attend. You know how it is."

"Yes, I do. Thanks for coming to get us." Our luggage had now been gathered up by the staff, who were headed into the palace.

"Yes," Sinclair said. "Thank you again for picking us up. That was a great ride."

Uncle Kris nodded. "Happy to do it." Then he climbed back into the sleigh and headed off. By land, this time. No need to make the reindeer fly when he was already in the NP.

"Mom, why don't you put Sinclair in the Crestfield suite?"

Her brows lifted a little as her lips pursed. "You mean the one across the hall from your apartment?"

"Yes. That one." I held her gaze. "Our cats like to hang out together. Having him so far away will make that tricky."

She tipped her head. "Your cats, hmm?"

Sin's expression said he was happy to keep the peace. "Wherever you want to put me is fine."

I ignored him. "Mom, there's nothing nefarious going on."

My mother's lips puckered up again. "It's not nefarious things I'm worried about. But I trust you. And you are adults, after all. The Crestfield suite is fine." She looked at Gregory, who was standing a respectable distance away, waiting on further orders. "Can you see to that?"

"Yes, Lady Frost."

I nodded at him. "Thank you, Gregory."

He bowed. "Just doing my job, Princess Jayne." He left to make that adjustment, leaving two underbutlers behind.

18

It wasn't necessary to thank the staff. That's something you learned early on as a royal. The family's thanks were implied. But in this case, I wanted to say it anyway.

My mother clapped her hands. "All right, let's head inside and get you two situated. I'm sure your cats would like to get out of those carriers."

I glanced at Spider. "I'm sure they would."

As we fell in behind my mom, Sin leaned in. "Should I be calling you Princess? And I know your mom said to call her Klara, but when should I call her Lady Frost?"

"No to Princess. Please, no. And only refer to my mom as Lady Frost when anyone who isn't family or staff is present." I almost shuddered. This was what I'd been worried about. That Sinclair would be overwhelmed by the formalities that went with life here in the North Pole. It was old hat to me, but I'd grown up with it.

To him it must seem like—

"It's another world up here." He looked around at the palace grounds, taking in the snow-frosted pine topiaries and the permanently frozen reflecting pond that mirrored the palace so beautifully.

"It is. Literally."

"I like it." He smiled. "It's very cool. No pun intended."

"Pun allowed. It's both cool and cool. So I'm

good with it." He didn't seem overwhelmed. Maybe I was worrying for nothing.

The two underbutlers marched along behind us, causing Sin to glance back once or twice. I wondered what he thought of it all. I hoped he'd tell me later. And I hoped it was good.

It took twenty minutes to get us to our rooms. Our things were already there, and Gregory was waiting on us. He wanted to have us unpacked, but I assured him that was something we could do ourselves. On occasion—like when I'd returned from college with a dorm room's worth of stuff, I'd let the staff help with that task, but this was nothing like that. I had one suitcase and one carryon that was all cat supplies. I could manage.

Sin had the same, and I was sure he wouldn't want strangers going through his stuff. It was way too early for that level of royal interference.

Gregory left, but a few minutes later, I heard knocking at Sin's door across the hall. I peeked out. It was Michael, another underbutler, with a cart holding all the things that had been added to the Montebonne suite for Sugar. Food and water bowls, a cat tree, a scratching post and the all-important litter box.

Sin answered and let the young man in to set them up. As Michael went past, Sin shot me a look.

I laughed to cover the nerves I was feeling. "It's a lot to take in, I know."

"And you've lived like this all your life?"

I nodded. "Sure. Except for college and Nocturne Falls."

He shook his head slowly. "I give you a lot of credit."

"For what?"

"For being so well adjusted. For not being completely spoiled and out of touch with the world."

"Thanks." His words made me both happy and sad. So I changed the subject. "Hey, you want to go into town? I'd love to show you around. We have the rest of the day and tonight to ourselves." Tomorrow there was a formal dinner in Sinclair's honor. Lots of dignitaries and such. Very official. I usually loved formal dinners, but I wasn't exactly looking forward to this one because I didn't want it to be a bad experience for Sin.

"That sounds really good. Maybe we could get something to eat?"

"Like breakfast? Because it'll be more like lunch when we get there. Physical North Pole time and magical North Pole time aren't the same."

"I'm fine with whatever. Lunch is good."

"Then I know a great food truck that has amazing tacos. Although I heard there's a new tandoori place in town that is crazy good."

He stared at me for a moment. "You have food trucks here? And tacos? And tandoori?"

"Sure. And pizza and sushi and burgers. It's the North Pole, not Mars." I needed him to see that life here wasn't that different. At least not outside the palace.

"I'm in. Let me just get Sugar's food out and I'm ready to go."

"Good. I'm going to change, get Spider set up, then I'll meet you in the hall."

He spread his hands. "Should I change too?"

He was in jeans, a thin gray sweater, and his black leather jacket. "No, you look perfect."

He smiled. "Thanks, Princess."

"Hey—" But he shut the door before I could complain.

I closed mine, too, and got myself ready. Then I went into my apartment's kitchen. All the apartments had them, but mine certainly didn't get used much. Mostly it was kept stocked with drinks and snacks. Nothing that needed actual cooking. There was a whole palace kitchen for that, complete with chefs, who unlike me, actually knew what they were doing in such a space.

A large box of my aunt's eggnog fudge sat waiting for me on the counter near the stove. That made me smile as I dished out a whole can of Chicken Party for Spider. "Here you go, baby."

He was sitting on the window sill looking down into the gardens at the back of the house. The centerpiece of the garden was a pond kept from freezing with a heating system. Because of that, it always had wildlife around it, mainly the talkative, black and white Muscovy ducks that my mother loved so much.

He seemed to be fixated on them, which explained why he hadn't responded to the food I'd put out. I went to stand by him, giving his head a scratch. His fur was so silky.

"Those pigeons are in the water," Spider said.

"Those aren't pigeons. Those are ducks. And ducks love the water."

"Ducks are dumb." He looked up at me. "Spider hates water."

"Yes, I know, but you love Chicken Party, and there's lots of that in your bowl."

"Spider loves Chicken Party." He jumped down and sauntered over to inspect the food.

I had changed into jeans, a long-sleeve T-shirt, and the galaxy-blue leather jacket Sin had gotten me for Christmas last year. Then I threw on a scarf. The new outfit was a lot more suited to running around town than the dress pants, blouse and long coat I'd worn. I'd picked the outfit because I knew my mother would like it, but also because I hadn't been sure who was coming to meet us when we landed.

Being a princess meant being appropriately attired at the appropriate times, something I'd struggled with when I was younger, but as I'd

23

grown older, I'd come to accept what being a princess was really about.

I had two lives. One lived for myself and one lived for the monarchy. Which meant my life wasn't always my own. Much of it was determined by the throne and responsibilities that awaited me.

I just hoped Sin would understand that too.

We walked together down the hall and through the corridors of the secondary residential wing of the palace. I'd moved here from the primary residential wing when I was sixteen. My parents lived in the primary wing. Essentially, that entire wing was theirs.

Sin did a lot of looking around, which I understood. It was an impressive place.

"You're going to have to give me the grand tour tomorrow."

"I'd be happy to. I'll have Gregory bring some Segways up."

"Segways?" He was on the verge of laughing.

"I'm serious. You want to see the whole palace? Then it's the only way. Too much ground to cover by foot in a day."

He whistled. "Crazy."

"It is, sort of. But a lot of the property is open to

the public and some of it is reserved for business use, and then there's all the staff that live here, so when you look at it that way, it doesn't seem so overwhelming."

"How many people actually live here?"

"About three hundred and fifty."

"In the palace?" He whistled again. "No kidding?"

"Honest. There are two people on staff whose only job is to keep the palace clocks wound and running. There's one particular maintenance person who only does paint touch-ups." My education in palace history and management were finally paying off.

He stared at me for a second. "This place is like a small city."

"It kind of is."

"That's surprising. But a lot of this is. I thought you'd have your own security, too."

I shrugged. "I could if I wanted, but there's never been a need. Plus, my magic makes me pretty capable of defending myself."

He nodded. "I'm aware."

We turned toward the private exit on the side lawn, where the personal vehicles were kept. The south exit was pretty much the one we all used to come and go by.

I didn't want a driver taking us into town, so we'd be in one of the crawlers, a large, high-tech

26

snowmobile hybrid with front skis and rear tracks that made any icy surface passable. In one form or another, crawlers were our basic form of transportation.

We stepped out beneath the south exit portico, and one of the valets popped out of the transportation office to meet us.

He tipped his hat at me. "Afternoon, Princess Jayne, and welcome home. What can I do for you today?"

"Thank you. We'd like a crawler brought up."

"Right away, Princess." He ran back to the office, where he called the garage on his radio.

Electronics don't work that great in the NP, but walkie-talkies seem to do okay over short distances. The staff in the palace and the elves who worked for my uncle all used them. Land lines did okay too.

In less than a minute, the crawler arrived. The valet who'd brought it hopped out and came around to present me with the keys.

"Thank you."

She bowed. "You're welcome, Princess."

Sin approached the vehicle with great curiosity. He trailed his hand over the sleek seating compartment that was sort of a clear, egg-shaped bubble cradled in gleaming white fiberglass. "This thing is very cool."

I dangled the keys. "Want to drive?"

His brows lifted. "Yes. But how about you get us into town and let me see how it works first? Then I'll drive back."

"You got it."

We got in, I started it up, and off we went. The crawler was quiet inside, letting us talk without too much engine noise.

Sin shook his head. "I still can't believe I'm here. This place is…I'm about to say cool again."

I laughed. "It's okay. It *is* cool."

"It must have been something growing up here." He was looking out the window.

Ahead of us, the palace gates were opening. I drove through with a nod to the guards. "It was great. I didn't always appreciate it, and sometimes, it felt like a prison, but now I love my home."

"Your kingdom," he said.

"Technically, my dad's kingdom." I smiled. "But yes, my kingdom too, since I am the Winter Princess."

His face went very serious. "And you'll be its queen someday."

"Yes. The Winter Queen."

"What would that make me? When we're married and you're crowned?"

When. I smiled. He was so optimistic. I let it slide, since he still had no idea what he was getting into.

I answered. "You will be the Queen's Consort.

28

Or the Prince Consort. Two versions of the same thing. It's an official position. You'd be generally known as Prince Sinclair and would be referred to as Your Highness."

The uncertainty in his eyes almost undid me. "That's…nuts."

I managed to hold on to my smile. "I know, it's a lot to process."

"I'm about the most unroyal person I know. I can't imagine anyone calling me Your Highness."

"You'd get used to it."

"I suppose." He went back to looking out the window.

He didn't seem so optimistic now. I swallowed, trying to keep my melancholy at bay. I drove the crawler across the Meltwater River Bridge and hoped the visit to town would lift the mood again.

I parked in the first spot I found, not bothering with the royal reserved parking near the factory. "Ready to eat?"

He nodded as we got out. "Sure. Although I'm okay to walk around a bit first."

"That's fine with me." My appetite wasn't all that great after our conversation, but I held on to my happy face. "There are lots of shops to look in, and with the town gearing up for the Tinkers' Tourney, there will be even more stalls and food trucks set up in Yule Square."

"Can we go that way, then?"

"I was planning on it." I tucked the keys in my pocket and took his hand. I narrated the walk by pointing out all the shops and interesting buildings along the way, but the walk was short since Yule Square was only five blocks away.

Music reached us before we saw the square, evidence of the festivities already going on.

Sinclair was smiling when we joined the gathering crowd, so I took that as a good sign. He looked around. "What is that delicious smell?"

I inhaled. "Could be one of several things. Kabobs, kettle corn, or candied chestnuts. There might also be some hot cider in there. Or some waffle cone sundaes. Could even be chili cheese fries, or fried cheese curds with gravy, or—"

"Okay, my stomach just rumbled." He laughed. "Those all sound good."

"Then let's grab something and eat while we wander."

"I'm in. Whatever we come to first is fine with me."

That just happened to be spaghetti and meatballs on a stick—one of my favorites, I can't lie. I love me some carbs. We got in line, but the people behind us quickly recognized me.

"Princess Frost?"

I turned, smiling. "Hi there."

My greeting was returned with bows. "Welcome home, Your Highness."

"Thank you. It's good to be home."

The people in front of us overheard. They moved aside. "Go ahead of us, please."

"No, I wouldn't dream of it. We're happy to wait in line."

They seemed unconvinced, but at the word *we*, all eyes shifted to Sinclair. The sly, knowing smiles followed. I knew they'd heard I had a boyfriend. As the saying went, royal news was everyone's news.

Such was my life.

We got our spaghetti and meatballs on a stick and meandered through the square, eating and shopping and mostly being left alone. Although I could hear the whispers as people spotted me. I was used to it, but I could tell Sinclair was bristling a little.

"It's no big deal," I said softly.

"Really? It doesn't bother you?"

"I'm used to it. And it's not like they're saying bad things. They're surprised to see me. I haven't lived here in a while, remember?" I was sure they were also talking about him. It was inevitable. He was with me, and he was incredibly hot. It was hard not to look at him.

He nodded in a thoughtful way, the wheels in his head obviously spinning. "If you're okay with it, then so am I. Not like there's anything to be done about it anyway, right?"

"Right." I shifted my spaghetti on a stick to my other hand, then looped my arm through his. "Let's go shop some more. And tonight, if you want, we can come back and check out the toys in the competition."

"They'll be here?"

"Yep. They'll be unveiled this evening in the opening ceremony of the tourney, then for three days, they'll be on display at the center of the square. Everyone can vote on which one they like the best, and the votes are considered, but the winner is chosen by a blind panel that may or may not include my uncle." I lowered my voice. "It does."

Sin nodded. "I definitely want to come back for that."

"Me too. It's a lot of fun. There's fireworks, and the tinkers demonstrate the toys, and the whole thing is like a street party."

He smiled. "It's already like a street party."

"Wait until you see it tonight, then. Most people are at work right now."

"I can't wait." He tipped his head toward the waffle cone stand. "And I really can't wait for ice cream. What do you say?"

"I say let's do it. Hey, you've probably never had a choco-cicle have you?"

"Since I don't know what that is, no."

"You can get one by itself or stuck in your ice cream, which is what I do. It's a chocolate icicle, basically. Hard chocolate shell with a gooey center of either fudge, marshmallow, or caramel."

He shook his head slowly. "The winter elf metabolism is something else."

We walked to the ice cream booth and got in line. When it was our turn, I ordered a chocolate-dipped waffle cone with rocky road ice cream and a marshmallow choco-cicle. Sin got the same cone with dark chocolate orange ice cream and a caramel choco-cicle.

The owners of the booth tried to wave away our money, but I insisted. I wanted to be treated like everyone else, especially in front of Sin. Getting stuff for free had never sat well with me.

We walked on, our ice creams disappearing. Sin stopped in front of a hat shop's window just as we finished the last of our cones.

He pointed to a green velvet brimmed cap with silver metallic ribbon trim and small silver rivet decoration on one side. "Think I could pull that off?"

"Sure. That's a fancy version of the everyday hat a lot of the builders wear."

"I am kind of a builder of doughnuts."

I grinned. "You could make it work. You could make anything work. It's one of your superpowers."

"You're very sweet." He slipped his arm around my waist. "I am incredibly happy right now. And that looks like the kind of hat an incredibly happy man would wear in a place like this. It's very festive."

"Then we should go in and you should try it on." I was bursting. Despite my fears about how Sin would react to my life in the North Pole, he was taking everything in stride and seemed to really be enjoying himself. Sure, it was early days. He'd only been here a couple hours and had yet to experience anything as formal as tomorrow night's dinner, but I had hope.

He took my hand. "Maybe we should get matching hats."

I followed him into the shop. "Let's not get crazy."

After a little more shopping (Sin bought the hat), a little more eating (peanut chicken kabobs, cheese curds, and chocolate mousse bombs drizzled with salted caramel), we headed back to the palace for a nap.

Sin drove the crawler, which he got the hang of immediately, and when we arrived at the portico to drop it off, I could tell he wasn't quite ready for his turn at the wheel to be over.

"You can drive it tonight when we go see the toy reveal."

"Yeah? All right. That'll be fun." He handed the keys over to the valet. "Kind of makes me wish Nocturne Falls got more snow. Although after what happened with the yetis, I probably shouldn't think that way."

He did a big pretend shiver as he looked around. "Where are the yetis, by the way?"

"Far, far away in the polar forests. You won't see them."

"Good. I'm yeti'd out."

We walked into the palace together, laughing at the memory. Our voices carried, echoing off the walls.

Sin looked around. "Where is everyone? I thought a palace would be busier."

"I promise it's plenty busy elsewhere. A lot of the staff are preparing for tomorrow night's dinner. My dad is in meetings, and my mom is probably in her office working as well. Same for my aunt and uncle. There is *so* much to be done this time of year."

"Maybe we shouldn't have come. I hate to think our visit is disrupting things."

"No, not at all. Christmas prep is an ongoing thing in the NP, but in October it really ramps up. Doesn't matter, though. This is standard operating procedure. A little visit from us isn't going to even register. This place thrives on being busy, I promise."

"Okay, if you say so."

"Also, I can assure you that the lack of people around us is totally on purpose. My family is giving us space, so you can take it all in without the pressure of company."

Light filled his eyes. "Really? That's very thoughtful of them."

"They really want you to like it here." As did I. So very, very much.

"I do, I promise. I especially like the eggnog fudge your aunt left for me."

I smiled. "I got some too. It's great for breakfast."

He made a face at me and laughed.

"Hey, I know we were going to take a nap since we got up so early and everything, but how about that tour? We could check on the cats, then I could show you around. We'd still have time for a little snooze before tonight's festivities."

"That sounds great." He took my hand. "Let's go see how the kids are."

I loved when he called our cats that. And it got me thinking about us actually having kids. Sin would make a great dad, I had zero doubts about it. But how would the citizens of the North Pole take it when they realized their next king or queen would be half winter elf and half necromancer?

The thought made me sigh.

"You okay?"

I blinked at Sin. "Hmm? Oh, sure. Just thinking."

"About?"

I smiled for his benefit and told a little white lie. "Which dress I'm going to wear for dinner tomorrow."

"I'm sure you'll look great in whatever you pick."

As we turned down the hall toward our rooms, the Segways I'd asked for came into view.

Sin laughed. "I almost thought you asking for those was a joke."

"You'll be glad for them. Makes getting around this place a lot easier."

"Good thing I've been on one before." He stopped in front of his door, giving the people mover a funny look.

"What?"

"I was just thinking I'm surprised there's no Segway tour in Nocturne Falls. I bet it would be a great business."

"You're right, it would be. Maybe no one's suggested it?"

"Or the Ellinghams don't want motorized tourists clogging up the streets."

"That could be too." I opened my door. "See you in a few?"

"You got it."

When I went into the living room, Spider was nowhere to be found. Not that unusual. "Spider? Mama's home."

No answer. His bowl of Chicken Party had been cleaned out, but there was still lots of kibble left and plenty of water.

I went searching. He wasn't sitting on any of the window sills or sleeping on the bed, but I finally found him on one of the shelves in the walk-in closet. "What are you doing in here, silly boy?"

He blinked and yawned. "Spider tired."

"Too tired to have Sugar come over?"

He sat up, almost conking his head on the shelf above. "Spider likes Sugar. Sugar can come play?"

"I know you like her. I'll see if she can come over. Do you need anything? I'm going back out for a little bit with Mr. Sinclair."

He casually licked a paw. "Spider likes treats."

"You just ate. Treats can wait until later." I scratched his head, then kissed it. "Love you, baby. I'll go see about Sugar coming over."

I left my leather jacket on the back of the couch as I went across the hall.

Sin opened the door, revealing he'd taken his jacket off as well. Sweet fancy Christmas, he was handsome.

I contained my inner gushing to focus on the needs of my talking cat. "Can Sugar come over? I think Spider would love that."

"She's sleeping, but I could wake her up."

"Um…" I looked around him at the precious little white cat sitting on the floor behind him. "I don't think she's sleeping."

Sugar mewed softly and Sin laughed as he turned. "Well, she was sleeping." He bent down and scooped her up. "Want to visit your boyfriend?"

39

She mewed again, making me wonder how much she understood. Just because she couldn't talk like Spider didn't mean she didn't comprehend what was being said.

Sin scratched her neck. "I'm ready to go anyway."

"Good. Me too."

We put Sugar in my apartment, then climbed onto the Segways and took off in the opposite direction we'd returned.

"This is surreal," Sin said, shaking his head in amusement.

"What is?"

"Riding Segways through a royal palace with my princess girlfriend."

"Well, I never thought I'd be in love with a necromancer so…"

"Point taken." He grinned and waved as we whizzed by a pair of housekeepers. "Where are we going first?"

"Service elevator, then down to the main floor. We'll do the big rooms first, see the kitchens, the gym, the pool, the bowling alley, the skating rink—"

"You have an *indoor* skating rink?"

"Yes. Does that seem odd?"

"Only that it's inside."

"We have one outside too. Skating's a popular sport."

"I can imagine all the winter activities are."

I smiled. "Kind of a natural fit."

We drove onto the service elevator, rode down to the main floor, then got off and started the tour. I took him from room to room, stopping in each one to tell him what was special about it, or what I loved about it, or who had last been entertained in it.

Sin, being Sin, had to take it a step further.

In the ballroom, he insisted on waltzing me around while he hummed a tune. In the library, he plucked a book from the shelves and read me a passage in a British accent. He bowled three frames in the bowling alley, and when we arrived at the skating rink, I already knew what he'd want.

He got off his Segway. "I love how it looks in here. It's got a 1960s cosmic vibe that I am totally down for."

"It's looked like this for so long we consider it historic." I parked my Segway, climbed down and pointed to the nearest wall cabinet. "There are skates in the cubbies behind those doors."

He laughed. "I'm good."

"What? You don't want to take a spin around the rink?"

"I have to confess, I can't skate. I'm willing to try, but I might break something."

I grinned and took his hand. "Wow, something the great Sinclair Crowe can't do?"

"Yes, you've found me out." He tugged me closer. "Do you still love me now that my shortcomings have been exposed?"

I leaned into him, still smiling. "I'll find a way to carry on."

And there, in the frosty blue light of the rink, he bent and kissed me, long and slow and soft.

My head spun in the most woozy, wonderful way.

"I'm glad," he whispered. "I'd hate to think that was a deal breaker."

"I'll teach you. It's not that hard." I wrapped my arms around him. The only deal breaker would be his decision on this life.

He sighed dramatically. "I suppose I'll have to learn. Skating is probably the national pastime. Or is that eating dessert?"

"Very funny." I did laugh. "There are skating lanes in the residential areas. It's actually a popular form of transportation."

"It's a small ask. I'm happy to learn."

I pulled back to look into his eyes, almost afraid to ask my question but needing the answer. "What do you think so far?"

"Of the North Pole?"

I nodded.

He smiled. "I love it. I love this enormous house you call home. I love you. And I know there is a lot more to see, but the early morning has caught up with me." He yawned. "I'm ready for that nap."

"So am I." He loved me *and* the NP. That was so nice to hear. "We can see the rest later. Let's head back."

On the Segways, the return trip took less than fifteen minutes, and when we arrived, we parked them in the hall where we'd picked them up.

I tipped my head toward my door. "You want Sugar back?"

"If she wants to come back. Otherwise, she can hang out over there. If you don't mind."

"Not at all, but let's see what they're up to. And what they've destroyed." I opened my door and went in.

Sin followed. "Hopefully nothing."

We found them curled up together on the sofa, which had had all its pillows shoved off. They looked like a furry yin-yang symbol, exhausted from slaying the pillows.

I glanced at Sin.

He shook his head and whispered, "Let them sleep."

I looked at the clock and whispered back, "Hour nap?"

"Sounds good. Text you when I'm up."

"Same."

He kissed me on the cheek and headed for his room.

Two hours and many texts later, we'd had naps and showers, gotten changed and were ready to head back out to town for the tinker toy competition unveiling. The crawler was waiting for us under the portico when we walked out the south exit.

Sin drove, smiling the whole way.

It amused me. I finished the piece of eggnog fudge I'd brought along to keep my strength up. "You really like this thing, don't you?"

"I do. I want one in Nocturne Falls."

"Sorry. This is proprietary NP property. But you can use one anytime you're here."

He shrugged. "I guess we'll just have to move here sooner."

I stared at him for a moment, not sure if he was kidding or not. Before I could ask, he spoke again.

"Believe it or not, I'm hungry again. Even after everything we ate earlier."

"I offered you fudge."

"I know. I was foolish to turn it down. I even thought about digging into my own stash and didn't. I'll learn your sugary ways, I promise."

I snorted at his silliness. "Well, there will be twice as many vendors tonight, so you're in luck. And you know me, I can always eat."

"One of many things I love about you."

Even though we were early for the competition, the crowds were already crazy. As a result, we took advantage of one of the reserved for royalty parking spots, then hiked toward Yule Square. A delicate drifting of snow had begun to fall, but the sky was still filled with stars. Obviously, my father's contribution toward making tonight even more magical.

Sin took my hand as we made our way through the throngs. "I suppose you've been to a lot of these."

"I have. As a matter of fact, I've even been the emcee several times."

He seemed surprised by that. "How come you're not the emcee tonight?"

"Because tonight, I'm just a citizen of the realm. And my cousin, Francis Snow—he's my aunt Martha's brother's son—has taken over since I moved to Nocturne Falls. Which I'm totally fine with, but I really hope he doesn't call me out or pull me onstage or anything like that. I just want to blend in with the crowd and enjoy the night like everyone else."

Sin's gaze went past my shoulder. "I think it's too late for blending in."

I looked in the direction he was staring and saw two older women standing in a shop doorway, watching us. And looking very judgmental.

Sin sighed. "I suppose they don't think I'm worthy of their princess."

I stared at them a second longer, giving them a look back that said I didn't appreciate their judging him. But I'd been afraid of this. So afraid I hadn't wanted to put it into words. There was a problem beyond Sin not liking the royal life.

The citizens of the North Pole, a few of them dyed-in-the-wool traditionalists, might not accept the Winter Princess marrying a man who wasn't an elf.

I pulled him aside next to one of the shops and out of the flow of pedestrian traffic. This wasn't the time or place I'd wanted to have this conversation—I actually didn't want to have this conversation at all—but we needed to talk about this. "Listen, I have to tell you something. About those women."

He nodded. "They don't think I'm the right guy for you."

I frowned. I couldn't pretend. "It's something like that. It's because—"

"I don't have pointed ears and blue hair and can't make snow fall from my fingertips."

I let out a long breath. Of course he knew. Sin was a smart guy and very perceptive. "I'm sorry. It's a very old-fashioned way of thinking, but yes, that's exactly it."

He smiled as he leaned in and kissed my forehead. "It's okay."

"It is? Because it's not okay with me."

"Well, not okay, but I get it. Not only am I a commoner, but I'm not a winter elf. If everyone accepted that with open arms, I'd frankly be a little suspicious."

"You would?"

"Sure. That would be too easy." He grinned, big and wide. "But I'm very lovable. I'll win them over."

I laughed, more relieved than I could say. "You are very lovable. And I'm sure you're right, you'll win them. But you have to know it's not going to happen instantly. This is a tough, old-school crowd."

"It's not a big deal. I promise."

I took a breath. I'd been so worried about so much, and all for naught. So what if his acceptance was an uphill climb? If he was okay with it, then to some degree, I would be too. I wasn't happy about the antiquated attitudes, but I wasn't going to let them rule my thoughts. "Still hungry?"

"Starving."

I looped my arm through his, and we headed back into the fray. I loved this sweet, sexy man so much. "How about steak-on-a-stick?"

He lifted his head and sniffed the air. "Is that what I smell?"

The meaty, charcoal aroma wafted over us. "Yes. And it tastes even better."

He hesitated. "It's not reindeer, is it? I'd feel weird about that."

"No!" I laughed. "It's beef. I swear."

"Good. I'm in. Is everything on a stick?"

"No. Well. A lot." I shrugged. "Makes for easy walking and eating."

"That it does."

The line for steak-on-a-stick was long, but we hung in there and ended up ordering two apiece. Hey, one for each hand. And they weren't *that* big. More like slice-of-steak-on-a-stick.

Of course, that meant we couldn't hold hands for a few minutes, but it was worth it, especially when we got to the hunk of bread under the steak at the bottom of the stick. By the time you got to it, the bread had soaked up all the yummy juices and was almost more delicious than the steak. Almost.

We found a spot near the front of the main stage along with a thousand other people and hung out, eating our steak and chatting.

Once, I could have sworn I heard the word *necromancer* whispered behind me, but when I turned, no one seemed to be focused on us. I decided it was just my overactive imagination. Or the slight breeze that had picked it up. Or a million other things.

How could anyone know that Sin was a

49

necromancer? I didn't think anyone in my family would have said anything, but then, it was possible that one of the staff had overheard them discussing him.

One thing I'd learned a long time ago was that household staff had ears and tongues and liked to use them. They were supposed to keep everything they heard to themselves, but they didn't. It was just elf nature to share the most interesting things gleaned in the palace. And everywhere else, really.

The North Pole was a huge small town. Gossip, rumors, and truth spread like a crack through ice on a warm day. A lot like Nocturne Falls in that way, but probably worse. That was a big part of why the most important meetings and conversations in the palace were done without any staff present.

And look, I wasn't saying those employed by the palace weren't trustworthy, but things happened. We'd learned to deal with it a long time ago. Like before my dad even took the throne.

So was it possible that the truth about Sin's background was spreading? One hundred percent. I hadn't done anything to hide it, and I wasn't going to, but I hadn't exactly broadcasted it either.

I got closer to Sin and bent my head a little so he couldn't see my face, then scanned the crowd around us as stealthily as possible. I caught a couple people looking our way, but I couldn't be sure that meant anything.

People liked to look at royalty. And I could only imagine how interesting it was to have a nice long look at Sin. The princess's beau. They'd want to know what he was wearing, what he looked like, judge if he was handsome enough, or if his ears stuck out, if he was too fat, too short, too tall, too thin. Everything about him would be scrutinized.

I was sure a full account of his public appearance would be written up in the *Pole Post*, probably in the News About Town section as a fluff piece. There was a slim chance he'd show up on the front page, but I was hoping the Tinkers' Tourney would keep him off it.

A little murmur went through the crowd, but this time it wasn't because of me or the man at my side. My cousin Francis had walked out onto the stage. The lights came up, illuminating the whole square. Then a spotlight found him in his navy-blue velvet suit trimmed in silver. He wore glittery, silver shoes that sparkled under the lights. Even his hair, nearly the same bright blue as mine, had been tipped in silver glitter.

He looked every inch the emcee.

Music swelled up, carrying over the crowd and announcing things were about to begin. I was glad. The competition would give people something else to talk about.

"Testing, testing…" My cousin tapped the mic, and the audience settled down. He waved and smiled, the perfect emcee, totally at ease. Seriously, so much better than I had been. "Good evening, ladies and gentlemen, elves of all ages. How is everyone in the North Pole tonight?"

Lots of hooting, hollering, and cheering answered him. We whooped and clapped a little ourselves.

Francis smiled, lightly touching his chest. "I hate to disappoint you, but I am not here to sing."

The crowd laughed.

"There is *something* else going on…" He put a finger to his chin and stared skyward like he couldn't remember. More laughter and a few people started to yell out reminders.

"What's that? The Thinkers Journey? The what?" He leaned in and cupped his ear like he was trying to hear better. "Oh! The Tinkers' Tourney! That's right." But his smile told everyone he was just teasing them, which of course, we all knew. "What an exciting night it's going to be too!"

More applause.

"I'm not going to keep you waiting. I know why you're here. So let's meet those tinkers and see their toys!" He moved to the side of the stage as the lights came on behind him, revealing the three competing tinkers and their covered toys.

With a big flourish, he pointed to the tinkers.

"Check them out! Let's hear how ready you are to see those toys too!"

A new round of cheers started. Man, he was good at getting people revved up. He should have had this job the whole time.

"Now you all know how this is done. With a drum roll and a countdown, the toys will be revealed at the same time. Then each tinker will be given a chance to demonstrate their toy and tell us about it."

Francis pointed at the audience. "Then you lovely people have three days to vote for your favorite until, at last, our secret panel decides the winner. Who's ready to see what these talented tinkers have brought us?"

We all hooted and cheered some more, Sin and I included.

"All right, drum roll, please."

The tinny jingle of bells came out of the speakers, causing the audience to laugh. Francis planted a hand on his hip and stared at the tech booth. "Does that sound like a drum roll to you guys?"

A real drum roll spilled out of the speakers then. Francis started to count down. "Three...two...one!"

The covers disappeared off the toys as the tinkers stood beside their creations. One was beaming, one was biting his lip, and the third was twisting her hands together nervously.

I studied the toys. There were signs on each display. The first toy was called Glitterskins and seemed to be a little machine that produced sheets of adhesive glitter that could be applied to anything. I immediately wanted that for the shop. Kids would love it. And so would parents, if the glitter stayed in one place.

The second was titled Mrs. Clucks-A-Lot and looked like a cute fluffy white chicken. Apparently, it laid eggs with prizes in them and could be taught to do all kinds of things. It also had a built-in alarm.

The third sign said Mega Chick and also seemed to be a mechanical chicken, but it was shiny and silver and looked a lot more like an android than a pet. Coincidentally, it also laid prize-laden eggs and had an alarm function.

"That's...odd," Sin said. "Two of them came up with robot chickens that lay eggs?"

"Well...chickens do lay eggs. Seems like a natural feature to include. But yeah. It's weird. I've never seen two toys so similar."

Obviously, we weren't the only ones who'd noticed. The whole audience was buzzing with it. The tinkers were just starting to realize what had happened. The woman with the Glitterskins suddenly looked a lot less nervous. Like maybe she thought this made her a sure thing.

Francis hadn't really looked at the toys yet, as his eyes had been on the audience, but he was figuring out something was amiss as the audience had stopped reacting the way they normally did. He followed the pointing and turned to see the toys.

"Jumping jingle bells. What the—" He ran a hand through his hair, smearing the glittered tips over his whole head. He laughed nervously. "I don't think this has ever happened before."

I sighed. "I don't think it has either." I glanced up at Sin. "This isn't good."

"I can imagine."

Francis pulled the mic away from his mouth so he couldn't be heard and started talking to the tinkers. There was a lot of head shaking and confused looks. Then Francis spun back to the crowd, smiling his big emcee smile again as he raised the mic. "Seems we've had a mix-up and need to figure a few things out. An announcement will be made. Thank you all for coming out and have a good night!"

The stage went dark, but there was enough light to see Francis direct the tinkers off stage.

"That is so weird." I couldn't imagine what was going on. How had this happened?

Around us, the crowd was demonstrably unhappy. Whispers turned to muttering, which turned to outright complaints of shady business.

"Something's up. Someone cheated."

"Tinkers don't cheat," another shouted back.

"They do now," came a fast response.

"It's bad magic, I tell you."

A couple heads turned toward us. Gazes focused on me. I stared back. What on earth did they expect me to say? I didn't know any more about it than they did.

A man near me shifted his gaze from me to Sin. "What do you know about it, necromancer? Because you might not be the only bad magic in town, but you're certainly the newest."

"What?" I glared at the man. "Are you accusing my boyfriend of being involved in this? What could he have possibly done? He just got here only today and has never been here before."

"He's not one of us," the man snapped back.

"How dare you?" I was trembling with anger. "Your small mind is not an indicator of his guilt. The fact that I'm with him should be good enough for you." I looked around at the crowd now circling us. Some of them shrank back as if they suddenly realized what they were doing. "For all of you."

Sin put his hand on my arm. "We should go."

I nodded, keeping my eyes on those around us. I'd never needed security in town before. Would life with Sin change that?

I wasn't afraid yet, but the man who'd started the whole thing wasn't ready to back down. He puffed out his chest. "If you're so sure of your boyfriend, Princess, maybe you should prove his innocence."

Another man jabbed a finger at him. "Don't speak to Her Royal Highness that way."

A kind interjection, but too little too late. My anger got the best of me. "I don't have to prove anything. I know he's innocent. But I'll do it anyway."

Sin drove us back to the palace, which was good, because I was too angry to drive. My hands were shaking, and my heart was racing, and I really wanted to hit something. I wasn't going to, that wouldn't solve anything, but the feeling was there.

What I needed was sugar. And lots of it.

Plus, a talk with my parents. I had to tell them what was going on. How Sin had been singled out. It was shocking, but at least it had only been by a small handful. I also had to tell them I'd said I would figure out what had gone so wonky with the tinkers and their toys.

My words had been a gut reaction. Pure emotion spilling out of me in a need to protect the man I loved. But how exactly was I going to determine why two tinkers had made nearly identical toys?

I sighed and put my head into my hands as I slumped down in the crawler's passenger seat.

"Hey," Sin said quietly. "It's going to be okay. I'll be out of here by morning if you just—"

"What?" I jerked upright again. "No. Leaving is not the answer."

"It's not the complete answer, but I think it might help."

"No, it wouldn't. People would think you were running. And they might take that as an admission of guilt."

"I realize that, but I also think if I left, all of the noise about me would disappear. Then you can figure out what's really going on and how those tinkers ended up with the same toy."

"Please don't go. I know the people here. You leaving would just complicate things. This will all get worked out, I promise." No clue how, but I was already invested. I was not letting this wonderful man take the blame for something he hadn't done.

"I'm sure it will, I just thought a little space might help."

"I would miss you terribly. In fact, if you go, I go."

He blinked at me. "You're willing to put your royal reputation on the line for me when your citizens think I'm bad magic?"

"Yes." I said it loudly while giving him my best reassuring look. "I know you're not bad magic.

And only *some* of the citizens think that. Very few, I'm sure. Just say you won't leave."

"I won't." Then he let out a weary sigh, eyes on the road ahead. "Necromancers are a misunderstood supernatural. People think all kinds of terrible things about us because of our connection to death. It happens so often I've come to expect it. Being accused of rigging a toy competition, though? That's a new one."

I sighed again, thinking of my ex Greyson and how he'd broken up with me because of my involvement with a necromancer. "Winter elves, like many other kinds of people, can be a superstitious lot."

"So...didn't you think my coming here might cause a bit of a problem?"

"I worried about it a little, yes. But I never thought something like this would happen. And I don't care. It doesn't change the way I feel about you."

He smiled as he drove through the palace gates. "I'm glad. It doesn't change the way I feel about you either. But that doesn't solve this problem."

"No, but the problem will get solved. You'll see. Just promise you won't leave."

"You have my word. I swear."

"Good."

He pulled under the portico. We got out of the crawler and headed inside.

I paused in the foyer. "We need to go to my dad's office and talk to him about all of this."

"Is your dad still in his office this late?"

"Probably. He'll be trying to get ahead of things so he can spend some time with us."

"Good man." Sin nodded. "Lead the way."

I turned toward the wing that housed the working area of the palace. It was a decent walk, but Sin and I were quiet the whole way. I was sure he was thinking about the tinker problem and the outburst in the square just as much as I was.

We entered my dad's office suite, and his office manager, Ezreal, greeted us.

Ezreal Zur'dar was only half winter elf. The rest of him was half ice troll, and he had the gorgeous deep blue skin to prove it.

He smiled warmly as he got up from his desk and came around. "Princess Jayne. I knew you were back, but it's so good to see you in person."

I hugged him. He wouldn't mind, and he couldn't do it first. Protocol and all that. "It's really good to see you too."

Ezreal looked at Sinclair. "You must be Mr. Crowe. I've heard so many good things about you. It's a pleasure to meet you, sir."

"Please, call me Sinclair." Sin stuck his hand out.

Ezreal laughed as he shook it. "Oh, sir, I can't do that. If and when you become the Queen's Consort, it wouldn't do for us to be that familiar. But I deeply appreciate the kind offer."

Sin blew out a breath. "I have a lot to learn."

"You've got plenty of time." I smiled at him before speaking to Ezreal again. "Is my father here?"

"I'm sorry, Princess, he just left for the evening. I believe he was headed to the royal residence to join Lady Frost in the private dining room for dinner. I'm only still here because I'm finishing up a letter."

"Okay, we can catch him there. Thanks." I started to leave, then hesitated. "Does he know about what happened in the square tonight?"

Ezreal's expression darkened, and his posture went rigid. "Yes. Ugly business. News travels fast."

"It does." I was tempted to chew on my bottom lip, but didn't. "Did he say anything about it?"

"He's extremely upset. As am I." Ezreal looked at Sinclair. "If I may be so bold, I assure you, Mr. Crowe, that the small-minded are not the majority here. They're just loud." He lifted his chin. "I've dealt with them a few times myself."

Sin smiled. "I appreciate that. Thank you."

I squeezed Ezreal's hand. "Yes, thank you. We'll let you get back to your letter so you can get home. Good to see you."

He gave me a little bow. "You too, Princess."

We left as he returned to his desk. We headed

for my parents' apartment, also known as the royal residence.

"He seems like a nice guy," Sin said.

"He is," I answered. "Very nice. One of the best, really. He's one of the few employees I'd trust implicitly. Him, Gregory, and a small handful of others."

"What did he mean that he'd had to deal with the small-minded himself?"

"He's half ice troll. That's why his ears point back instead of up and where he gets his deep blue skin. And what he's referring to is the minor dustup that occurred when my father first hired him. But that's long past, and Ezreal is the loyalist of loyal. Hard worker, efficient, and close-mouthed." Ice trolls were also excellent mimics, but that seemed neither here nor there in this conversation. "I hope he's still around when I become queen."

"A dustup? Because he isn't a hundred percent winter elf?"

"To some extent, yes, but also because he was the reigning North Pole boxing champion, and people didn't think a brawler was the right sort for the Winter King's office manager."

Sin's jaw dropped open. "Ezreal is a boxing champion? I mean, he looks very fit, but..."

I laughed softly. "Yep. Underneath that proper suit and tie is a lean, mean, tattooed fighting machine. I'm sure he could still beat the snowflakes out of just about anyone. I think that's partly why my dad hired him. Office manager and security all in one."

Sin nodded thoughtfully. "Ezreal seems like such a cool guy. And your dad is a smart man. Hiring him was brilliant."

"It was. I hope I can be half as good a leader as my father. I also hope my turn doesn't come for a very long time."

Sin slipped his hand in mine. "Me too. I like your dad. I like both your parents. Honestly, your whole family is really great."

That warmed me up, and in combination with our talk with Ezreal, I was feeling pretty good.

I knocked on the door to the royal residence, and a moment later, my mom answered. "Hi, honey. Hi, Sinclair." Her smile was sympathetic, but her eyes held a little righteous indignation, telling me she'd been filled in on what had happened in the square. "Come in. We just started dinner, but there's plenty if you're hungry."

"Thanks, but we really came to talk."

She nodded. "I know, but you're still welcome to eat. We're having one of your father's favorites. Linguine carbonara with garlic bread. And there's crème brulee for dessert."

My traitorous stomach growled. "That sounds great. I guess a little dish would be okay."

Sin snorted, so I jabbed him lovingly with my

elbow. He held up his hands. "Hey, it does sound good." Then he looked at my mom. "I just hate that we're interrupting your dinner with this."

My mother's gaze rose to meet his. "Sinclair, this issue affects us all. An accusation against you is an accusation against all of us. Jayne has brought you into our life, and through your own actions, you've made yourself a valuable part of it. So long as you two are together, the circle of protection that surrounds this family has officially been extended to include you as well."

He put a hand to his heart. "That's…more than I expected. I'm overwhelmed. Thank you."

"It's just what we do." She moved aside. "Now come in. The food's getting cold. We'll talk while we eat."

We entered and followed her to the dining room. With a few words, she directed the household staff to set two additional places and serve us. In minutes, we were lifting forks filled with creamy pasta goodness.

My dad's plate was almost empty, but he waved away a second helping, a sign he was upset. With a sigh, he leaned back in his chair. "What happened at the square tonight is unacceptable."

I swallowed my mouthful of garlic bread. "I agree. How did two tinkers end up with essentially the same toy? And why on earth would anyone think Sinclair had anything to do with it?"

"I don't know, but I'm putting out a statement in the *Pole Post*'s morning edition. I won't stand for accusations against Sinclair." My father looked at Sin. "We stand with you as a family. I'm sure Klara told you, but I wanted you to hear it from me as well."

"Very kind of you," Sinclair said. "I had no idea my visit would create such chaos for you all. I'm sorry about that."

"It is what it is," my father said. "And there's nothing for you to apologize for. We're going to deal with it. But I'm sorry you've had to experience it. We were hoping your visit here would be one that showed you what a great place the North Pole is to live." He frowned. "Obviously, that's not what's happened this evening."

Sin glanced at me. "No place is perfect. And what happened tonight hasn't ruined my opinion of your beautiful kingdom."

"That's very generous."

Sin twirled his fork in his pasta. "Growing up as a necromancer, I learned to deal with people's predisposed opinions about me. People are scared of death, and that makes it easy to be scared of my kind. Of what we do. Anyone who can control the thing you're most afraid of either earns your respect or your hatred. It's just human nature. And, it seems, elf nature too."

"You have a better handle on this than I do, then." My father shook his head. "As far as the tinker situation goes, my brother-in-law, Kris, and I agree that it feels like much more than a coincidence."

I thought about that. "Do you know both tinkers? Would either of them be the kind of elf to do something underhanded to get ahead?"

He stared at his plate, thinking. "They're both good men. One's only been a tinker for two years. He's eager to prove his worth, but that's natural. The other has been a tinker for nearly fifty years and has been in the competition numerous times."

I leaned in. "That gives both of them motive to tip things in their favor. One to win, one to keep winning."

"I agree," my dad said. "But that also leaves us with a lot of unanswered questions."

I put my fork down. "I can help. In fact, you have to let me."

My father's brows lifted. "I *have* to?"

"Yes. Sin's been accused of being a part of this, which is ridiculous, but I want to prove just how ridiculous by finding out what actually happened. Let me talk to them both. Let me do some digging."

"Jay, I appreciate the offer, but this isn't Nocturne Falls."

"Even more reason I should handle this. *Because* it's the North Pole. The kingdom I will one day rule. If I can't fix this, how am I ever going to take the throne? There will always be a stain on my past. This blemish that I can't erase. And worse, this incident will forever color the way our citizens see Sinclair. Because of that, he has to help me with the investigation."

My father pursed his mouth in objection. "Jay, I don't think that's a good idea."

My mother dropped her napkin onto the table. "I do. I think it's a terrific idea. Jayne is right. Sinclair has to be a part of the solution. He deserves to clear his name of this stupid and irrational accusation."

"Klara, now listen—"

"No, Jack. I'm putting my foot down. How would you feel if someone had accused me of something? You'd be the first to defend me."

He smiled. "I would."

"Then let Jayne do this. And let Sinclair help her. She's already proved how good she is at sorting out such messes in Nocturne Falls. She should be even better at it here."

My father sighed, letting out a little stream of icy vapor that showed how high his emotions were. "Your mother has spoken, Jayne."

"Does that mean I can dig into this? And Sinclair too?" I was happy, but also realized what I had just gotten myself into. If only I could fly Birdie up here.

My father nodded. "I give you royal dispensation to go where you need to go and do what you need to do. Just...be prudent."

I did not jump up and down in my chair, even though I felt like it. Getting this permission had saved me from explaining to my parents I'd told the crowd at the tourney that I was going to handle this. "Of course."

"Your uncle is speaking to both of the men in his office at nine A.M. tomorrow. I'll send him word that you're joining him."

I also did not squeal in excitement. "Thank you."

"Yes," Sinclair added. "Thank you."

My father nodded. "Now let's eat some crème brulee. I am in desperate need of sugar."

I barely slept. Most of the night was spent thinking about what questions I would ask of the two tinkers. I knew those questions would depend on what information they offered. I assumed they'd both have an explanation for how they each ended up with a robotic chicken as their entry.

How similar those explanations were remained to be seen.

Dawn came early, and for that I was glad. I fed Spider, took care of his litter box, then got myself showered and dressed. I hadn't really brought interrogation-appropriate clothing, so I dug around in my closet to see what clothes I had that might work. Very little of my standard North Pole attire had come to Nocturne Falls with me since what I wore in the NP was mostly winter clothes.

The bulk of my Nocturne Falls wardrobe now

leaned heavily in the shorts and flip-flops direction. Gotta love Georgia in the summer.

What had remained in the NP was extensive. I found some navy dress pants and a navy cashmere sweater with ivory trim at the neck and wrists. I added simple pearl earrings and my rainbow obsidian bracelet, which I always wore, plus a pair of charcoal-gray suede low-heeled boots. The look was crisp and classic. Probably not as intimidating as black jeans, black leather jacket and skull earrings, but it would do.

I didn't own skull earrings anyway.

But I did have some other impressive jewelry. More items I hadn't taken to Nocturne Falls, but a few I had borrowed for the Black and Orange Balls. I opened the safe in my closet. The jewels in here were exclusively mine and therefore could be kept in my apartment safe, as opposed to the family vault.

I selected my diamond and sapphire House of Frost broach. It had belonged to my grandmother and her grandmother before her, one of the first Winter Queens to take the throne.

I pinned the intricate snowflake to my shoulder and took a look. It was a not-so-subtle reminder of who I was and the history of my family. Whether or not that would impact the tinkers, I had no idea, but it should.

A knock at my door stopped me just as I was

about to add a touch of perfume. I went to open it, not surprised to see Sin. "Good morning. How did you sleep?"

"Morning, sweetheart. I slept as well as can be expected, I guess." He leaned in and kissed my cheek. "You look nice. Very royal. I like it. Has a don't-mess-with-me-I'm-a-princess vibe."

I laughed. "I'll take that. You look like I was hoping to. Which is to say, appropriately intimidating."

"Yeah?" He spread his arms as he walked in. He was in black slacks, fitted gray sweater and his black leather jacket. A thick silver rope encircled one wrist. He looked like who he was. Someone powerful. And closely connected to death. "Not too much?"

I shook my head. "Nope, it's perfect. You can be bad cop." I squinted at him. He was such a nice guy. I'd seen him angry, but not for a while. "Do you mind being bad cop?"

"Not at all."

"Good. Because it's kind of hot." I winked at him, causing him to smile. "Let me just grab my jacket, and we can go."

He hooked his thumb over his shoulder toward the hall. "Do you want to put Spider in my apartment? I figured he might like to hang with Sugar over there today. Plus, it would be a change of scenery."

"Good idea. Spider, Sinclair is here," I called out. "You want to spend the day with Sugar?"

Spider came running out of the bedroom, meowing all the way, making us both laugh.

I shook my head. "Spider, use your words. It's okay to talk in front of Mr. Sinclair."

He just sat there, staring at me. Stubborn little thing.

"He'll, uh, talk when he's ready, I'm sure," Sin said, giving me that look that said I was adorable even if I really believed my cat could talk.

"He *can* talk."

Sin nodded. "Oh, I know. Totally." He smirked and tipped his head toward the hall. "Come on, Spider. Sugar's waiting on you."

Sin went across the hall to open his door, and Spider darted right in.

With a sigh, I slipped on my leather jacket, which was perfect with this outfit, and we were off to pick up the crawler.

"We're headed to the factory, right? The big Christmas-tree-shaped building?" Sin asked.

"Yes. You actually need clearance for that, but we have it thanks to the badges my uncle messengered over." I pulled them from my jacket pocket and handed Sin his.

Sin's face was incredulous as he looked it over. "You need a badge to get into your uncle's toy factory?"

"No, well, parts of it. These give us full access."

"I had no idea it was such a secure place." He tucked the badge in his pocket. "Is there a reason for that?"

"There is. Years ago, an elf went rogue and tried to sell some toy ideas to a human manufacturer. It didn't go well for him, but the upside was our security improved."

He nodded, then went silent a moment. "Anything new about last night?"

"You know, the *Pole Post* wasn't delivered to my apartment this morning. So I'd say yes, there's a story. And it's one Gregory, or someone, thought I shouldn't see. Probably Gregory." I exhaled, a little cranky at that realization. "I appreciate him looking out for me, but I need to know what's happening."

"Should we go back?"

"No. We're already here, and the transportation office will have one."

Sin held the door for me, and out we went. I marched past the approaching valet and right over to his booth. I could see a copy of the paper on the seat he'd vacated. I reached through the window and grabbed it.

When I flipped it over, I immediately saw why Gregory had kept it from me. The morning's headline read, *King Defends Death's Presence*. The nerve of them putting that headline on my father's statement. Sin wasn't Death. There were a few smaller headlines like, *Will Death Rule Us?* and *Tinkers' Tourney Tainted By Dark Magic.*

Red edged my vision. This negativity was so unlike what I was used to. Had things changed so much in the time I'd been gone? "What a load of garbage. Unsubstantiated, lying, foul garbage. How dare they?"

Sin looked over my shoulder. "Seems about right based on the reaction last night."

"No, it doesn't. Not to me. You might be used to this, but I'm not."

"Does the paper normally give the royals a kid-glove treatment? Because most papers like to sensationalize the news. Sells better. Sad, but just how it is."

"The paper doesn't necessarily provide a lovefest for everything the royals do, but this is uncalled for." I tossed the paper back into the valet booth and addressed the young man trying to hand me the crawler keys. "Send a message to Gregory that I expect a copy of the *Post* in my apartment when I return. Today's copy."

The young man nodded. "Yes, Your Highness."

"Good." I took the keys and headed for the crawler with Sin at my side. My mind was spinning with one thought after another. "You know what I think we should do? If you're up to it, that is."

"What?" Sin asked.

"Give the *Post* an interview. After I give them a piece of my mind, naturally. But let them see for themselves what a wonderful, non-scary guy you are. What do you think?"

"I'll do it. I should change first. Be less bad cop, more good boyfriend."

I smiled as much as I could manage. "Perfect. I'll have Ezreal set it up when we get back."

"You think they'll go for it? And if they do, what's to keep them from putting their own spin on my answers?"

"They'll go for it. They can't say no to a royal request. And they'd better not spin the answers if they want to stay in business."

"You mean your father could shut them down?"

"He could take away their funding. The paper isn't privately owned."

We got into the crawler. I was driving today since Sin had only been close to the factory, not actually to it. Not that it was so hard to find. You could see the building from just about every spot in town, because it rose above everything.

I slammed my door without meaning to. "Sorry. I'm a little wound up."

Sin winked at me. "You have every right to be."

"You bet your snowballs I do." The crawler engine was already on, so I pushed my foot down and took off. I drove too fast, but it felt good. And got us there in record time.

The guard at the factory gate greeted me with a kind smile. "Morning, Your Highness."

We showed him our badges. "Good morning."

He started toward the guard shack to lift the gate, then hesitated. "Just want to say I don't believe nothing the *Post* is saying." He leaned down to see Sinclair better. "Me and the missus think it's great you and the princess are in love."

Sinclair gave the man a nod. "Thank you. That's nice of you to say."

I looked at the man's name tag. "Yes, Mr. Bunting. It's very nice. And the support is appreciated. Thank you."

He pushed the button to lift the gate, smiling. "You two have a good day now."

"Same to you." I drove through and took a breath. "That was brave of him to say. And kind. Proves that not everyone is against us."

Sin reached over and took my hand. "It *was* nice to hear. Just like that man who spoke out for you in the crowd last night."

"Yes." I parked in the private lot next to my uncle's cherry-red crawler and we got out. "You'll need your badge for this entrance too."

"Okay." Sin fished his from his pocket as we walked in.

There was a small steel and glass foyer inside, but the metal door that led to the rest of the building was locked. A guard sat inside a control booth behind a sliding glass window that was currently open. He stood as soon as I entered. "Good morning, Princess Jayne."

"Good morning. We're here to see my uncle." I showed my badge to the guard, then Sin did the same.

The guard nodded. "Of course." He hit a button on the desk, a small chime sounded, and the door blocking our entrance slid out of the way. The hall before us was as simple and austere as the foyer, but that décor would change soon enough as we got deeper into the building.

"Thank you." I took Sin's hand as I went through, wanting to feel his strong grip. It was reassuring. Not that I was in any particular need of reassurance. But it was nice.

"I know you said security was increased a while back, but this place still has better security than I imagined it would. And yet..." Sin glanced around as we came to the elevators.

I pushed the up button. I couldn't wait to see what Sin thought of the ride to the top. "And yet what?"

"None of the guards carry weapons of any kind."

I laughed. "They don't need to. They can freeze you solid with a flick of their magic."

He chuckled. "Yeah, that would do it. I forget winter elves can do that sometimes."

The elevator doors slid open, revealing the plush interior that hinted at what was to come.

Sin ran his hand along the tufted burgundy velvet walls as we got on. "This is more like what I thought this place would look like."

The gold trim and dark wood panels added to the luxurious feel. I tapped the S button. "The parking lot entrance is the only one that's sort of plain. You'll see."

"Oh?" He was still checking out the elevator. "I like the big mirror."

"It's not a mirror. Not really." The doors shut, and we lifted. I tipped my head toward the back wall of glass. "Watch."

He did just as the elevator rose out of its metal base and opened up to a view of the first level of the factory floor. Thousands of elves toiled away at worktables, creating the toys that children around the world would find under their Christmas trees. The speed and efficiency with which they worked filled the air with the shimmer of magic.

Sin's mouth came open, his eyes widened, and he leaned in, fingertips on the railing in front of the glass. He breathed out a soft sound of wonderment.

The view improved as we rose, allowing even more levels to be seen. On each one, different toys were being made. Dolls on one. Wheeled vehicles on another. Blocks and connecting toys on a third.

Higher and higher we rose. Sin continued to be captivated. "Are they…singing?"

"Yes. We do that while we work."

"I thought that was just a myth."

"Nope. Helps the time pass and keeps the mood light. It's fun."

He snorted. "Sure, if you can sing."

"All elves can sing. Some better than others, but all reasonably well." I squinted at him when he looked at me. "What? It's one of our things. I'm sure there's a trait all necromancers have."

He blinked twice, then shook his head. "Not that I can think of."

I pointed at the window again. "You're missing it."

As we ascended farther, the slides started. It was one of the most common ways to go from floor to floor. Elevator up, slide down. Unless you were carrying a lot of stuff, traveling down a *lot* of floors, or my uncle. He had his own private elevator that allowed him to move quickly to wherever he needed to go in the factory.

Also, he'd gotten stuck on a slide once. That was the end of that.

Sin laughed. "Okay, I have to do that. Can we? Or is that an elves-only thing?"

"We can do it. Later, though. When we're done with the interrogation."

"Sure." He went back to watching the factory.

"This place just keeps getting better."

I smiled, my heart light with those words.

Finally, the elevator stopped at the top floor. The Santa floor.

The doors opened and out we went. Mamie, my uncle's receptionist and secretary, wasn't at her desk, but the door to his office was open, and I could see there was already a crowd in there.

"C'mon," I said to Sin as I started forward. "Might as well join the fray."

My uncle stood by a big worktable with several other elves, builders and confectioners, by the looks of them. They were all going over some papers that were spread out. He glanced up at the sound of my voice. "Jayne! And Sinclair! Welcome to the factory."

"Thank you," Sinclair said. His face still held the look of wonderment it had in the elevator.

Thankfully, no one in the group seemed to care that Sinclair was who he was. Or if they did, they were smart enough not to show it in front of my uncle.

I walked around the desk and gave my uncle a hug. "Hi, Uncle Kris. I hope we're not interrupting. This looks important."

He looked at me over his wire-rimmed glasses and tapped the papers. "These are the blueprints for the new confectionary. We're taking your aunt Martha's eggnog fudge international, and once the website launches, we're going to ship worldwide."

"That's awesome. But how are you going to get a website to work up here?"

He grinned and pointed at one of the elves, a young man with bright green eyes and a shock of reddish-purple hair. "Meet Ingvar. He's our new IC guy."

Ingvar worked hard not to smile. "IT. I'm the new tech guy."

I stuck my hand out. "Nice to meet you, Ingvar. I have to ask. How are you going to get all of that stuff to work up here? IT has never done that well up here."

He sank into himself a little, like the sudden attention was overwhelming. "Mostly landlines, some heavy insulating, and a strong dose of magic. The electromagnetics here are not conducive to good connections, as you know, but my team has been working on it, and I believe we've come up with a solution."

"Excellent." I looked at my uncle again. "Finally joining the rest of the world, are we? I like it."

"Your aunt told me if she couldn't get better access to something called Pintermost—"

"I think you mean Pinterest."

He waved a hand. "Whatever it is. She likes it and it's only on the interweb, apparently."

I rolled my lips in to keep from laughing outright. "Well, good for you for making her happy."

He sighed. "It's easier." He went back to the plans and the elves in front of him. "Expand that office, add a third-floor breakroom, and let's break ground."

"You got it, Santa." The elf in charge rolled up the plans, tucked them under his arm, then directed his crew to the elevator.

Ingvar gave a little wave as he left. I waved back, then turned to my uncle. "All right. We're ready to interrogate."

He looked at his pocket watch. "Your timing is perfect. The tinkers should be waiting."

"Lead the way."

Uncle Kris straightened. "They're in the mezzanine focus group rooms. At least, they should be. Let me check." He went to his desk and pushed a button on the intercom. "Mamie, are you here?"

Mamie's voice came crackling back at him. She was eighty-five if she was a day, but winter elves who never left the North Pole tended to age very slowly. Spry was Mamie's middle name. (Actually, I think it was Belle, but you get my drift.) She had been my uncle's secretary since before I was born, but her real claim to notoriety was that she'd been married seven times. Or eight. Hard to keep track. "Yes, sir, I'm here."

"Good, good. Have the tinkers arrived?"

"I just checked them in."

"We'll be down. Go on ahead and meet us there."

"Yes, sir."

He held up a finger to Sin and me. "Just a moment. I would prefer if you let me speak to them first. You can watch and listen, but I need to talk to them first. See what I can get out of them. Mamie will record it all for reference."

"Of course," I said. "Going to use some of that Kringle intimidation?"

"Possibly." He sighed. "I'm hoping I won't have to."

Sin's brows rose, and his expression turned skeptical. "You seem too nice to be intimidating. Which I mean as a compliment."

Uncle Kris put his hands on his belly and laughed. "I understand. But there's more to me than just being a jolly old elf, I promise."

Sin held his hands up. "I believe you. No one builds an empire like this without being able to bring the hammer down on occasion."

Uncle Kris tapped the side of his nose. "Exactly, my boy, exactly."

We followed him to his personal elevator. He pushed the call button, and the doors opened immediately. This car went wherever he wanted. We got on, then he pushed M and down we went.

He crossed his arms over his belly. "I called Constable Larsen. I figured we ought to have her on hand, just in case one of the tinkers confesses."

Sin spoke right up. "You think that's a possibility?"

"I think anything is possible, but I don't really expect a confession. Having the constable there will add an extra layer of officialness to the proceedings. Her presence will also prevent any future questions about how things were done. Not that I expect that sort of thing, but one can't be too careful. We've never had anything like this happen before."

The elevator came to a stop, and the doors opened, but my uncle made no move to get out. "Both of these tinkers are good men with bright minds and strong work ethics. They wouldn't be tinkers otherwise. But something isn't right." He sighed as if a great weight pressed down on him. "I don't want either of them to be guilty of cheating, but we have to get to the bottom of this."

I put my hand on his arm. "We will. And who knows? Maybe it really is just the biggest coincidence ever."

Uncle Kris smiled weakly. "It's not, Jayne. We both know that."

I returned the weak smile and added a limp shrug. "I know."

Pain etched his gaze, and I hurt for him. He was, after all, the most famous tinker who worked here. I knew how deeply this had to cut him. Beyond any other kind of elf who inhabited the NP, the tinkers were his people.

Proving Sin was not to blame was big. But putting the smile back on my uncle's face was also important. Christmas was coming. Santa had to be happy.

He headed toward the focus group rooms, and we followed behind. Sin shot me a concerned look and tipped his head at my uncle like he was asking if Uncle Kris was okay.

I shook my head. He wasn't. And he wouldn't be until this was fixed.

Constable Larsen met us in the focus group area. The rooms were mostly used with kids to test out prototype toys, so while the bright colors worked in that regard, it made for an odd place to question the tinkers about possible cheating.

Larsen had her thumbs hooked in her uniform belt. She looked good in the dark gray outfit. Better than her predecessor, Constable Ray. He'd gotten quite the paunch over the years and had started to look more like a snowman than an officer of the law. Not all elves had the metabolism of a hummingbird. My uncle was proof of that.

Ray had lost interest in the job too. He'd been successfully encouraged to take an earlier retirement. Something that hadn't actually taken a lot of encouragement.

Larsen, on the other hand, was three years into the job and still very eager. She'd been on the force for nearly eighteen years, so she wasn't a rookie by any means. Very by-the-book and on top of it. I was glad to see her. I had a feeling she'd be all over this investigation considering how little actual crime happened in the NP.

"Constable Larsen, nice to see you. This is my boyfriend, Sinclair Crowe."

He put his hand out. "Constable."

She gave him a quick once-over as she took his hand. "Sinclair. I've heard about you. Pleasure to meet you."

"I'm sure everyone has heard about me by now. I promise, I'm not bad magic. Nice to meet you too."

Her expression remained the same. Mostly neutral, but with a hint of cynicism. "Everyone's innocent until proven otherwise." She squinted at Sin a little. Like she was reevaluating her first impression. Or something. "But I'm sure Princess Frost wouldn't associate with anyone whose character was less than exemplary. You're not high on my suspect list."

I stared at her. "I wasn't aware there was a suspect list. Other than the two tinkers."

"Always be prepared," she said. "That's my motto."

I had always liked Constable Larsen, but she was starting to rub me the wrong way. I knew it was because of her crack about Sin and the suspect list, but really, how had she expected me to react to that? "That's the Boy Scout motto, actually."

My uncle cleared his throat. "Mamie should be here..."

"Right here, boss." She walked out of the first observation room, her standard narrow skirt and sweater set in a monotone rose pink. A slim strand of North Pole crystal beads, a gift from Uncle Kris on her fiftieth anniversary of employment, sparkled at her throat.

"Good, good." My uncle rubbed his hands together. "I'm going in to speak to the tinkers, one at a time. Mamie will go in with me to take notes. You three can watch from the observation room, and then we can discuss going in to talk to them further."

"I've already taken their statements," Larsen said.

Uncle Kris stared at her, the reddening of his cheeks a sign of his unhappiness. "I left specific instructions that no one was to talk to them until I did."

Larsen stared back, unapologetic. "This is a serious matter. I deemed it in the best interests of justice to take official statements before anything happened that might color their memories of the incident."

Uncle Kris's cheeks now bore two spots of bright apple red. "Color their memories? I wasn't going to feed them stories to tell you. My plan was to get their side of things without any interference."

Larsen nodded. "And I did that. I'll have the reports typed up and messaged over to you as soon as they're done."

Uncle Kris leaned in and, in a very controlled voice, simply said, "You are on the naughty list."

Mamie's brows shot up as her mouth puckered.

Larsen went very, very pale. "Sir, I didn't mean—"

"You knew what I wanted to be done, and you did what you wanted instead. I do not appreciate that. I expect those reports immediately. You're dismissed."

The muscles in her jaw twitched, and you could almost hear her teeth grinding. She wasn't happy, but she knew when to keep her mouth shut. With a nod and a glance at us, she left.

Mamie cleared her throat, her steno pad and pen in hand. She took a long look at the three of us. "I guess we should get on with it."

I lifted my index finger and shot her a quick "hang on" look. My uncle's temper wasn't something to be trifled with, but I felt I had to say something. Plus, I had more leeway there than most. "Um, Uncle Kris? Do you really think you should have done that? Sure, she went against your orders, but I mean, she is the law around here. I don't think we should make an enemy of her, you know?"

His stern expression held on for a second longer, then suddenly melted away as he sighed. "She made me angry. But you're right." He turned toward Mamie. "Send Constable Larsen a pound of chocolate mint fudge and a note telling her I spoke in haste, and I apologize. She's not off the hook, but I won't put her on the naughty list."

Mamie's sharply arched brows stayed skyward as she scribbled in her steno pad. "Consider it done."

"Mamie, this is my boyfriend, Sinclair Crowe. Sinclair, this is Mamie Wynters, my uncle's secretary and the woman who helps keep this factory running."

Mamie smiled and offered her hand. "Pleasure to meet you, Mr. Crowe."

"Likewise." He shook her delicate little hand.

Uncle Kris settled his hands on his hips. "Mamie's more than my secretary." He nodded at her. "I couldn't get on without her. Now, she and I should head in and see what these tinkers have to say for themselves."

She tapped her pen against her steno pad. "Ready when you are, sir."

"Jayne, take Sinclair into observation room one. We'll start with..." He looked at Mamie. "Which one is in that room?"

"Terrance Whitley. He's the young man who presented Mega Chick."

"Very good. We'll start there." He nodded at me. "Go on."

I gave him the thumbs-up. "See you in a few."

I grabbed Sinclair's hand and led him to the observation room, flicking the lights on as we went in. "They can't see or hear us in here."

He glanced up. "Is that why the lights are low?"

"Yes. Helps keep shadows off the one-way glass." I took a seat in one of the big comfortable chairs positioned toward the mirrored wall, but Sin stood there, looking through to the focus group room.

On the other side of the mirror, Terrance Whitley sat in a gray metal chair at a small folding table, both of which had been brought in for the questioning. The table was one of those with the metal legs and fake wood top. A second metal chair was tucked under the table. In the bright yellow room with red and blue stuffed ottomans, the setup was glaringly out of place.

"He looks nervous. And a little afraid," Sin said.

"Understandable. He hasn't been a tinker long, and this great opportunity has suddenly turned into a big mess. I'm sure he's freaked out."

"Or guilty," Sin said. He glanced back at me. "Not saying he is, but it's a possibility." He came over and sat next to me.

"He could be."

My uncle walked in with Mamie behind him, and Terrance went rigid. "Mr. Kringle, sir, I just want you to know that I'm very sorry about what happened, but Mega Chick was my idea. I s-swear."

Mamie sat on a bright blue stuffed ottoman by the door, but Uncle Kris took the other folding chair at the table. He nodded thoughtfully. "I appreciate you coming in today."

I snorted. "Like he had a choice."

"He could have run," Sin said.

"Into the forest with the yetis? I don't think so."

Uncle Kris folded his hands on the table. "I know you've given your statement to the constable, but I'd like to hear it from you. Why don't you tell me about your inspiration for the toy? How did you come up with the idea?"

Mamie had her steno pad and pen poised.

Terrance took a breath and hesitated. Probably gathering his thoughts.

"In your own time," my uncle said.

Terrance exhaled and began. "It was just something that came to me, really. I've always liked chickens."

"Why is that?"

"My mother is a baker, and when I was little, the egg man invited us out to see his farm. My mother thought it would be a good idea, so we went. When we got there, the peeps had just hatched. They were so cute. All yellow and fuzzy. And the mother hens were so smart, the way they took care of their broods. I guess I was at an impressionable age, and those chickens made a lasting impression."

"Have you designed chicken toys before?"

Terrance shook his head. "No, but I did make a wind-up penguin two years ago. Thought I might make it into the Tinkers' Tourney with that, but I realize now it was too simple. Cute, but wind-up toys are pretty common."

"So a robot chicken was the next step?"

Terrance blinked a few times. "I had a dream about a giant chicken that came to the North Pole. It wasn't like one of those monster movies or anything. It was a nice chicken. It laid eggs filled with candy. I'm sure that was part of my inspiration."

"When did you have this dream?"

He chewed at the inside of his cheek. "I could check my notes—I journal everything. Probably right after the last Tinkers' Tourney? I've been working on Mega Chick for nearly twelve months, so that seems about right."

Uncle Kris glanced toward us. I wasn't sure if he was trying to say he believed Terrance or not. Then he focused on the tinker again. "Is there anything else you can tell me that might help us sort this incident out?"

Terrance swallowed. "Just that I swear I would never do anything to cause a problem like this. As much as I would love to win the tourney and see my toy produced, I would never resort to cheating. I have many years of tinkering ahead of me. I hope, anyway. And that means many opportunities to get into the tourney again."

"True," my uncle said. "We'll need you for a few more moments. I'll send someone in to dismiss you when we're through."

"Yes, sir." Terrance went back to looking miserable as my uncle got up and left with Mamie.

The door to the observation room opened, and they walked in.

"What do you think?" my uncle asked.

I sighed. "He seems sincere. I guess it's plausible that he could have had a dream about a giant chicken."

Uncle Kris looked at Sinclair. "What do you think, son?"

"He seems sincere to me too. Totally freaked out and scared, but honest."

Uncle Kris nodded. "I think so too. I guess we'd best go see what Stanley Kinder has to say."

There wasn't much else we could do at the moment. "And if we don't learn anything new from him?"

Uncle Kris sighed heavily. "Then I'm going to have to turn this investigation over to Constable Larsen."

I frowned. "I understand, but I can't see her letting me and Sin help."

"I don't suppose she will since that's not procedure." His eyes narrowed. "But I know you pretty well, Jay, and I don't think you'd let a little thing like lack of permission get in your way."

I snorted. "Yeah, but still. She's the law."

He shook his head. "And you are the Winter Princess. Heir to the throne. With your title comes the unique ability to accomplish things others can't. Investigate. Dig. See what you can uncover. No one, and I mean no one, is going to stop you."

At the table on the other side of the observation room glass, Stanley Kinder sat with a resigned gaze, a relaxed posture, and his hands resting lightly on the table's surface. Okay, he was frowning a bit, too, but mostly he seemed calm. And why shouldn't he, considering everything I knew about him?

He'd been a tinker for a *long* time. He was trustworthy. A hard worker. A perennial producer of solid toys. He'd won numerous awards for his excellence, and innovation, and had twice created the toy of the year. The Pocket Pets that we'd sold out of last Christmas? Those were a Kinder Creation.

I know you've seen that brand. Or at least you've heard of it. That was one of the awards bestowed on him by my uncle—having his own label. He was one of three tinkers who'd earned that distinction in the last decade.

Stanley Kinder was not a cheater. He had no reason to be. He was already golden.

So yes, I was going into this interrogation with some bias. I didn't dislike Terrance, but Stanley just seemed like the most improbable candidate of the two to be involved in something shady.

As Sin and I once again settled in to watch from the observation room, I couldn't keep my opinion to myself. "There's no way Stanley is guilty."

"No way? He does look sure of himself. A little nervous maybe. No, stressed is probably a better description. And who wouldn't be? But he's not on the verge of losing it like Terrance was." Sin shot me a curious glance. "Is that why you're so convinced?"

"That and because I know him. Everybody does. He's one of the old-school tinkers, been here a long time, won a lot of awards, and is already known for his skills. His reputation speaks for itself. He doesn't need to prove anything."

"Even against a young up and comer like Terrance? Are you sure?"

"Yes." Then I thought about that. "Well, I was sure until you put it that way. But I just can't believe Stanley has it in him to do anything so sneaky as to steal Terrance's idea. Or anyone's idea. Besides, Stanley has to be getting close to retirement. Why would he do something to jeopardize that?"

"Maybe he was looking to pad his nest egg. No

pun intended. But I see what you're saying." Sin seemed to ponder it all a bit more. "When did Stanley last have a big win?"

"Last Christmas, actually. He came up with Pocket Pets, which were huge. We couldn't keep them on the shelves."

Sin nodded. "I think I bought some of those for my nieces." He glanced through the glass at Stanley. "A plush robot chicken isn't really that far away from the Pocket Pets, is it? They're still animals."

"Not so different in the world of toys, no. But that could go either way. It's either a great way to explain Mrs. Clucks-A-Lot as his new idea or a great way of covering up stealing the idea by saying it was the next logical step." I slipped down in my seat, feeling perturbed.

I'd been so sure Stanley was the innocent in all this, and now I was doubting that assumption. And I hated that. I didn't want either of the tinkers to be guilty of anything, but how else was a coincidence like this possible?

And until we proved what had actually happened, we had no definitive proof to offer the citizenship that Sinclair was not bad juju.

My uncle and Mamie entered the focus group room, and just like before, Uncle Kris sat at the table while Mamie stayed in the background to take her notes.

Sin and I leaned in, as if that was going to make a difference in what we heard.

Stanley nodded at my uncle. "Kris. How are you?"

My uncle chuckled softly. "I should be asking you that."

Stanley shrugged. "I've had worse days. Not many, but a few. This will all be cleared up soon, I'm sure. What can I tell you to make your job easier?"

That was Stanley. A giver. A true tinker's heart to ease the minds and moods of those around him.

My uncle let out a long breath. "Tell me about your toy. How you came up with it. What your inspiration was. Anything that might explain how it came to be."

Stanley took his glasses off, pulled a cloth from his vest pocket and began to polish the lenses. "Last year, I had Pocket Pets."

Sin gave me a little nudge as if to say we'd guessed what his explanation would be.

"Of course," my uncle said. "One of our best launches ever."

"Yes, a big toy. Hard to top. But I wanted to. It was a challenge. I started right after the New Year. I thought and thought and thought about how to make a toy that was even better." He folded the polishing cloth into a neat square before returning it to his vest pocket. "For a long time, I came up with nothing."

My uncle listened intently as Stanley continued.

"A few months go by. Spring comes. Still no good ideas. Just lots of frustration." He put his glasses back on and smiled. "Then my granddaughter, Lyla, she says to me, Grandpa, why can't Easter be every day? I wish I had a rabbit that laid magic eggs whenever I wanted."

Uncle Kris smiled. He loved children, obviously, but making their dreams come true was his life's work.

Stanley laughed, his gaze far away in the memory for a moment. "So what does any good grandfather do? I set to work on that very thing."

He leaned in, suddenly very amused by something. He held his thumb and forefinger up, pinched together but not quite touching. "I was this close to having a working prototype, and you know what she says to me? Grandpa, our class went to the farm today. Rabbits don't lay eggs, but chickens do. And I met the most beautiful chicken in the world. She has fluffy white feathers and can count to ten by pecking her beak on the ground."

He sat back, arms wide. "This chicken was all Lyla talked about. So for her, I changed the rabbit to a hen. A fluffy white hen who knows her numbers and lays magic eggs." He sighed and shook his head. "And then Terrance steals my idea."

My uncle stiffened, and all traces of amusement vanished off his face. "You know that for sure? That he stole your idea?"

Stanley shrugged. "How else would he come up with that thing? It's so much like mine. Could it be a coincidence? I guess. But I don't think so."

My uncle sat back. "Did he ever come to your workshop? Was there ever a time he would have been alone with your plans? Or had an opportunity to see what you were working on? Maybe caught a glimpse of something through the door as you were both locking up for the night?"

Stanley's eyes narrowed in thought. "Not that I recall. And our workshops are on opposite sides of the lab floor. I see him on the elevator headed to lunch sometimes, but not much more than that. Although I suppose if he was going to do something like steal an idea, he'd do it on the sly. Wouldn't he?"

"I suppose he would. But maybe he was in your workshop for another reason and just happened to see your plans?"

I leaned toward Sin. "It's not unusual for younger tinkers to be mentored by the more experienced, or even just to spend some time with them learning new techniques."

Sin tilted his head toward me. "So it wouldn't be out of place for one tinker to be in another's work space?"

"Not if they were invited. But the toy competition is sort of a sacred thing. It's a given that the secrecy around a tinker's new toy is respected."

"Interesting. Would there be any security footage to review? To check if Terrance did get into Stanley's shop?"

I shot him a look. "In the North Pole? No."

He grinned like he'd already known the answer to that question. "Didn't hurt to ask." He sighed and looked forward again. "We have nothing to go on. No real proof of Terrance doing anything. So we're back to this being a coincidence. Not that I think it is."

"There's always room for some investigating."

Sin glanced at me. "What are you suggesting?"

What was I suggesting? I said the first thing that came to mind because it seemed like the logical place to start. "We go visit both their work spaces. The lab floor. Now. While they're here."

"Do we have permission to do that? Don't we need a search warrant or something?"

I shook my head. "Master tinkers are given a private work space here in the factory, and that is truly where the bulk of their work is done. And while it's their private space, it's also company property."

"They don't work at home?"

"They can work on personal things at home, but anything meant for production is generally produced here on factory grounds. There's some special exceptions granted, but most don't like to take work back and forth from home anyway. Toys in the prototype stage can be fragile. And moving a toy can mean letting people see it before it's ready."

He put his hands on the arms of the chair. "Let's go, then."

I got up. "Let me tell my uncle where we're going. He can give me their work space numbers. Then we're off."

A few minutes later, we were back in the elevator headed to the penultimate floor. The tinkers' work space was one floor below my uncle's penthouse office. It was also restricted space, but Uncle Kris had assured me our all-access badges would get us in.

He was right. Swiping our badges through the card reader lit up the button for the lab floor. I'd never been able to push that button before, even though I'd tried a few times when I was younger. I might have been able to get under the door with my Santa Slide ability, but Uncle Kris had told me the doors were proofed against that.

Pretty sure now he'd been making that up, but I hadn't wanted to test it then, or now.

"Wow, this is cool." Sin looked around as we stepped out of the elevator. "And very, very quiet."

The space had been a collaboration between the builders and the tinkers. Rivets trimmed the doors, and on each one, backlit glass plates held a perfectly etched number. Well below the number plate was a wide mail slot with a hinged cover.

The walls were brushed bronze with leather panels, and thick ivory wool carpeted each hall floor, absorbing footsteps. Edison bulbs dotted the ceiling, while color-changing LEDs along the baseboards washed the walkways in color. The space managed to mix old-world charm with modern tech in a way that worked remarkably well. It looked like the kind of place where amazing inventions came to life.

"It is cool. And the quiet is on purpose." I took a good look around myself. "I've only been here a few times in my life with my dad and uncle. Never by myself, though. I've never had clearance before."

Sin seemed taken back by that. "Really?"

I nodded. "The tinkers' work space is a safe, sacred area. They are never disturbed while they're here. Not even the cleaning crew has access."

"Maintenance?"

"If there's an issue, it gets called in, then a special work order is granted."

Sin's eyes widened a little. "I feel odd being here now."

"It's okay. We're not going anywhere but to Terrance's and Stanley's labs. And for good reason."

He nodded. "How many tinkers have labs here?"

"I believe there are seventy-five in total, but only about seventy have been allotted."

"Still a lot."

"Fortunately, we only need two. Three and sixty-seven."

Sin's gaze narrowed. "Terrance's is sixty-seven, isn't it?"

"Yes. How did you guess that?"

"Stanley's been around longer. I'd assumed that means he'd have a lower number. One of the earlier ones assigned."

"You're right. And we have a little walking to do." I pointed down the hall as we moved forward. "Interestingly, the spaces can be passed down from one tinker to another in a family so long as that tinker is a registered master. Stanley's mother gave him his."

Sin made a little noise of appreciation. "Are there a lot of women tinkers?"

"A good number."

"Do tinkers ever share spaces?"

"Sometimes. Again, that really only happens in families." I gestured to the door ahead of us. "Sixty-seven. Terrance's space."

I slid my badge through the reader, and the lock clicked open.

Sin put his hand on the knob to open the door, then hesitated. "You're sure this is all right?"

"Yes. We're looking for evidence to clear your name and figure out how this coincidence happened. Or if it even is a coincidence. I don't see what other choice we have with no new info from the tinkers."

"I know. You're right. It just seems like, I don't know, we ought to have the constable here."

I hesitated. "We could reach out to her. But I'm not sure if she'd even respond to us today. And if we wait too long, any evidence that's in here could get disposed of."

"Good point. Let's do this." He pushed the door open, and in we went.

Terrance's space was clean and well organized. Drawers and cabinets were labeled, tools were hung on a peg board and outlined so that there was no question as to what went where. Bins filled with parts and materials were spaced evenly on the shelves. Even the project on the large worktable, a truck of some kind, was laid out in a tidy manner. The trash bin was empty, and a white smock hung on a peg next to the door.

Sin looked around. "He likes things a certain way."

"I'd say. But a lot of tinkers are like that." I went for the large wall cabinet. "Let's see what's in here."

"I'll check out some of these journals, since he mentioned them."

"Sounds good." I opened the doors. The top half of the cabinet was shelves. The bottom half had three filing drawers side by side by side. The labels on the drawers were Current Projects, Completed Projects, and Future Ideas.

I went for Completed Projects, hoping to find a history on his Mega Chick. Didn't take long. It was in the first file, but I only figured out it was for Mega Chick when I thumbed through the papers inside. The file was named Eggcellent Idea. "Cute."

"What's that?" Sin asked. He looked up from a notebook on the worktable, keeping his finger on the spot he'd been reading.

"Terrance called Mega Chick an Eggcellent Idea on the file. I didn't peg him as the punny type." I held it up for Sin to see. "But the plans are all here. And dated back to..." I shuffled through the paperwork. "April seems to be the first time the chicken was really a chicken. Before then, I think it was more of an actual robot."

"Like C-3PO?"

"Is that the tall gold one from *Star Wars*?"

"Yes." Sin snorted. "Have you really not watched *Star Wars*?"

"Eh. Space shmace. I like romcoms better. And no, not a robot like that. More like the laundry hamper on wheels one." I turned the file around so he could see the drawing.

Sin rolled his eyes and chuckled. "That would be R2-D2." He walked over to inspect the sketch. "Why the change from this basic design to the chicken? All because of that dream?"

"If we believe him, then yes."

"But it's not provable. The dream, I mean."

"What are you thinking? That it's just an excuse to cover his change in ideas? Sure is convenient, isn't it?"

Sin nodded. "Very."

"April would also be about the same time Stanley said he went from a rabbit to a chicken."

"Which only makes Terrance's change seem more suspect. To me, anyway."

"No, I agree. The timing is so close. We need to look at Stanley's work space. Make sure there's something to back up his claims as well. But first…" I reached for my phone, then remembered I didn't have it on me. Not much point in carrying one in the NP, so I generally didn't. "Snowballs."

"What?"

"I don't have my phone and I want to take some pics of these notes. Do you have yours?"

"I do." He produced it from his inside jacket pocket and handed it over. "I know I can't make calls up here, but it's a habit."

"I'm glad. I should start carrying mine. Especially if Ingvar gets the web working up here. Anyway, I should still keep it on me. Never know when you might want to document something. Although, technically, no photos are allowed on this floor. But this is a special case, so I think we're good." I snapped a bunch of pictures of the files, then gave the phone back and returned the file to the drawer. "All right. Let's see what Stanley's been up to."

We locked up and went to Stanley's lab.

The difference between his space and Terrance's was as easy to see as the stack of papers threatening to topple off the workbench.

Almost every inch of the space was covered. Sketches tacked up, tools scattered about, materials heaped in bins and piled in corners, papers stuffed in every nook and cranny... It was a chaotic, but energetic mess. There were also jars of candy here and there. *Many* jars. This was my kind of work space.

"Now this looks like the shop of an inventor," Sin said. He ran his finger over one shelf and came away with a little smudge of dust. "You said the cleaning crew doesn't have access, so I imagine tinkers are responsible for their own housekeeping?"

"Yes. But keep in mind that Stanley and his family have occupied this particular work space for over a century. There's bound to be a little buildup here and there."

Sin wiped his hands off. "You really don't want Stanley to be guilty, do you?"

"I don't want either of them to be guilty." I sighed. "I don't want to be biased toward either of them either, but that's not working so well, is it?"

"The way you feel is understandable."

"But not fair. You have to keep me fair. Keep this investigation fair."

"I'll do my best."

I smiled at him. "Thanks." I tipped my chin toward the shelves of bound journals. None of which were labeled. Nothing was labeled in here. Well, not much. A couple of the glass jars of candy were labeled Candy, which seemed unnecessary to me since they were *glass* jars. "You want to skim through those journals while I poke around in the cabinets over here?"

"Will do. I'll start with the ones that look the newest."

"Cool."

We dug in. And I do mean dug in. If Stanley had a method for organizing his stuff, it wasn't evident. The filing system seemed to operate in such a way that the newest stuff was up front. That was about all I could figure so far.

"This might be something."

I turned. Sin had one of the journals open on the worktable. It was propped on a box of Pocket Pets and a leather pouch of tools. He pointed at the page in front of him. "Robo Rabbit. Right there. But nothing else that shows the bunny becoming a chicken."

I came over to look at the page, then turned to see what was on the next one. More drawings of the rabbit, and a few for a carrot that doubled as a remote control. "I really like this rabbit. I think it's cuter than the chicken. And seems to be more fully thought out."

"If he really changed midstream to accommodate his granddaughter, then this all makes sense."

"Except we haven't found anything chicken related yet."

Sin looked around. "I'm sure it's in here. But finding it might take some doing. There is stuff everywhere. Guess we'd better get back to it."

"Yep." I pushed my sleeves up. Cashmere seemed like a bad choice now, especially since we hadn't even gotten a chance to talk to Terrance or Stanley.

Ten minutes later and I hadn't found anything else in the filing cabinets that was remotely related to the rabbit or the chicken.

"Hey," Sin said. "Is this anything? Or just a fancy cigar box?"

I looked over my shoulder. He was holding up a red velvet box with a brass lock on the front. The fabric was a little worn on the corners, and the lock showed tarnish in the crevices. I might not have access to this floor as a rule, but I knew what that was. "That's the tinker version of an interoffice memo."

"Meaning?"

"Tinkers use those boxes to send things back and forth to each other."

He shook the box. "Can't tell if there's anything in here. Should we open it? What if Stanley and Terrance were using this as a way of talking to each other?"

"Could be. We should open it." I glanced around. "Finding the key in this mess is highly unlikely."

"I could break it open. Probably."

"No need." I smiled. "I have some lock-picking skills."

His brows lifted. "Do you now?"

I shrugged one shoulder. "Princesses need to know all kinds of things."

"Apparently." He handed the box over as he came to stand beside me. "And when exactly did you decide you needed to learn to pick locks?"

"Around fifth grade. Which was when the cooks locked the candy pantry to keep me from raiding it."

"The palace has a candy pantry? Never mind, that seems absolutely reasonable. Just like the fact that candy is the reason you learned to pick locks." He grinned. "I could not love you more."

"You'd better." I laughed and gave him an affectionate hip bump. "And listen, when we leave here, I really need something to eat."

"Deal. I'm pretty hungry too."

I balanced the box on the stuff on the worktable, then pushed my sleeves a little higher. "Here goes."

I pulled up my magic and twisted two narrow slivers of ice from my fingertips. I downshifted my body temp to near freezing so the ice would keep its form longer. Now, standard ice—the kind you'd find in nature—would snap if you tried to use it to pick a lock, but this was winter elf magic. This ice was as strong as steel. Until it started to melt. Which meant even with my body temp lowered, I had to work at a good pace.

"Very impressive," Sin said.

"Thanks." My breath curled out in little puffs of icy vapor. I slipped the picks into the brass lock and manipulated the insides until I finally heard the click I was waiting for. "There you go."

I brought my body temp back up and dropped the picks into the trash bin. They'd melt and leave no trace, other than some dampness, but that was unlikely to be noticed in the midst of this disorder.

Sin didn't move. "You should open it."

"I just thought because you found it..." I shrugged. "Okay." I lifted the lid. "Nothing."

Sin looked inside, tipping the box toward him. "Hang on." He reached in and pulled out a strand of white fiber.

I peered at it. "What is that?"

"I have a guess, but let's see if I'm right." He twirled it between his fingers, and suddenly, the strand fluffed out. "I'm right. It's a piece of a feather."

"That's pretty interesting. Could it be a chicken feather?"

"That I don't know. But there's got to be a way to figure that out." He put the fragment back in the box, closed it, then turned it in his hands. "How can we find out who sent this to Stanley?"

"We can't. There's no tracking on the boxes."

"How do they get delivered?"

"Tinkers just slip them through the mail slots on the front of the doors."

He glanced at the door. On this side of it, a wire basket sat under the mail slot to catch anything that might get pushed through. "So this isn't much good to us. Except that someone might have sent Stanley a feather, or something with feathers."

"Right."

He let out a long sigh. "I feel like that should mean something, I just don't know what."

"Me either. I was hoping we'd get further today."

"Me too." The disappointment in his voice was obvious.

And honestly, I felt it as well. I'd thought we'd come here and uncover some clues that would lead us to an answer. I wasn't ready to give up yet, though. "Let's go see Stanley. Talk to him about the feather in the box. Maybe he'll tell us what it's all about. And who sent it."

Sin nodded. "I'm in if your uncle will let us."

"He will, especially once we tell him about this. Grab the box, and let's hit the elevator."

Sin tucked the box under his arm. "Got it."

I locked up and we walked toward the elevator. My stomach growled as we approached.

Sin tapped the down button, looking amused. "I heard that. You want to eat first?"

"Yes, but no. This is more important. First Stanley, then we'll grab something. We can even eat here if you like."

The doors opened, and we got on. I pressed the Mezzanine button.

"Here?" Sin asked.

"The cafeteria. Food is awesome. And the desserts are amazing. Sugar being the fuel that keeps us going and all."

"I can imagine. You think…I'd be welcome there?"

My heart hurt that he'd even be motivated to ask that question. I smiled brightly. "Of course."

But the truth was, I couldn't be sure.

"What can you tell us about this box?" Sin and I sat across from Stanley in the focus group room. As I'd suspected he would, Uncle Kris had turned things over to us once I'd told him about the memo box and what we'd found inside it.

Now he and Mamie sat in the observation room just like Sin and I had. Only, Mamie was taking notes.

Stanley took hold of the box like it was an old friend. "This is what tinkers use to send messages back and forth to each other on the lab floor."

I nodded gently. "I know that. But what can you tell us about this box specifically? We found it in your work space."

He looked at me then, eyes filled with concern for one long moment. Then he sighed and sort of collapsed in on himself as he let the box drop to the table. "I shouldn't be surprised you were in there. I knew you would be."

"We didn't disturb anything. We were just looking for…"

"Proof?" He smiled, a little weakly but sincerely all the same. "I know. It's all right. You're just doing what you need to do."

His gaze went back to the box. His fingers brushed the lock and tested the lid. It lifted slightly, as we hadn't locked it. "You opened it."

Sin glanced at me as if to say, *Here it comes.*

I answered Stanley. "Yes. It was empty except for the small fragment of a white feather. What can you tell us about that?"

Stanley's mouth firmed into a thin line. "Truth is, I was wavering. On changing the rabbit to a chicken. I knew Lyla wanted the chicken, but I had done so much work on the rabbit already. It was close to being ready. And it was good. Cute. Cuddly. Magical. The kind of toy kids respond to."

He looked at us with a confidence that surprised me a little. "I have enough years of experience to know when a toy is good. When a toy has all the right components to make it a hit." He pointed into the air. "The rabbit had that."

He went back to staring at the box. "But Lyla was obsessed with the chicken. The farm even sent her a stuffed chicken in the mail. I guess she'd won it as a prize when she was there. That only made her more determined in her efforts to convince me to make her a robotic one that laid eggs."

He stopped talking like he was lost in his thoughts.

"But something happened," Sin prodded gently. "You made the change."

Stanley nodded. "The memo box showed up. And it was filled with the most beautiful soft, white feathers. They were snowy and fluffy and so perfect that I took the arrival of them as a sign that I was indeed supposed to turn my rabbit into Lyla's chicken."

Sin and I looked at each other. The coincidences were piling up around us like snowflakes in a heavy blizzard. Although this gift of feathers felt more like a blatant manipulation.

I asked the question I knew had to be on Sin's mind too. "Who sent the feathers?"

Stanley shrugged. "I have no idea. The box didn't come with a note."

Sin frowned. "Kind of odd, isn't it?"

"For tinkers?" Stanley shook his head. "Not that odd. See, we send things to each other all the time. Sharing a new tool. Encouraging with a thoughtful note. Or a favorite kind of sweet. Gifting a bit of inspiring material. That's all I thought this was. Someone with spectacular timing. But I didn't think it was odd. After all, I'm known for my Pocket Pets. Animal toys have kind of become my area. And I'd talked about doing something larger for a while."

He hadn't really explained the issue of not knowing the sender. "But to get a box of feathers without a note?"

"A couple months before the feathers, I'd gotten another box with two yards of the best fake fur you can imagine. Also no note. That fur was top quality. I'd already patterned it out for the rabbit, in fact." He leaned back and put a hand on his stomach. "And six months before that, I got a pound of your aunt's eggnog fudge. One of my great weaknesses."

"All anonymous?" Sin asked.

Stanley nodded, smiling a bit. "After I won the tinker competition last year, I got quite a few boxes. Most had notes, I'll give you that, but not all. We tinkers can be a forgetful group. Too focused on our toys. So sometimes, notes get left on workbenches. Or not written at all. It's not a big thing."

It felt like a big thing to me.

Stanley pushed the box away and folded his hands on the table. "I'm sorry for the mess this has caused. I wish I could help you more."

I was a little mad at him. His attitude was great, but if he really wanted to help, why hadn't he told us about the box and the feathers sooner? "Is there anything else you can tell us? Anything else about this whole chicken business that you think we should know? Even something you don't think is that important?"

He shook his head slowly. "No. I should have mentioned the gift of the feathers sooner. I just didn't think it meant anything. I'm sorry about that." He hesitated. "There is one other thing."

I sat up a little straighter. "Yes?"

"I want you to know that my wife and I don't think any of this was caused by Mr. Crowe's presence here. We don't think he's bad magic. At all."

Sin bowed his head slightly. "Thank you."

I stopped being mad at Stanley. Yeah, my bias was showing again. Frankly, my emotions were currently about as organized as Stanley's office. This was hard.

I stood, ready for a break. "Thank you for your time, Stanley."

He got to his feet, nodding. "Of course, Princess."

"We'll be in touch soon. I'm sure we'll have more questions."

"I'm always available. And I want this sorted out as much as you do, I promise."

"Glad to hear that." I glanced toward the one-way mirror and my uncle, who was somewhere behind it in the other room. Then Sin and I headed for the door.

Uncle Kris was waiting on us in the hall. For a large man, he could move with lightning speed. He wrung his hands together. "We have nothing. I have to release them both. They've been here for long enough already."

I nodded. "I agree. There's nothing to hold them on." I wasn't sure if that was good or bad. It felt like both. "This has been a very frustrating day. One question. How long are our badges good for?"

"For the length of your stay here in the NP. For both of you."

"Thanks." I tucked a strand of hair behind my ear and blew out a breath. "I wish I knew what to do next."

"Let's go eat," Sin said. "Maybe the distraction will help us think of something."

My uncle patted his stomach. "Hmm. I could eat. Let's go to the cafeteria. Mamie, what's on the menu today?"

Mamie answered without hesitation. "The specials today are chicken pot pie, tater tot casserole, and enchiladas. The desserts of the day are banana pudding and French silk pie."

My stomach growled again. That all sounded so good to me.

Sin didn't look swayed by that list of deliciousness. "That's quite the menu, but I don't know if I'm up for the cafeteria and all those people."

Uncle Kris put his hand on Sin's shoulder. "Son, I understand how you must feel. But I think it would be good to show your face. The elves that work here are good people. They're not the ones who think you're to blame for all this. And you'll be with Jayne and me and Mamie. You'll have our support."

Mamie nodded, her steno pad clutched to her chest.

Sin's gaze remained impassive. "If it's not the elves here, who is it?"

"Most likely a small group of mostly snow elves. They've always been a stubborn, cantankerous lot." Uncle Kris shook his head as he took his hand away. "But they're a minority, I promise."

Sin turned a curious expression toward me. "Snow elves?"

"I'll explain later." I slipped my hand in his. "I'm so sorry you feel this way, but maybe being around some more of the elves here would help you see just how great the people are. Look at the guard at the gate. Look at Stanley. Most of them are like that."

"Was that Jim Bunting at the gate today?" my uncle asked. "He's a good man. Jayne is right. Those are the kind of people that work here. You'll see."

"Okay, I'm game," Sin said. "Let's eat."

After my uncle dismissed Stanley and Terrance with the rest of the day off, the four of us walked to the elevator and went down to the cafeteria. Despite Sin agreeing to go, I could see by the tension in his stance that he was prepared for the worst.

I squeezed his hand, which I was still holding, and gave him a smile. But inside I continued to hurt for him. This was not the North Pole experience I'd wanted for him, and no matter how much he insisted everything was fine, I had my doubts.

To make matters worse, we had nowhere to go with the chicken incident. I was really afraid that leaving it unsolved and continuing to call it a giant coincidence would mean terrible things in the future.

Sure, my uncle was right that the snow elves, who were most likely to be upset by this, were a small group, but they were very vocal. If they continued to think that Sin was somehow responsible for this chicken incident, their dislike of him would color everything. Including our marriage and my eventual rule. The unrest would fester over time and create a rift.

Oh, those prickly snow elves.

Our ancient history, which was built on a blend of truth and myth, said that once upon a time, the North Pole was all there had been of the world, and the elves that lived here had been divided into two groups: the snow elves and the ice elves.

Each side thought the other should join them and all become one, but which side? No decision could be reached, and a civil war had broken out. The magic used by both was so strong and so devastating that the North Pole cracked in two, and the Meltwater River was formed.

Shocked by what they'd done, the elves decided they would all be known as winter elves from that day on, and a monarch was chosen to keep peace over the new kingdom. And that's how the first Winter King came to be crowned.

Or so the story goes.

A few who were descendants of the snow elves liked to cling to their heritage. I understood that, I really did. Being proud of who you were was a good thing. But not at the expense of someone else's happiness and peace. There had to be a balance.

But occasionally, things tipped heavier in one direction. Then balance had to be restored.

Uncle Kris and Aunt Martha's marriage was supposed to have done that. Aunt Martha was a snow elf, although I think most people tended to forget that. It certainly wasn't something I thought a lot about. If ever. At least until now.

The delicious smells from the cafeteria floated over to us as we stepped off the elevator. I was starving, but for once my stomach could wait. I grabbed Uncle Kris's hand and stopped him. "Listen, if you really think it's a group of snow elves stirring up trouble against Sinclair, then maybe Aunt Martha should say something. Put a statement in the paper. Something."

He nodded very thoughtfully. "That's a good idea. You know, I sometimes forget Martha's a snow elf."

"We all do."

He kissed my cheek. "We'll get this sorted out, Jaynie. You'll see."

"Good."

Sin slipped his arm around my waist. "Come on. I know you're hungry. You can go back to fighting my battles once you're full."

I smiled at him without effort. "You are absolutely the right man for me."

He grinned back, winking. "I know."

I laughed. "Do you also know I'm getting both of today's featured desserts?"

"If you didn't, I'd be concerned."

We strolled in, hand in hand, and the buzz in the cafeteria gave way to an ear-piercing silence that almost pushed me right back out the door.

Heads turned, and all eyes were upon us. Then the elves did something that brought tears to my eyes.

They stood up and applauded.

I blinked back the tears and laughed, waving to the workers. "Thank you all."

I wasn't sure if they were applauding for Sin or for me or for us as a couple, but whatever the reason, it was incredibly sweet and touching and wonderful.

My uncle raised his hand, and the room went quiet again. "Ladies and gentlemen, your support is much appreciated. Let me be the first to officially introduce you to Princess Jayne's intended, Mr. Sinclair Crowe."

The cheering started up again.

But I was still stuck on the word *intended*. Obviously, I hadn't agreed to marry Sin yet, but Uncle Kris made it sound like a done deal.

Sin nudged me and whispered, "Don't worry, I won't hold you to that."

I struggled for a response. "He probably thought boyfriend sounded too informal for an official introduction."

Sin nodded as he waved to the workers. "It's okay. Whatever his reason, I know what's what."

I really couldn't love him more. And I wanted to say yes with every fiber of my being. So long as he was sure he could handle this life. Which clearly wasn't without its ups and downs.

A cafeteria employee came to us, bowed, then ushered us to my uncle's booth. It was in a corner that looked out over the factory floor, but was also *very* visible to everyone eating.

That visibility was purposeful, but I was starting to question if coming here had been such a good idea. Fish in a fishbowl? That was us right now. But while I was a little uncomfortable and worried about how Sin was feeling, the workers were all smiling at us and seemed happy about our presence.

I guess my uncle had been right. Sin showing his face here was a good thing. Unless this level of attention freaked him out, and then not so much. I glanced at him, and he seemed...okay. A little strained maybe. This kind of attention could do that to a person.

We laid our jackets on the booth seats, then got in line for food, letting Mamie and Uncle Kris go ahead of us. There was no special treatment in the cafeteria for anyone, outside of my uncle having a reserved booth. I liked that.

We picked up our trays, utensils, and drinks (Dr Pepper for me, because of course) and shuffled by the food.

"What are you getting to eat?" Sin asked.

"Tater tot casserole. You?"

"Chicken pot pie."

"Don't you think eating chicken right now is a little too much?" I teased.

He laughed. "Proves I'm not afraid."

"Good attitude."

We got our food and headed back to the table. I slid in toward the center with Mamie (who'd gotten clam chowder in a bread bowl, a cafeteria standard), while Uncle Kris (chicken pot pie) and Sin took the outside spots.

We dug in, and I watched the crowd for a bit, wondering if anyone would approach us. Didn't take long.

A man in a tinker's apron came up and made a short bow. "My apologies for bothering all of you, but I was asked to deliver this to Princess Frost. It came to my work space this morning in a memo box. There was another note with it, telling me to be sure it got to you, but that was all." He placed a small cream-colored envelope on the table.

Sin let out a soft snort. "Let me guess. You have no idea who the sender is."

The tinker looked mortified. "No, sir, I don't. I'm sorry."

"It's all right," I said. "Thank you for delivering it."

"You're welcome, Your Highness." He bowed again and backed away, returning to his table.

I picked up the envelope by its edges and turned it over. There was no writing on it other than a J on the front. The ink was black and otherwise unremarkable. I opened it and took out a folded sheet of paper in the same color.

One sentence was scrawled across the middle. *There's no such thing as coincidence.*

I showed it to Sin, then to Mamie and my uncle. "The plot thickens."

My uncle frowned. "It had to come from another tinker. No one else has access to that floor. As you know."

Sin put his napkin on the table. "But we had access. So there are other people allowed up there."

Uncle Kris looked at Mamie.

She flipped open her steno pad and scanned the page. "Not today. Only you two, King Jack, and Santa." She looked up at us. "You two were up there. Did you pass anyone in the hall? See anyone in the elevator?"

Sin and I both shook our heads.

Mamie shut her steno pad. "Then it had to be another tinker."

I glanced at the note. "I'm keeping this. It's evidence."

"True," Sin said. "And proof that someone wants us to keep digging. Doesn't mean they're on our side, though, so we need to keep that in mind." Then he made a face. "Or they're rubbing our faces in it. Sending a note to show that they can."

Uncle Kris grimaced. "Sounds like whoever sent that note thinks they're smarter than the rest of us."

Sin nodded. "That it does."

I stabbed a cheese-laden tater tot and let my mind wander into the possibilities. I ate the tot and thought while I chewed, repeating the procedure over and over. Tater tot casserole was pretty powerful stuff. I hoped it could help shake my thinking process loose. I wasn't sure how much time passed before Sin's voice brought me out of my reverie.

"Hey, you've gone awfully quiet. You okay?"

"Hmm? Oh, yes. Just thinking."

"Come up with anything?"

"Maybe." I let the mind-wandering continue a few seconds longer. "Regardless if this person who sent the note wants us to keep digging or is trying to show off how smart they are, we should still keep looking for answers. But where, right? I mean, there are a lot of directions we could go in. Maybe the best place to start is at the beginning."

Sin leaned in a little. "Meaning?"

"We can't prove or disprove Terrance's dream. But Stanley's change from the rabbit to the chicken has a trail." I turned to Mamie, the source of all things NP. "I think I already know the answer to this, but which farm would the children have visited?"

An hour later, full of delicious food and tasty desserts, Sin and I were back in the crawler headed to the eastern zone of the NP. Farmland. Granted, it wasn't the kind of farmland most would picture. Because of our climate, most of our farming was done in giant greenhouses and enormous, acreage-covering bio domes. Everything from plants to livestock used them.

The farm we were going to was Sweet Acres, a small exhibition farm that raised chickens and tundra goats, and grew two of the most important products in the NP: sugar cane and sugar beets.

As you could imagine, the greenhouses were especially important for those crops.

The greenhouses sparkled in the afternoon sun as we approached. The bio dome here was smaller than most, having only to house chickens. Tundra goats didn't need a bio dome, or anything else, to protect them from the weather. Although I was sure they got put into the barn at night to guard them from yetis.

"Okay, this is not something I expected to see," Sin said.

"How did you think we produced our food?"

"I honestly didn't think about it. But this is amazing. I imagine there's a good bit of winter elf magic at work here too. Am I right?"

"You are." I parked the crawler. "Let's go see Farmer Brown."

"I also can't believe that's actually the name of the man and family that runs this place." He laughed as he got out.

Farmer Melton Brown met us as we approached the barn. He wore olive-green twill overalls with a red flannel shirt and navy ball cap that bore the name Sweet Acres in white stitching. He pulled the hat off as he walked toward us. "Princess Jayne. It's a pleasure to welcome you to Sweet Acres."

"Thank you. I was here years ago when I was in school. Came for the tour like all the other kids."

"Well, in that case, welcome back."

I gestured to Sin. "This is Sinclair Crowe. My guest."

Farmer Brown nodded and shook Sin's hand when he extended it. "Pleasure to meet you too, sir."

"Thank you. I've never been to a farm like this. Really fascinating. It's all so neat and clean too. You must love your work."

Farmer Brown preened. "I do. It's my family's business and has been for many years. Did you want to take a tour?"

I realized Farmer Brown didn't know what we'd come for. "Not today. We just don't have the time unfortunately. But I would like to ask you a few questions."

"I'd be happy to answer them. What would you like to know?"

I glanced behind him at the barn. "I don't suppose you have an office?"

"Of course! I'm sorry I didn't offer. Please, follow me."

We did, and he led us into the barn. The interior was as neat and tidy as the rest of the farm. Which wasn't to say it was pristine. It was a farm after all. But it wasn't covered in muck and grime and gross stuff. Mostly pine shavings and chaff from the sugar cane.

The barn was an enormous structure with a loft over the half that was divided into goat stalls. The other half held some large equipment and an office that was walled off into its own little room. That's where we were headed.

Inside was a desk and an old floral sofa covered with a fleece blanket. There were a few hairs on the quilt. Dog or goat, I couldn't tell. Farmer Brown took the desk chair. Sin and I took the sofa.

He swiveled toward us. "What can I help you with?"

"Sometime back in March or April, you had a class come through. Fourth-graders." That's the grade Mamie had told me Stanley's granddaughter was in.

Farmer Brown nodded. "March and April are when we do all our school tours. That's when we have the most peeps and kids." He smiled. "Baby chickens and baby goats."

I nodded. "Right, makes sense the kids, er, I mean, children would visit then. I'm wondering if you remember one specific child. Lyla Kinder. She would have been in Mrs. Mint's class."

Farmer Brown's gaze narrowed as he thought. "I remember Mrs. Mint, of course. But that's a lot of kids. I might not have even given that tour. My whole family pitches in on tour days. Could have been my wife or my son or one of my daughters."

"Well, Lyla won a contest while she was here. Ended up getting a stuffed chicken as a prize? You must have a record of that, at least, since it was mailed to her."

He scrunched up his face. "A contest? Must have been something the school was doing. Or maybe Mrs. Mint herself. We don't do anything like that. We do have a gift shop. My oldest daughter runs that. I can ask her if we have any stuffed chickens. I think we sell something like that." He grinned suddenly. "If we don't, we ought to. Stuffed goats too. They're a might cuter, I must say."

"No, we were told this was a contest here at the farm."

He shook his head. "We don't do those. I promise. We have enough going on with thirty children trying to catch the goats, put peeps in their pockets, and playing hide-and-seek in the sugar cane. Giving one of them a prize and the rest of them nothing? I'm a brave man, Princess Jayne, but I'm not that brave."

I laughed. I liked Farmer Brown. "I understand. So no contest, no stuffed chicken?"

"Not to my knowledge, Your Highness. But if you'd like, we can walk over to the gift shop and ask my daughter about it."

"That would be great."

We followed him next door. The gift shop was pretty much a large shed that had been annexed. There was a whole wall of goat-milk products, like soap and hand lotion, a glass-front cooler with drinks, a couple shelves of packaged snacks and candy, more shelves with books on farming, some cookbooks, and some T-shirts and ball caps like the one Farmer Brown was wearing.

There was also a large display of stuffed toys. Chickens, peeps, goats, and a smiling stuffed sugar beet.

Farmer Brown leaned on the counter and tipped his head at the young woman behind it. "This is my daughter Greta Ann. She manages the gift shop. Greta Ann, this is Princess Jayne and her guest, Sinclair Crowe."

Greta Ann made a deep curtsey, almost disappearing behind the counter. "Pleasure to meet you, Princess, and Mr. Crowe."

She had a sprinkling of freckles across her nose that made her seem younger than she was, but I guessed her age around thirty. "You too. We're trying to find out if you remember one of the school children that was here last March or April by the name of Lyla Kinder? She apparently won a contest while she was here and was sent a stuffed chicken after the visit." I pointed to the rack of toys. "Probably like one of those white ones."

"We don't run contests, but I did send her a chicken. A woman came to the farm a day after that school visit and had me send it to her. Said it was Lyla's birthday and she'd wanted it and it was to be a surprise."

I looked at Sin.

He nodded. "Good thing we dug deeper."

"For sure." I looked at Greta Ann again. "What can you tell me about this woman?"

She shrugged. "Not much, I'm afraid. She was average build. Short, medium blue hair with a few silver streaks. Maybe midsixties? Pretty sure she had glasses too. She paid cash. Handed me Lyla's address on a slip of paper. And a sealed note to go with the chicken."

"Did she say who she was?"

"I assumed a relative. She talked a lot, I'll tell

you that. So much so that I couldn't do much but nod and take some notes."

"Probably so you couldn't ask questions," Sin said. "What did she talk about?"

"All sorts of nothing. The weather, how much she liked animals, how much she liked sugar, how pretty the farm is, what fun it must be to live here, lots and lots of small talk."

Clearly the woman had known what she was doing. "Do you have anything that might help us find her? Or figure out who she is?"

Greta Ann pursed her lips. Then she ducked down and came up with a big accounting journal. She ran her finger down the tabbed edge, found what she was looking for and flipped it open to that section.

From a small pocket on that page, she removed a little bundle of papers, and from that she separated out a small, creamy piece of paper and handed it over. "This is what she gave me with the address."

I pulled out the note I'd been handed at lunch and compared the two.

The paper was a match.

We hightailed it back to my uncle's office. Not to see him, but to see Mamie, who I had started to think of as Birdie's North Pole equivalent. I bet the two would get on famously, despite being worlds apart. Hey, they both even had blue hair. Although Mamie's was more silver now, and Birdie's was just a rinse. And really, with Birdie, that blue could be pink by the time we got back to Nocturne Falls.

Chaos reigned in my uncle's office when we stepped off the elevator. Supervisors from every department jostled for position in front of Mamie's desk, desperate for her attention. And, I'm sure, access to my uncle. She was speaking with one of them, but not getting very far from the looks of things.

At the chiming of the elevator, some in the crowd looked our way.

My name was uttered, and a few more of the group shifted in our direction. Followed by *all* of the crowd shifting in our direction. I was starting to wish we hadn't come back here.

"Princess Frost," one of the builders began as he sketched a short bow. "Have you seen this?" He thrust the afternoon edition of the paper under my nose.

"I...no." I took the paper from him. Instantly, I saw what the outrage was all about. Or at least what had caused it. The headline read *Incoming Administration Could End All Worker Benefits.*

Now I was angry. I shook the paper in the air. "This is pure speculation. Actually, it's a flat-out lie. This is several lies, really. First of all, there is no *incoming* administration. Not in any immediate future sort of way."

"They mean your new boyfriend," someone in the back shouted.

"I know what they mean. But they're wrong. He's not incoming any more than I am. My father has many, many years left on the throne."

A few grumbled responses, but some of the fight seemed to leave them. That was a good sign, because it meant they could still understand what was fact and what was fiction. But I wasn't done.

I shoved through the group to stand beside Mamie's desk. "Secondly, no one's benefits are getting ended or diminished or cut or changed in any way. Understood? That's my word on that. And I can guarantee that's my father's word on it as well. I'm sure my uncle will back me up as well."

A couple of nods in the crowd. They were listening now.

I dropped the paper in the trash. Where it belonged. "And speaking of my uncle, he's who handles worker benefits. Not me, not my father, not the monarchy in any way. So any changes would come from Santa himself. *Not* the Winter King or Winter Queen. You all know that. You've lived here all your lives. Nothing's changed."

I shook my head and tried to make eye contact with each of them. "Don't you see you're deliberately being spun up? Why would you suddenly think after all these years that things are going to be different? They're not."

The remaining anger drained from their faces. In quite a few, it was replaced by embarrassment or a little shame.

Good. They needed to feel that so they'd remember this and think twice the next time. But I had more to say. "Whoever wrote that piece clearly has an agenda. One against the monarchy. Or maybe just my relationship with Mr. Crowe. I'm not sure, but I plan on getting to the bottom of it. In the meantime, if any of you has something to say about my father's rule, me, or my love life, here's your opportunity to speak up."

I tapped my pointer finger on Mamie's desk for emphasis. "Right now. I'm listening."

Silence. Just as I suspected there would be.

Then a foreman from one of the building crews stepped forward. "I'm very sorry, Princess. We don't have anything against any of you. We lost our heads, is all. Seeing that article..." He shrugged. "We won't fall for that a second time. And I'm embarrassed we did the first time."

"Thank you. I appreciate that." I looked behind him. "Anyone else have anything to say?"

Fedina Berry, one of the head bakers, tentatively raised her hand. "I'm sorry too, Princess. I hope you don't hold this against us. I, for one, am very happy you've found a...*friend* like Mr. Crowe. You deserve happiness. And for the record, I'd be thrilled to bake your wedding cake."

That sent a ripple of gentle laughter through the crowd and a rush of heat into my cheeks. "That's very kind of you, Fedina. We're, uh, not quite at that stage of the planning yet, but I'll keep that in mind."

Sin was grinning wildly. "Yes, very kind. I like chocolate."

More laughter. The incident was well and truly over.

I softened my tone. "Now, if the rest of you could please spread the word about these unfounded rumors and calm your crews down, that would be greatly appreciated. Will you do that for me?"

They all nodded, and a few more came up to personally apologize as they filed out.

When the last one had left, I turned to Mamie. "What in the snowballs was that? I've never seen them like that."

She shook her head. "Neither have I. That article…" She sighed. "We are living in strange times, Princess." She picked up a pen and notepad. "Did you want your uncle? He's not in at the moment, but he should be back very soon."

"No, that's okay. I actually want to ask you something." Then I would deal with this inflammatory article.

"Oh?" She blinked at me, setting the pen and pad down to rest her hands on the desk. "What is it?"

I pulled out the note from lunch, then the slip of paper with the address on it. "These two pieces of paper look exactly the same to me, but I figured if anyone knows about office supplies, it's you. So are they the same? And where in the NP would you get this kind of paper?"

She adjusted her desk lamp and looked at the two pieces for a long, thoughtful moment. She gently ran her fingertip over each surface. Then she held both up to the light and nodded. "Just as I thought. Not sure why I didn't see it earlier on the note from lunch."

"You didn't really get a chance to examine it then. What do see you?"

She tapped a spot on the paper. It was a square drawn three dimensionally like a toy block with a T in it. "That's the tinkers' watermark. This is the paper supplied to their floor. All the disciplines have their own stationery with distinctive watermarks, just like the palace has its own."

"You mean this paper is what's supplied to the factory floor where the tinkers build the toys?"

She looked over her spectacles at me. "No, Princess. This is the stationery given out to master tinkers. It's what's used on the lab floor. The one with restricted access."

I heaved out a breath and frowned. "I might not be an actual detective, but I've figured out enough things while living in Nocturne Falls to know that this isn't just another coincidence. We're being led down a path. Or pushed down one. And I don't buy it."

"Me either," Sin said. "Using the tinker's watermarked paper feels very much like an attempt to pin the blame on a tinker. It's too deliberate."

I nodded. "It is. Which is why I absolutely believe that this whole thing is a setup. We just have to figure out who's behind it."

Mamie lifted her chin. "I am ready and able to assist."

"Good, because we're going to need someone with your exceptional skills to help us." I tapped the lunch note. "I want to know who could get their hands on this paper besides a master tinker. I would assume the printers and whoever works there, but who else? And that salacious article in the paper—I'm getting to the bottom of that too. It's the second time something slanted against my family and Sin has been printed since we arrived. There must be something going on there, because it's not like them to print such blatant lies like that."

Mamie got a little twinkle in her eyes. "You should head right over there and have a word with the editor. August Woolsey. He's a real piece of work."

"In what way?"

"He's a snow elf. Took over two years ago after the last editor retired. Been at the paper a long time, though. Wouldn't be surprised if he wrote that article himself. Although, there's no byline which is odd. Of course, if I'd written that, I wouldn't want my name attached to it either."

"No one would."

Her eyes narrowed. "In fact, I was thinking about calling him up and asking him if he had written it. Not sure he'd tell me, though." Her mouth puckered like she'd just licked a lemon. "He's gotten so crotchety in his old age. The old fool."

I'd never seen Mamie so riled up. "I take it you know him well, then."

"You could say that." She practically growled the words. "He was my first husband."

The crawler's engine purred as the vehicle cut through the snow. I was driving again, since Sin didn't know the way.

"What do you think is going on?" he asked quietly.

"I'm not sure of the why, but obviously someone has an ax to grind with me and my family, and they're using your presence here as a way to dig that ax in further."

"I'm sorry." He was staring out the window, looking very contemplative. "This wouldn't be happening if I wasn't here."

"We don't know that. If this is a plot to take down the royal family, they'd find another way to come after us. You just happen to be a useful tool in their grudge against the monarchy. It happens every great while, but it hasn't in my lifetime so I guess we were due." I glanced at him. "This is all going to get fixed, Sin. It will. I swear." I sighed long and hard. "I hate all of this, I really do. I wanted you to have such a good time while you were here."

"All things considered, I am." He gave me a quick, guarded smile and went back to staring out the window.

The sight of his handsome face in profile almost made me want to weep with how lucky I was to have such an amazing guy. Smart, sexy, skilled, and a wizard with doughnuts. Who wouldn't want to marry him? Of course, I'd never answered his question.

A sudden chill went through me.

Did he have any idea how I felt? I wasn't sure, but I needed him to know. "I know I never answered you, but I do want to marry you, you know. I'm just not sure I can say yes yet."

His lips parted, but no words came out for a moment. "I know. And it's important to me that when you say it, you say it with no reservations. I want you to be absolutely sure."

"I will be. I love you. So much. We're really good together." A new realization hit me. One that thrilled me and scared me in the same heartbeat. "I could abdicate. When the time comes, obviously."

He stared at me for a few breaths. "That's crazy. And amazing. And a huge sacrifice. *Huge*. But I don't want you to do that. You shouldn't have to. It wouldn't be fair. You've prepared your whole life to be queen. You deserve to wear that crown."

I smiled. "That's sweet, but I could be happy with our life in Nocturne Falls."

"Could you?"

I thought about it. Our life there was good. No, our life there was great. It could absolutely be enough for me. But I would miss this place. This life. My family here. The people here—despite everything that was going on—were good. I would miss them too. "I could."

"But you'd miss the North Pole. You can't deny it. You lit up the moment we touched down. It's obvious you love it here."

"I do, but we could visit."

"Sure, but it wouldn't be the same." He kept watching me, but the look in his eyes had changed. Like a good part of him was deep in thought.

"What is it?"

"Who would take your place on the throne if you abdicated?"

"My cousin."

"Francis. The emcee."

It wasn't a question, but I answered anyway. "Yes."

His eyes narrowed. "Funny that the man with the most to gain from you being discredited because of your relationship with me was the emcee of the competition that started this whole mess."

I gripped the wheel a little harder. I knew exactly what Sin was saying. "Francis wouldn't...at least, I don't think he would." I chewed on my lip a second. "Son of a nutcracker, what if he did?"

"Could he? I mean, is he capable?"

I had to breathe openmouthed for a second. "We've never been best buds or anything, but we've always been friendly. I can't imagine he'd be the one behind all this."

"Then who could you imagine it would be?"

"I don't know." I frowned as I thought. "He does stand to gain a lot if I abdicate. But he's assuming that I *would* abdicate."

"True." Sin's brows lifted ever so slightly. "Or he's counting on you being discredited. Either way…"

"He gets the throne." I pulled into the *Pole Post*'s parking lot and shut the crawler off. "That's a lot to count on. But having the paper behind him would certainly help."

"It would."

I stared at the building. "Let's go have a chat with August Woolsey. Then it might be time to go see my cousin."

August Woolsey was a tall, wiry man who'd been a champion sled racer back in the day at Edmund Snow High School. I knew that because of the photos on his office wall. There were also a number of journalism awards and certificates, but considering what he'd allowed to be printed in the *Post* recently, those were a lot less impressive.

August wasn't in his office at the moment, but I'd told his secretary that Sin and I would wait in there anyway. One of the perks of being royalty meant she couldn't say no. Sure, she'd wanted to. I could see it in her eyes. But she hadn't said it.

Maybe she would have, if not for how obviously upset I was. Sin had even commented on it once the office door was shut and we'd taken seats to wait.

He was still looking at me now. "I know you want to destroy this guy, but you catch a lot more flies with honey."

"I'm not going to bite the man's head off. Not at first."

Sin smirked. "Good. And look, if he's responsible, he deserves what's coming to him, so I'm not going to feel too bad. But are you going to give him a chance to explain himself?"

"I suppose." I exhaled while drumming my fingers on the arm of the chair I was in. "Yes."

"I think that's wise and fair and very diplomatic of you."

"Thanks. But you know he'll probably publish another article about the monarchy overstepping its boundaries or bullying the little man or some such thing because of us being here."

Sin shrugged. "Maybe he won't."

"Why wouldn't he? He's already done it twice. But I don't care. It'll just prove my point that he's a sneaky snake."

"Maybe being confronted with his lies will put an end to it."

"I'd love for it to be that easy, but I have serious doubts." I shook my head at the commendations on the wall. "I just need to have some face time with him and see for myself what kind of man he is."

"I agree," Sin said. "He must think he's really untouchable to publish such lies about the family that's responsible for his job."

"I'm sure he—"

The door swung open, and a very flustered

August Woolsey rushed in. His tie was slightly askew, and the sheen of perspiration shone on his forehead beneath a few wayward strands of steely blue hair. He swiped at the hair and shut the door. "P-Princess Frost."

He did a little bow as I stood. "Mr. Woolsey." That bow was not going to sway me. "I'm sure you know why I'm here."

"Yes, and I'm very sorry." The wrinkles around his eyes deepened as he spoke. "Those articles, those terrible articles—I printed a notice saying they were editorials and do not reflect the views and opinions of the *Pole Post*."

That sort of stopped me short. "Then why were they published? And why were they on the front page?"

He went red. "Because the editions I approved for printing were changed without anyone knowing about it. Those articles should *not* have been on the front page. They were not approved for the front page. They were not approved at all. They weren't even written here. If they had been, they never would have been given headline space. At best, they would have been in the Op Ed section. But honestly, they're not even appropriate for that."

I stared at him. Of all the scenarios I'd imagined, this wasn't one of them. "Then why did it happen twice?"

A look of deep mortification came over him. "Because I didn't think it would happen twice. I am ashamed I made that assumption and was so very wrong."

I wasn't quite sure what to say to him in that moment. He'd messed up. Big-time. But he knew that.

He exhaled an utterly worn-out sigh. "I know you're here to fire me. And I accept that. But I want you to know that I am deeply sorry. I had planned on sending you a letter of explanation and apology, then I thought perhaps I should come see you in person, then I wasn't sure you would see me, but I suppose it's too late for either of those things."

Behind him, Sin leaned over and shot me a questioning look.

I shrugged. Woolsey could be making this all up, but he seemed genuine. And he looked like a man worn thin by stress. That wasn't as easy to fake. "You said there was a notice printed about the articles being editorials and not approved?"

"There was. I put it in the afternoon edition, but I sent a copy to the palace as soon as I had it written up, but I don't suppose that ever got to you or your father."

"I've been gone all day."

"Again, I am deeply sorry. I love my job. At least, I did." A little noise somewhere in between a groan and a sob slipped out of him.

154

I started to worry about his immediate health. "Mr. Woolsey, please sit down. I'm not here to fire you."

For the first time since he'd entered the office, he lifted his head. "You're not?"

"No. But I am here to get to the bottom of this." I took my seat again, ready to ask more questions and see if any of the answers gave us a clue as to who was behind all this.

He nodded and sat behind his desk. "I'm happy to help. Happy. These articles are sullying the paper's reputation too. Whatever you need, just ask."

"Good. You said you were going to write a little note of explanation. Why don't you start by explaining who wrote the articles?"

"If only I could." The lines on his forehead deepened. "I have no idea."

Sin snorted. "You're the editor in chief, are you not?"

I lifted my hand toward Sin. "This is Sinclair Crowe, Mr. Woolsey. The man someone seems to think is going to be the end of the North Pole as we know it. In case you hadn't already figured that out."

Woolsey's hands were trembling a bit. He nodded. "Very good to make your acquaintance, sir. I have to say I do not share that person's view. And yes, I am editor in chief, but what I approved for print was changed after hours. Between the time I approved the final layouts and the time they went to printing, someone added those articles."

Sin crossed his legs, sitting back. "How did that happen?"

Woolsey straightened his name plate. "I talked to my layout people, my printers, even the security guard. None of them know how it happened, other than someone gained access and made the changes unbeknownst to the rest of us."

Sin glanced at me before his next question. "Who has access to this building besides those who work here?"

Woolsey frowned. "Not many people. Even amongst those who work here, only a handful have keys."

That wasn't unusual. Still, if the building had security…

Sin had picked up on that too. "Not even your security saw anything?"

"No, but in their defense, I should point out that the paper has never had any kind of security issues before. At least not since I've worked here, and that's been a long time. The North Pole is a very low-crime area. Almost nonexistent, really. I'm sure Princess Frost can attest to that. And the newspaper just isn't a place anyone would want to break into. Why would they? There's nothing much of value here. Our worth is in what we produce, not what's in the building. Although that worth seems rather questionable now that our content can't be trusted."

He looked miserable. So much so that I felt for him in a way I hadn't expected. Before I could say anything, he opened the folder on his desk and took out a large piece of doubled newsprint. "This is the current working layout. It's what's running tomorrow."

He unfolded it and showed it to me.

The headline read *The Post Apologizes*.

I nodded. "I like that. I assume there's an article to go with it?"

"Yes. I'll be happy to get you a copy right now. And I want you to know, I plan on staying here until this edition goes to print to be sure there's no tampering."

"What about your security team?" Sin asked.

Woolsey chuckled sadly. "Team? The paper has one security guard. Mort Deerman is ninety years old and is probably the only elf who's worked here longer than I have. Ninety isn't that old in elf years, but I have a feeling he naps on the job from time to time. I can't let the sole responsibility of watching over this edition fall on him."

Suddenly, Woolsey's eyes bulged. "Please don't fire Mort. This isn't his fault."

I leaned forward. "No one's firing anyone. But why don't you hire a couple other guards to help out?"

"We've never needed more guards before. But I did put a request in. I'm sure approval will take a few days. I know His Majesty is very busy."

"He is." But I also knew my dad wasn't a slacker. "When did you put the request in?"

"Just this morning. Right after the first article about..." He glanced at Sinclair. "When the issue with the tinker competition appeared."

I crossed my arms as I sat back. "And the one with the write-up calling Mr. Crowe death?"

Woolsey fiddled with his collar and answered softly, "Yes."

"Mr. Crowe is a necromancer. He's not death. He's not a reaper. He simply has the power to temporarily overcome mortality." He also had the ability to mark someone with his death touch, leaving a wound on them that could only be removed surgically, but sharing that was not going to help.

Woolsey shifted in his seat. He was now actively avoiding eye contact with me and Sin.

"Does that make you uncomfortable, Mr. Woolsey?"

He took a breath. "It's not something I'm used to."

I supposed a lot of people felt that way. I tried to soften the tone of my voice to be more understanding. "What do you think is most disconcerting about his being a necromancer? What have you heard people say that bothers you?"

If Woolsey could have left, I'm sure he would have. He almost looked at Sin. "It's been said…" He coughed nervously. "That a necromancer's touch causes death. That is rather unsettling. As I'm sure you can imagine."

Sin sighed. "I'm sure it is. To say that a necromancer's touch causes death isn't exactly true. Not unless you're a vampire. But my touch doesn't cause death any more than the touch of a winter elf does. Do you go around freezing people to death, Mr. Woolsey?"

He snorted. "No."

"Nor do I use my gifts so carelessly. Now, are there any vampires in town that I need to be aware of?"

He shook his head rapidly. "No, no vampires. Just us winter elves, some ice trolls, the occasional snow nymph, you know." He laughed in an anxious but relieved kind of way.

I laughed too, to help put him at ease. "Mr. Woolsey, if Sinclair's touch caused instant death, do you think I'd still be sitting here? I hold hands with him all the time. We walk arm in arm. And we've kissed."

"On more than one occasion," Sin added proudly.

I almost choked as I continued speaking to Woolsey. "And I look pretty alive to you, don't I?"

He laughed again, this time without reservation.

"Yes, Princess, you look very much alive. And happy too. Despite the rumors that have been spread. People don't think things through, do they?"

"No, they often don't." I smiled at him.

He touched a silver pen on his blotter. "I've been guilty of believing things I shouldn't as well. I am deeply sorry about that. I will strive not to let it happen again."

"You're forgiven. Why don't you do an interview with Mr. Crowe? Ask him some questions. Dispel some of the misunderstandings the folks in town have. It would mean a great deal to me if the truth about Mr. Crowe was able to rise above the rumors."

Woolsey nodded. "I agree. An interview would be great." He finally made eye contact with Sin. "Would you be willing to do that, Mr. Crowe?"

Sin grinned. "Absolutely. If people are going to talk about me, let's give them something real to talk about."

"Excellent," Woolsey said. "I need a little time to prepare my questions. And we should get a good photo. Maybe two. What do you say about tomorrow morning?"

"Perfect," Sin said. Then he glanced at me. "Unless there's something else scheduled I don't know about."

"Nope," I said. "That's a good time." I put a hand on Woolsey's desk. "We'll be here right after breakfast. And I'm going to look into that request for additional security as soon as we get back to the palace."

"Thank you, Princess Frost."

I stood. Sin and Woolsey followed. I extended my hand. "I'm grateful for your time and your explanation, Mr. Woolsey. We'll be in touch soon."

He shook my hand. "Excellent. I appreciate you taking the time to listen. And not firing me."

"Of course."

Sin stuck his hand out as well. "See you tomorrow."

Woolsey hesitated for half a second, then snorted softly and shook Sin's hand. "Yes. Tomorrow. I'll see you then, sir."

As we headed for the crawler, Sin took my hand.

I peered at him. "Do you think you should have explained your death touch to him more thoroughly?"

"Do you?"

"No. It's not his business."

"Good." He shrugged. "It's not as if I keep it a secret, but it's not something I readily share. And it's not like it's going to happen accidentally. The time it happened at the Black & Orange Ball was a one in a million."

"I know." We'd been frozen in place so that thieves could strip all the valuables from the crowd at the ball. Sin had been using his abilities to try to unfreeze himself, and one of the thieves had brushed against his hand, making contact and taking the brunt of Sin's power. That small touch had resulted in a mark that required medical attention to remove it and stop the death from spreading. "I don't think it's anything anyone needs to know about."

"Good, because unless it becomes more of an issue, I'm keeping it between us." He held the door open for me, and we went back out into the bright sun of the parking lot.

"Fine with me." I smiled, ready to change the subject. "That was a pretty productive meeting."

"It was. I think we can eliminate Woolsey as a suspect."

"Yes, but not my cousin." I sighed. "You know who would have access to the *Post* building?"

"I'm guessing royalty. Including your cousin."

"Yes and—" A new thought occurred to me. I glanced at my watch. "Speaking of royalty, we might be in big trouble."

"Why?"

"Because the formal dinner is in less than two hours, and we haven't started getting ready yet."

"It won't take me long. I'm assuming that's not the case for you?"

"For a formal dinner? It's going to take a little longer than usual. I'm sure my team is already in my suite waiting on me." I dug out the crawler keys from my pocket.

Sin's brows rose and amusement danced in his eyes. "You have a team?"

"Yes. That's what it takes to get a princess ready." I really wanted to tell him he'd have one as well when he became the Queen's Consort. Instead, I dangled the crawler keys as we approached the vehicle. "You need me to point the way back to the palace from here?"

"Nope. I got it." He grabbed the keys out of my hand, laughing.

"Good. Just drive fast, will you?"

"Like you have to ask."

Sin got us home in record time, but as I'd suspected, my team was indeed waiting on me. But they were in the hall, not my apartment. That was new. Maybe because I'd brought Spider to the NP with me? I doubted any of them wanted to be the one who let my cat escape.

And it seemed there was a small team waiting on Sin as well. I guess years of service had taught Gregory how to perfectly anticipate guests' needs, and he'd understood Sin wouldn't have welcomed more than a valet and a barber, so that's exactly who Gregory had sent. I was thankful for that small team, and for Gregory being keen enough to know what Sin might find overwhelming.

Sin took the additions to his prep in good stride, kissing me on the cheek as we parted ways in the hall and went into our apartments to get ready.

Our late arrival meant things were a little

frantic, but as my lady's maid, hair dresser, makeup artist and jeweler all started talking, I held my hands up for silence.

"Okay, I'm late. It's not a big deal."

"But, Princess," Allene began. She had been my lady's maid since I was twelve. "You haven't even picked out a dress."

She gestured to the rack near the window. At least a dozen dresses hung there, ranging from all shades of blue to deep purple and emerald green.

I walked over and gave them a quick look. There wasn't time for more. "The emerald green. I'll wear the tanzanite jewelry and my hair down, but pulled back."

I turned and smiled at my team. "Good?"

Allene nodded. "Excellent, Your Highness. We'll get everything ready while you shower."

"Great." I went to change and shower. I wasn't washing my hair again. Nesto, my hair dresser, had taught me a long time ago that freshly washed hair was harder to style anyway.

Twenty minutes later, I was in a robe and sitting in the styling chair in my dressing room. Nesto was working on my hair, Benna was working on my face, and Allene was steaming my dress.

Davide had gone to the vault to get the suite of jewels I'd requested.

I wondered how Sin was making out. I was sure that once I'd picked out my dress, his valet had been informed so the appropriate accessories could be supplied, even though Sin had brought his own suit. His valet would probably offer him a tie and pocket square that had some green in them, and Davide would show him a selection of cuff links that complemented my jewels.

Sin's valet would also make sure his suit and shirt were pressed and lint free and his shoes were shined.

I hoped Sin was okay with all of that. Royal life was an odd thing. I mean, I was used to it, and it seemed strange to me at times. How crazy would Sin see it? Would he think it was invasive? Because it was. But these people were just doing their jobs. Jobs that they'd always done.

Jobs that Sin might think completely unnecessary.

"Princess?"

I stopped staring into space to look at Benna. "Yes?"

She held a makeup brush aloft. "You're frowning."

"Sorry. Just worried about how Mr. Crowe is going to take all this fussing."

Nesto took a curling iron off the dressing table. "He seems like a man's man. He might not like it. But then, your father is a man's man and...well, your father isn't so fond of all this either."

We all laughed. Allene shook her head. "Sometimes I think it would be nice to have all this help, and sometimes I don't know how you do it, Princess. So many people in your personal space."

"Well, I don't do it when I'm in Nocturne Falls. But when I'm here, I'm used to it." I closed my eyes. Nesto's hands in my hair were almost putting me to sleep.

"Does Mr. Crowe like the North Pole?" Nesto asked.

"Mm-hmm. Although not all of the North Pole likes him, it seems."

The team went quiet, and I realized some of them might have reservations about the man I loved as well.

"Your Highness," Benna started, "I think… people just need to get to know him. If you love him, then he has to be a good man, and everyone else will come to love him too."

"I hope so." I sighed at Nesto's bliss-inducing touch. "Tomorrow, the *Post* is doing an interview with him. That will help people get to know him and understand who he is and what the truth is about necromancers."

The door to the suite opened and closed. Davide called out, "Just me."

I opened my eyes as he came in carrying two large black cases. He set them on the dressing table and opened them to show me what he'd brought.

"First, Princess, the tanzanite suite as you requested. I also brought the amethyst, the emerald and some strictly diamond pieces."

The tanzanite set was simpler than most of the royal jewels, but then, the stones were fairly large. The gems, which shifted from blue to purple depending on the light, were accented by a few smaller diamonds and set in platinum. "The tanzanite will be perfect. I think the ring and necklace are all I want."

Davide opened a second, smaller case. "With a pair of more streamlined diamond drops perhaps."

I looked at the earrings he'd brought. "Yes. That middle pair is just what I want."

He smiled. He'd anticipated my mood perfectly. "I've also brought your snowflake tiara, but I'm guessing you'd rather the diamond circlet."

"You guess right. The snowflake tiara is too much for this dinner. The circlet is better."

Davide lifted the thin band of diamonds in platinum. "Nesto, are you ready for this yet?"

"I am," he answered.

Davide handed the circlet to Nesto, then spoke to me again. "I'll lay everything else out on your vanity table."

"Thank you."

Nesto went to work fastening the circlet into my hair, allowing me to close my eyes for a few more minutes. I thought about my cousin Francis and tried to picture him as the one behind all of this chaos.

He did have the throne to gain. But he'd never seemed interested or envious of that position at all. Was he just that good at hiding it?

He'd also seemed genuinely surprised and flustered by the reveal of two nearly identical toys at the tourney. Was he that good of an actor?

I thought back to family Christmases and birthdays. I could remember him being a little less than happy when Aunt Martha had given him a wooden desk set instead of the new boots he'd asked for, but then, we'd been kids. And kids didn't hide their disappointment well.

As soon as possible, which probably wasn't going to be until much later this evening, Sin and I had to talk to my dad about our suspicions. Maybe he'd have some insight on Francis that could move us forward.

"All done, Princess," Nesto said softly.

I opened my eyes and saw my reflection in the mirror. My hair and makeup were perfection, but then, that's what my team did. "You and Benna both did an amazing job. I look like a princess. Which is to say, a lot better than usual."

He laughed but shook his head. "You are always beautiful, Your Majesty."

"Thank you." I turned my head side to side to get the full picture of what he'd done. "And thank you for such great work."

Allene clapped her hands. "Everyone out to the living room so I can get the princess dressed."

Nesto, Benna, and Davide quickly did as they were told. Allene had that way about her.

I shucked my robe and stood there in my underwear and strapless bra while Allene helped me into the dress and zipped me up. I turned to face the full-length mirror. "What do you think?"

"A very good choice. The color is a subtle but unusual choice for you, and the cut of the dress shows off your figure beautifully. You look appropriately royal."

The dress had an off-the-shoulder neckline and small cap sleeves, then it hugged my shape until it flared out at my knees in a bell shape. Other than the shine of the deep green silk, the dress had no embellishments. "I do usually wear things that are a little fancier."

"The jewelry will be the perfect touch." She lifted the necklace and fastened it on me.

"You're right." I touched the diamonds and tanzanites sparkling at my throat. "With the earrings and ring, I'll be good to go."

While I put the rest of my jewelry on, including the rainbow obsidian bracelet Sin had given me, Allene laid out three pairs of shoes—black satin heels with silver buckles, shiny silver kitten heels, and dyed-to-match ballet flats.

I chose the latter, slipping my feet into them with a smile. "I'm going with comfortable tonight. Or at least as comfortable as I can be at a dinner like this."

"I don't blame you." She put the rest of the shoes away. "You look gorgeous. Understated and elegant."

"Thank you. I can't wait to see what Sin looks like."

Allene smiled. "Me too. Mr. Crowe is a very handsome man. If you don't mind me saying that."

"I don't mind at all. Let's go see if he's ready." Her kind words gave me such a warm feeling. If Allene could accept Sin as my boyfriend, and possible husband-to-be, then there was hope for the rest of the palace staff. She would make sure of it.

And those who refused to accept him?

I wasn't sure what would happen to those staff members. But if they couldn't hide their feelings toward Sin, they would probably end up looking for jobs elsewhere. And not just because I'd become queen and let people go.

It would be because I'd married Sin, and my father would be unwilling to tolerate those who weren't accepting of his new son-in-law.

I walked into the living room, and my team smiled. Benna clasped her hands in front of her. "Absolutely chillacious."

I laughed. "Thank you."

Davide nodded. "Agreed."

Nesto, who was leaning against the sofa, pursed his mouth. "One of your best looks ever, Princess."

"Thank you all. Now, who would like to come meet Mr. Crowe with me? I'm dying to see how he looks. And we should be getting down to the dining room."

"I'm in," Benna said.

Davide and Nesto picked up their cases, nodding. "Ready."

"Excellent. Let's go." I went across the hall to knock.

The valet Gregory had assigned to Sin opened the door. He bowed. "Princess Frost, you look lovely."

"Thank you. Is Mr. Crowe ready?"

"I am," Sin said as he rounded the corner from the bedroom.

"Wow." That was all I could come up with at the moment. Sin had never looked quite so polished. It was something else. He looked utterly regal. From his smoothly coifed hair to his impeccably fitted suit to his sparkling cuff links.

There was a fire in his eyes as he took my hand and leaned in to brush his lips against my cheek. "Wow to you too."

I smiled. And then remembered that my team was standing behind me. I introduced Sin to all of them, and while he greeted them, I checked around the apartment for Spider and Sugar. No sign of either of them.

My team dismissed themselves after the introduction, as did Sin's barber and valet, and Sin and I were once again alone.

Except for the cats. Which I still didn't see. "Where are the kids?"

"Sleeping in the closet. Neither one was a fan of the company. Spider can stay, if that's all right with you."

"It's perfectly fine with me. No point in waking either of them up. Are they all set on food?"

"I made a point to put out fresh water and two new bowls of Chicken Party before the dinner prep began." He took my hands in his and looked into my eyes. "You really do look amazing. It's moments like this where I can absolutely see you as queen. It's a little intimidating, if I'm honest."

"I don't mean to intimidate you."

He gave me this sly little smile. "I have a feeling I'll get used to it." He lifted my face toward his with his fingertips under my chin. "It's also a little sexy. Which I didn't anticipate. I guess I like being involved with a powerful woman more than I knew."

He pressed his mouth to mine before I could answer, kissing me with the kind of soft pressure that said he was in no hurry to end the kiss.

I leaned in, letting my head swim with the pleasure of it.

At last, he broke the kiss, but not the contact, keeping his forehead to mine. "I suppose we should go down to dinner."

"I suppose we should. Too bad. I'd much rather stay here now."

He laughed as he straightened. "Don't get me in trouble."

"Wouldn't dream of it."

He offered me his arm. I took it, and we headed for the door.

He looked over his shoulder. "You kids behave. We'll be back."

We were nearly to the elevator when I felt compelled to ask, "Are you nervous?"

He sighed as he pushed the call button. "Yes. Are you?"

"A little. Mostly because I'm not sure I'll be able to be civil to my cousin."

"That sounds like you've already convicted him."

I sighed. "You're right. That's not fair of me. Thank you for reminding me of that."

"You're welcome. Of course, it'll be interesting to see how he behaves toward you. If he shows any signs of being jealous."

"It will be. That might not be easy for him if he's really doing all this scheming. And all we have to do is pretend we don't know anything."

With a soft chime, the doors slid open. We got on.

"Well," Sin said. "We don't know much."

"No, but I have a feeling that's all about to change."

We didn't actually go to the dining room. That's not how formal dinners worked. We all gathered in the drawing room first, then we went into dinner.

Of course, we had to be announced first. Gregory took care of that, meeting us at the door as a footman opened it. "Her Ladyship Princess Frost and our guest of honor, Mr. Sinclair Crowe."

Then we went in. My parents and Aunt Martha and Uncle Kris were there, as were a few of my other aunts and uncles and cousins, although Francis had yet to arrive. Also in attendance were the members of my father's council and their spouses. The mayors of each neighborhood and their spouses were also present. Several committee members and organizations had been invited too. With their spouses, naturally.

All in all, I tallied the guest list, family included, at around fifty-three people.

A pretty standard dinner party for palace life, but I could see that after fifteen minutes of introductions, Sin was looking weary.

I found a moment and a far corner of the drawing room and made some space for us. "Are you okay?"

He nodded, but didn't quite shake off the dazed look. "How often do you do this?"

"A formal dinner? Probably once or twice a month."

"You're really good at it. All the small talk and remembering people's names and asking about their work and families."

"I've been doing it all my life. And it's easy when you're the one who's royalty. It's not such a big deal if I mess up. Know what I mean?"

"Sure." He glanced over his shoulder. "This is going to take some practice for me, I can see that. But I'll get the hang of it."

"Practice? So you'd like to have more of these?"

He whipped around, a slight look of panic in his eyes. "I meant—" He laughed when he saw the amusement on my face. "You're a rotten person."

"I know. But you love me, so now you have to deal with the consequences."

He snorted and went back to looking over his shoulder. "Your cousin just came in. Who's the woman with him?"

I looked. "That's Umelia Pine." Her deep blue

hair was in a sleek updo, showing off her diamond earrings. "Nice girl. Her father is in paper design, and her mother is a Master Bow Maker. They're decorators."

"You don't mean interior design, do you?"

"Gifts. Packages. Presents. Large or small, they wrap it all. That is literally the decorators' motto."

He laughed and shook his head. "Of course. I keep wanting to equate everything here to something I already know, but this place just isn't like any other, is it?"

"Nope.

His smile held on. "I suppose decorating is a big thing here."

"Pretty big. Gifts are kind of our bread and butter. That's what all the toys are for, after all."

"Is there a competition for that too?"

"There is. There are competitions for just about everything here. Granted, the Tinkers' Tourney is the biggest, seeing as how without toys this would all just be weird."

"Makes sense. So are he and Umelia engaged?"

"Only just. As in he proposed on the summer solstice."

Sin squinted. "Which was in June sometime, right?"

"Right. The twenty-first, I believe."

He let out a long, thoughtful breath. "Seems like there's a whole other competition going on."

"You think he proposed to her because you proposed to me?"

He shrugged, eyes on me now. "How long have they been dating?"

"On and off for about three years."

"Why on and off?"

I glanced at Umelia. I didn't know her that well, but I knew what the rumors were and what the family talk was. "He wouldn't commit."

"Then we happen, and he finds a way." Sin pursed his mouth. "Since we're all about coincidences lately..."

"It does seem like interesting timing."

"She's from a good family?"

"Very."

Sin nodded. "I assume she'd make a good royal consort, then. Probably one much more easily accepted than me."

"Sin—"

He shook his head. "Not placing any blame or judgment. Just stating a fact. That I expect you to answer honestly."

I frowned. "Yes. To some people." I looked at the young couple again. "They seem happy."

"And why wouldn't they be? She's got the ring she was after, if she was indeed after it, and if he is guilty of orchestrating all of this, he's doing a fine job of hiding it. And getting his way."

"True. I hope he doesn't notice how closely we're watching him tonight."

"And if he does? What's he going to do about it?"

"Good point." I put my hand on Sin's arm. "Let's go see my dad. Now isn't the right time to give him or my uncle the full rundown, but I want to see about that request for more security at the paper."

"Okay."

I placed my hand on the inside crook of Sin's arm and together we walked over to my parents. My mother was sipping a predinner cordial, probably wintermint, judging by the pale green tint. "Hi, Mom, Dad."

"Hi, honey." My mom leaned in and kissed my cheek, then smiled up at Sin. "You both look so handsome. I mean, pretty. Well, you look pretty, Jayne. Sinclair looks handsome." She giggled.

Sin grinned. "You look beautiful, Lady Frost."

My father slanted his eyes at her. "Klara, how many of those cordials have you had?"

"Oh, you hush. Just one." She smiled, her cheeks bright. "I'm happy. Are you happy, honey?"

"I am." Mostly. "You look very pretty too."

"Thank you." Something distracted her. "Oh, your aunt Cecelia is waving at me. Excuse me, won't you?"

She went in my aunt's direction, leaving Sin and me with my father, which worked out perfectly.

I watched her for a moment. "Aunt Cecilia is Francis's mother," I told Sin.

Sin nodded in understanding.

I turned back to my father. "Dad, do you remember seeing a request for more security at the *Post* come across your desk? August Woolsey said he just submitted one, and I'm personally asking you to fast track it. Actually, I'm asking you to give it instant approval."

He frowned. "I don't think the *Post* is in any position to be asking for favors, but I'm more surprised to see you as their advocate. What don't I know?"

"That August isn't responsible for those terrible articles. Someone got into the paper and made the changes after the day's work had already been approved for print. He needs the extra security because it's happened twice now, and he only has one guard."

My father took a moment with that. He looked at both of us when he spoke next. "You feel confident he's telling the truth?"

"I do."

My father looked at Sin. "You too?"

He seemed pleased to have his opinion considered, and I loved my father for that. "Yes. He looked genuinely upset by the whole thing. I'm doing an interview with him tomorrow in hopes of dispelling some of the rumors circulating about me."

My father nodded. "Good. I like that. I'll send a footman with a note to Ezreal immediately that the additional security for the paper is approved."

"Thank you." I smiled at him. He was a good king. I wanted to tell him about Francis, but this wasn't the time for that conversation.

Before any of us could say another word, the dinner chimes sounded. We all turned like the well-trained subjects we were. Sin went along with the crowd.

The dining room doors opened behind the footman with the chimes. "Your Majesty, esteemed guests, dinner is served."

My father and mother went first, then my aunt Martha and uncle Kris, then Sin and me, then the rest of the royal family and guests.

Seats were assigned with small place cards written in elegant calligraphy. As I approached my seat, I realized I should have explained to Sin ahead of time that we wouldn't be sitting together.

My father was at one end of the table, while my uncle was at the other. I was at my father's right, and my mother at his left with Sin beside her. The Mayor of the Tinkers was at my right, while the man's wife was seated farther down the table. At Sin's right was another of the mayors.

More family members and guests were interspersed around the table with precise effort to ensure a good mix and lively conversation. At least that was the way it had been explained to me by my mother many years ago.

It was her job (with help from her secretary and some input from Gregory) to arrange all these seats. The undertaking was no small feat. She had to be aware of moods and opinions, personal relationships, even allergies sometimes.

The task would eventually fall to Sin as consort, but I wasn't about to broach that subject now.

I studied him from across the table. He looked so handsome and regal that he fit in perfectly. On the outside, anyway.

I had no idea how he was feeling on the inside. And I was too far away to talk to him about it. Naturally, I would have rather been at Sin's side, but once I noticed that Francis and Umelia could barely see each other due to a floral centerpiece, I felt better. Maybe my mother had done that on purpose. She was pretty savvy when it came to all this social intrigue business. Made me proud of her, if she had. I guess I was petty like that.

And a little stuck on the whole competition thing Sin had brought up. It really did make it seem like Francis was positioning himself for something grand.

And what was grander than the throne?

Growing up together, he'd tried to one up me on several occasions. Was he really trying to do that again?

I knew Sin would tell me I was judging Francis unfairly again, but that didn't stop me from scowling. Lightly, so my mother wouldn't fuss at me later about making such a face at the dinner table. Of course, he never noticed. He was engaged in some fascinating conversation with the Mayor of the Decorators, a large woman with small pearlized bows in her blue curls.

I'm sure the decorators were on his side. After all, those were Umelia's people. Wouldn't they love to see one of their own as the royal consort?

Hmm. That started new wheels turning in my head.

"Jayne. *Jay.*"

"What?" I looked at my father.

"I asked what you and Sin have planned for the rest of the day after the paper tomorrow."

"Oh. Sorry. Nothing in particular, why?"

"I thought you might like to tour the new peppermint plant with me. Your mom thought Sin would enjoy seeing something like that since he's a baker. I realize confections are not the same thing, but it's in the vicinity."

"That would be great. I'm sure he'd love that." I glanced at Sin. The Baking Mayor at his elbow seemed to be enjoying her spot next to him and was talking very earnestly about something.

But then, my mother had arranged for Sin's dinner companion to be someone he could have a conversation with. And one who wouldn't have an ounce of compunction about being seated next to him. Another big, fat, sugar-coated point for Klara Frost.

I would have smiled at her in thanks, but she was speaking with one of the footmen at the moment.

So I went back to looking at Sin, who was, no doubt, being his usual charming self. I hoped he wasn't bored stiff. There was no getting out of these dinners.

"Worried?"

At the sound of my father's voice, I made eye contact with him again. There was little point in hiding what I was feeling, so I just smiled thinly and said, "Yes."

He lowered his voice, making sure the conversation stayed between us. "I wish I could offer you some tried and true advice, but your mother came to this life having already been fully immersed it in. We both did."

I nodded. "I know. It's okay."

"Sinclair is an intelligent man. He pursued you, after all. Give him more credit. I'm sure by now he's got a decent grasp of what he's getting into."

I sighed. "Maybe. I don't know. His reception here hasn't been exactly what I'd hoped for."

"That will all be resolved. And if he loves you as he seems to, this life, the one you're so worried is going to scare him away, is only going to strengthen his resolve to love and protect you."

I smiled at my dad. Sometimes he really did have the best answers. "Thank you."

He smiled back. "Anytime, Jay."

A battalion of footmen walked through the dining doors carrying silver trays.

Dinner was served.

Sin shook his head as we stepped off the elevator. "I'm just saying it's shocking news. And I'm not sure I can marry you now."

I laughed at his teasing, very happy that dinner was over and that it had gone so well. "We *must* have some kind of doughnut in the North Pole. I feel like doughnuts were a big part of my life growing up. I've had to have eaten them here before."

"Not according to Mayor Crumb. Cookies, cakes, pies, pastries of all assortments—even a fried dough that could be described as doughnut adjacent, but nothing that she claims is a genuine, honest-to-goodness doughnut. It's a real shame. Think of the children."

I snort-laughed at his mock outrage. "I suppose you'll just have to spearhead some kind of doughnut project, then. Bring honest-to-goodness doughnuts to the North Pole once and for all."

He shot a sideways look at me. "That, missy, would require me having a reason to be here for more than a week."

I knew what he was getting at. His proposal. And my nonexistent official answer. But as we rounded the corner and walked down the hall toward our apartments, the sight of Allene, Davide, and Sin's valet awaiting us brought an end to that conversation.

Sin held up his hands. "I appreciate it, but I can undress myself."

Davide smiled patiently. "I'm just here to collect your cuff links, sir."

"Ah." Sin lifted his arms to glance at the forgotten jewelry. "I'm ready for you to collect them too. What are these worth again?"

Davide held his black cases at his sides. "Their worth is not my purview, but I can tell you that they are each three and a half carats of exceptional tanzanite with another half carat each of white diamonds set in platinum, and they were once part of Princess Frost's great-great-grandmother's personal collection as a brooch. She had it taken apart and turned into cuff links for her husband. I trust they did their job for you this evening."

"If their job was to make sure I matched the princess, then they did it beautifully." There was an edge to Sin's voice. A strained quality I wasn't used to hearing.

As we stopped in front of our doors, he looked at me, and I could see the frustration in his eyes. He'd expected us to come back, get comfortable and hang out. We still could, it was just going to take a little longer.

I smiled at him. I should have told the team they could have the rest of the night off. "With Allene's help, I can be over in less than ten minutes. Sound good?"

"Yes." Then he looked at his valet. "I know you're just doing the job you were sent to do, but I'm going to undress myself."

"Sinclair," I said gently as I gave him a meaningful gaze. "I'm sure your valet would be happy to wait in the hall for your suit. So he can take it to be cleaned for you."

Understanding lit in Sin's eyes, and he nodded to let me know he got it. "That would be fine." He looked at the valet again and smiled. "Be right out."

"Very good, sir." The valet stood waiting.

With one last glance at the team, Sin unlocked his door and went in.

I unlocked mine and did the same with Allene and Davide behind me. "Thank you for not waiting inside. That might not have gone over as well if Sin had walked in to see his valet already in there."

Allene snorted. "That's what we thought too, so we just stayed in the hall."

189

Davide set his cases on the coffee table. "He'll get there. It's just a matter of—"

Sin came barreling into my apartment, eyes glinting with anger. "Jayne."

"What's wrong? Are Spider and Sugar okay?"

"The cats are fine. But someone was in there. In my apartment. And I don't mean housekeeping. There's a package on the coffee table."

I bit my lip. "Gregory, I'm sure. He does that when there are deliveries. I'll tell him it's not okay."

Davide spoke up. "Princess? There's a package here on the coffee table for you too."

"There is?" I turned to see Davide holding up a box about the size of a salad plate wrapped in white paper and tied with doubled lengths of sheer gold ribbon.

Sin pointed at it. "Mine looks just like that."

Davide weighed it in his hands. "Could be chocolates."

I wasn't interested in anyone's guess, just being alone with Sin to discuss this. "Davide, Allene, get this jewelry off me." I started fussing with the circlet, loosening it from my hair. I was sure Nesto wouldn't be happy with me destroying his coiffure, but I had other things to worry about.

They dashed over, taking the gems off me and securing them. Allene waited at my elbow after handing the earrings off to Davide. "And your dress?"

I looked at Sin.

He waved a hand. "Get changed, then come over and we'll figure this out."

"Okay," I said, but my tongue almost stuck to the roof of my mouth. I knew he was mad. I didn't blame him. To anyone not used to it, having someone in your personal space felt like an invasion of privacy.

With a terse nod, he started to go, then stopped and turned back, holding out his hand to Davide. Diamonds sparkled on his palm. "Your cuff links."

Davide took them with a gracious bow. "Thank you, sir."

I'm sure Davide would have also liked to explain that they were not *his* cuff links, but the jeweler had been in service long enough to know when to keep his mouth shut and who to keep it shut around.

Sin left.

Allene had the zipper down on my dress before the door finished closing. Davide locked his cases and gave me a respectful nod. "Princess, as always it has been my pleasure to serve you."

"Thank you, Davide."

He left too.

I sighed with impatient frustration.

"Now, now," Allene said softly as I stepped out of the dress. "It's going to be all right. You'll see."

"I hope so." I toed the ballet slippers off.

With the dress already folded over her arm, she scooped up the shoes and made for the door. "Have a good night, Princess. And be well."

I nodded. "Thank you. You too."

As she left, I yanked off my strapless bra, threw on a more comfortable one, along with a big sweatshirt and yoga pants.

Thirty seconds later, I was at Sin's door in my bare feet with the wrapped package in my hand. The valet was still in the hall. He bowed at me and, as a credit to his training, didn't blink at my very casual outfit. I nodded back as I knocked.

Wasn't long before Sin opened the door. He was in sweatpants and a T-shirt. He handed the suit to the valet. The young man took it and disappeared quietly.

I stood there, searching Sin's face for any sign that his mood had changed. It seemed to have softened a bit. "You okay?"

"Yes." He raked his hand through his hair, destroying the sleek styling his barber had done and returning it to the wilder look he usually sported. "I'm just not used to all this, Jayne. I'm not."

"I know. We can fix it. Lay some ground rules. Make sure the staff knows—"

"No." He exhaled. "That's not necessary. I don't want to be a problem."

"Sin, it's okay. Especially if it helps. And you're

not a problem. Palace staff is here to serve the family. If the method of service needs to change, that's perfectly fine."

"Well...maybe a little. But this is what you're used to, isn't it? Which means it's what I'll have to get used to as well." He managed a weak half-smile.

"You really don't have to. Adjustments can be made. Adjustments *will* be made. It's not even up for debate." I tipped my head toward the space behind him. "Are you going to let me in?"

"Sorry." He moved back, making room for me to enter. I tossed the package onto the couch. "I don't want to be the exception. I want to adapt to your life. This life."

"But until then, there's no reason we can't take things slow."

He stared at me. Hard. "You mean with us?"

"No." I put my hands on his beautiful face. "With certain protocols. With standard procedures. That kind of stuff. Okay?"

"Okay." He turned his head and kissed the palm of my left hand. "I'm sorry I lost my cool."

"You have nothing to apologize for."

He pulled me into his arms and just held me for a few seconds. "I can't believe you grew up like this. But I'll get there. Be patient with me."

"That's what love is supposed to be. Patient. And I can do that. Especially with you."

"Good." He kissed the top of my head. "You want to see what the gifts are? And hopefully who they're from?"

I pulled back, laughing a little. "Yes, for sure. Don't you?"

"Yeah. I am a little curious."

We went over to the living room area. I picked up my package from where I'd tossed it on the couch, and sat cross-legged on the middle cushion. He took his off the coffee table and sat next to me.

I nudged him. "You go first."

He pulled at the ribbon. "Do you get gifts all the time? Is this standard operating procedure?"

"There are a fair number of gifts involved in being part of the royal family."

His brows lifted, but he just kept unwrapping. Inside the white paper was a simple brown box, but it bore a familiar mark. A square with a T in it. "The tinkers," he said.

"Yes."

He didn't open it. "Do you think this is more competition nonsense? Should we maybe have someone here?"

"I...don't really know. I could call my dad. Or the constable."

He stared at the box.

"Just open it," I said. "We'll figure out what to do based on what's in there."

"Okay." He lifted the top off. There was a slim,

red leather collar inside. It had an odd-shaped bell attached to it. A note in the same creamy paper we'd come to recognize as also belonging to the tinkers sat on top. He opened the note and read what was written inside.

"Dear Mr. Crowe, I was told you and Princess Frost both have cats. I hope you enjoy this gift. It's still in the early development stage, but should work well enough to entertain. All the best, Stanley."

Sin looked at that. "How about that? He sent us a present. After everything that happened today." He took the collar out of the box. "What do you suppose it does?"

"Let's put it on Sugar and see."

Sin laughed. "You realize I'll have to wake her up for that. She and Spider are still passed out in the closet."

"I can fix that." I hopped up and went over to Sin's stash of cat supplies, grabbed the treat bag and gave it a good shake.

Two streaks of black and white came barreling into the room seconds later. The cats skidded to a stop by my feet.

"See how easy that was?" I laughed and tossed a few treats down.

While the fishy morsels were being gobbled up, Sin came over and put the collar on Sugar. "There. Now what?"

I shrugged. "Not sure."

Spider ate the last treat. Sugar looked up at us expectantly. "More."

I looked at Sin. "You heard that, right? That was an actual word, not a meow."

He nodded, a little dumbstruck. "Did Stanley develop a pet collar that allows pets to talk?"

Sugar put her front legs on Sin's knee. "More more more, food man."

We burst out laughing, and I nodded. "I think that's exactly what he did. And I'm not sure the world is ready."

He looked at me in dismay. "Is that what she calls me? Food man? I have to admit, that's a little disappointing."

I rolled my lips in to keep from laughing. "Well, that does kind of describe you, doughnut guy."

He narrowed his eyes at me, but couldn't keep the smile off his face. "Not you too."

"Speaking of…wanna raid the kitchen? Formal dinners never serve enough food to fill me up."

"Never change, Princess. Never change." Sin just shook his head in amusement. "But before we go anywhere, you should open your present and see if you got the same thing. I realize it's implied, but you never know."

"True."

"Hey, you don't think Stanley sent us these gifts as a bribe, do you?"

"No. He knows better than that. I think he just wants to show there's no hard feelings." I went back to the couch and grabbed mine, yanking the bow free with a little less care than Sin had.

As the ribbon came free, a piece of folded paper fell to the floor. Sin bent and picked it up. "Weird that your note was on the outside."

"I didn't see it. Must have been on the bottom. I guess Stanley forgot to put it in the package."

Sin unfolded the paper. "This isn't from Stanley. At least I'm betting it's not." He turned the note so I could read it.

You're going to lose the throne.

I could hear my heart thumping in my chest as I read those words a second time. "Is that a warning or a threat?"

Sin shook his head. "I don't know. But it looks like the same handwriting as before." He nodded at the partially unwrapped gift still in my hands. "Open that and see if there's a note from Stanley in there like mine had."

My hands were shaking a little as I tore the rest of the wrapping off. "Note and collar, same as yours."

I collapsed onto the couch with the box in my hands. "It's Francis, isn't it? That note is a threat. A taunt, maybe. Who else could have slipped that paper into the wrapping of a gift that found its way into my apartment? Who else would know to do that? It had to be him. And he was late coming to dinner."

Sin sat and put his arm around me. "Or it's someone who really wants it to look like Francis."

"Are you having second thoughts about it being him?"

He went quiet for a moment. "I watched him as much as I could tonight. Never once did I see a malicious look on his face. He seemed happy to be at the dinner and genuinely in love with his fiancée. He doesn't strike me as a man with overreaching ambitions. But you know your cousin far better than I do."

I thought about that. "You're a good judge of character. I didn't notice anything odd about him tonight either. And I kind of thought the same way you did—that I'd at least catch him shooting eye daggers at one of us. But I didn't. And you didn't either. So where does that leave us?"

"We could talk to your father or your uncle. Or the constable. Or Francis. If you really want to go there."

"No, not yet. I think we should stick to my dad, Uncle Kris, and Constable Larsen. We need to fill them in anyway. But maybe that's what the note is trying to get us to do. React."

"So…do you not want to react?"

"I do. I just don't know how." I tipped my head back against the couch cushion. "Chocolate cake would help me think."

He laughed. "All right. Get some shoes on and let's go down to the kitchen."

But I stayed where I was and took the collar out of the box, turning it in my hands. "This will be a great cover for Spider's ability to talk. Not sure how he's going to feel about it, though. He's not much of a talker in front of anyone but me."

"Apparently. Maybe this will change that."

"I'm sure it will, and even if it only works half the time, can you imagine how these will fly off the shelves? I mean—" I sat up, collar still in my hand, and blinked hard a few times before turning toward Sin. "Why on earth would Stanley enter that robot chicken when he's sitting on a collar that translates your pet's voice? It's not a toy in the strictest sense of the word, but it's close enough. What kid wouldn't want to be able to talk to their pet? I realize he made the chicken for his granddaughter, but he could have just given that to her. This collar is amazing."

Sin put his arm up on the back of the couch. "Those are very good questions. And ones you should probably ask him."

"We will. Right after your interview at the *Post*."

"Do you know where he lives?" Sin asked.

"No, but that's easy enough to find out."

"Good." Sin stood. "Because I don't think those questions should wait until the morning."

"You're serious?"

"Yes. Let's do this. Let's figure this out. So what if we wake him up? You're heir to the throne. I see the kind of power you have. Let's put it to use."

I jumped to my feet. "You're right. Let's do it." I held my finger up. "But not in these clothes."

Our first stop after changing was Ezreal's apartment in the staff wing of the palace. He was up and happy to help. "Come in."

"I'm glad you haven't gone to bed yet."

"No, no. Just finished sending a notice to August Woolsey at the *Post* that his request for additional security was approved." He waved us in.

"That's great."

"Your father had me send it with one of the palace guards. He's starting watch at the paper until they can hire their own additional people."

"That's my dad." Ezreal's place was nice. Small, but well appointed. My father had offered him a larger place a few years ago, but Ezreal had turned it down, so my father had given him a budget for redecorating instead. I wasn't an expert by any means, but it seemed to me Ezreal had used that budget wisely.

Ezreal nodded. "He never does anything in half measures. What can I help you with?"

"I need Stanley Kinder's address. Any chance you might have that?"

"I think so. Follow me."

He led us into his home office. One wall held a shelf of boxing trophies and photos from his fighting days. Sin went over and started looking at them.

"Give me just a moment." Ezreal veered toward a set of ledgers that took up one long shelf above his desk. "This is a few years old, but I don't believe the Kinders have moved." He pulled down one marked Tinkers and paged through it.

Sin glanced around at some of the other boxing memorabilia in the office. "You did all right in the ring, didn't you?"

Ezreal looked up and smiled. "I did. Still train three days a week in the palace gym if you ever want to spar."

"For real?" Sin rocked back on his heels. "I would actually love that."

"Please," I said. "Don't break my boyfriend."

Ezreal laughed. "I wouldn't dream of it."

"Hey, now," Sin said. "I don't want special treatment. I can survive a black eye or a fat lip."

Ezreal tapped the page. "Found them. Seventeen Cranberry Lane."

I stuck my hands in my jean pockets. "Old neighborhood but very nice. Thank you. We'll get out of your hair now."

"It's never an inconvenience, Princess. Mr. Crowe, I'll be happy to supply you with a beatdown whenever you're ready."

Sin barked out a laugh and stuck out his hand. "I like you a lot, Ezreal. I'll be in touch about that beatdown."

We left and went straight to the crawler. The transportation valet was not as schooled at keeping the surprise out of his face as Sin's valet had been. His eyes rounded when he saw us, but then he quickly regained his composure. I'm sure we were the last people he expected to see at this late hour.

He gave me a little bow, then asked, "The crawler, Princess Frost?"

"Yes, thank you."

It took a little longer. Apparently, they'd garaged all the crawlers for the evening already. But a few minutes later, we were on our way toward the Tinkers' Village, often affectionately referred to as Toy Town.

Cranberry Lane was a beautiful street of older townhouses. It was no real surprise that the Kinders lived here. They'd been tinkers for a long time. If I had to guess, I'd say the house had been in the family equally as long.

I parked, and Sin and I went up the steps to the door. The front light was on, but so were the front lights of most of the townhouses. Didn't mean the Kinders were awake. I rang the bell and hoped for the best.

It took a few minutes, but Mrs. Kinder came to the door, dressed in a flannel robe and a nightcap, instantly making me feel bad for disturbing them so late.

"I'm sorry to bother you—"

She dropped into a curtsey far lower than I would have expected from a woman of her age. "Princess Frost."

"Yes, ma'am. I was wondering if we could talk to your husband, Stanley."

As she rose, he appeared behind her. He was still in his work clothes. "Princess Frost, what an honor to have you at our home."

"I'm sorry about the late hour, Stanley, but we really need to speak with you."

"Of course, come in." He moved out of the way, concern filling his gaze. "I hope the gifts I sent weren't out of place. I just thought—"

"No, no. They were great. But they are a big part of why we're here." The Kinders' home was charming, cozy, and neat as a pin. It looked picture perfect. Like a photo out of *Tinker Life* magazine. (Yes, that's a real publication.) I took that to mean Mrs. Kinder didn't allow the kind of chaos that existed in Stanley's work space. "Can we talk somewhere?"

Mrs. Kinder gestured to the room behind us. "Please, use the sitting room. I was just making some hot chocolate. I'll get some for everyone."

"That sounds wonderful," Sin said.

"It is," Stanley said. "Gracie grew up in a confectioners' household. She's a whiz with sweets." He led us into the sitting room.

I took a spot on the couch. "I'm more of a whiz at eating sweets."

Sin sat beside me.

Stanley chuckled. "That's more my area of expertise too." He took one of the easy chairs. "What can I help you with?"

Sin glanced at me, giving me a little nod. I smiled at Stanley. "Those collars you sent over are really something. We already tried one of them on Sinclair's cat, Sugar, and it worked like a charm. It was amazing."

He smiled back. "Thank you. I'm glad you like them."

"We love them," Sin said. "Sending them was a very thoughtful gift."

"It was," I added. "But it made me think. When you have something that amazing, why didn't you enter the collar instead of the robot chicken in the Tinkers' Tourney?"

Stanley shrugged. "The collars are really prototypes. They're not ready for mass production yet. And Mrs. Clucks-A-Lot was my gift to Lyla. Her inspiration, my creation. I was hoping that seeing her idea come to life would inspire her to be a tinker."

Mrs. Kinder walked in with a tray of steaming mugs. "There's no shame in being a confectioner, Stan."

"No, honey, of course not. There's no shame in

any profession. But there's no shame in me wanting to sway her a little either."

Mrs. Kinder handed out the mugs of hot chocolate. Fat, snowflake-shaped marshmallows floated on top. No doubt also homemade. She shook her head. "Our son became a builder, and it looks like his three little girls all want to pursue baking or confections. Stan is the last of a very long line of tinkers in the Kinder family, so it's been hard."

The thought of that squeezed my heart. "Oh, Stanley, I'm sorry. I didn't know."

He stared at his hot chocolate. "I don't know what happened, but none of them want to make toys." He looked up at us, attempting to smile. "I'll be okay. But after me...no more Kinder Creations."

"There will always be Kinder Creations." But I knew that wasn't true. At some point, that label would be retired.

He smiled a little more. "That's kind of you to say, Princess." He let out a long sigh. "Maybe one of them will change their mind and decide to make toys after all."

I sipped my hot chocolate. It was exceptional. "How old are they?"

"Three, six, and nine."

Sin laughed softly. "Still lots of time for them to figure out what they want to do in life. I have two nieces—a seven-year-old and a thirteen-year-old.

They've already been through about a dozen careers already."

Stanley's smile seemed more heartfelt after Sin's words. "Children do change their minds, don't they? I was just hoping a good showing at the tinker competition would help with that. But now...I guess there won't really be a tourney this year."

I sighed. I was letting my frustration show, but I didn't care. "I'm sorry we bothered you so late. And I'm sorry we haven't gotten much further in figuring out what happened at the tourney. I wish I had answers, but I don't."

Stanley nodded. "They'll come. I hope."

Since we were here, I decided to ask a few more questions. "Do you have any enemies, Stanley? Anyone who'd want to see you fail?"

He shook his head. "Not that I know of. I certainly hope not, anyway."

We fell into silence until Sin chimed in. "Mrs. Kinder, this is the best hot chocolate I've ever had." He lifted his mug. "What's your secret?"

She smiled profusely. "A little touch of cinnamon and a vanilla bean that's been soaked in bourbon. Oh, and a dash of sea salt."

He laughed. "I think it's that bourbon-soaked vanilla bean that does it."

She blushed a little. "I'm sure you're right."

He took another sip, then looked at me. "Maybe you should tell them what we learned at the farm."

I thought about that. "I guess I could. What have we got to lose?"

Stanley sat forward. "Tell us what?"

I glanced at Mrs. Kinder before answering him. "First, let me ask you when Lyla's birthday is?"

Mrs. Kinder answered me. "September twenty-sixth."

I shook my head. "So that part was a lie."

Stanley frowned. "I don't understand."

"You know how you told me Lyla won a stuffed chicken in a contest? There was no contest. But a woman did come into the gift shop and send a stuffed chicken to Lyla after the class field trip. She said it was for Lyla's birthday."

"But the note said it was because she'd won a contest. What woman was this?" Mrs. Kinder asked.

"We don't know." I wrapped my hands around my cup. "We have a description, but that's about it."

"Tell us," Stanley said. "Maybe we can help."

"All we know is she has an average build, short, medium blue hair with a few silver streaks, and was about midsixties. And she wore glasses. Could be anyone."

Stanley looked at his wife, then back at me. "Sounds like a lot of women in the North Pole."

"I know." I drank the last of my hot chocolate, resisting the urge to use my fingers to retrieve what was left of the marshmallow, and set the mug aside. Then I remembered something. "Hang on…"

I dug into my purse. I pulled out the note from the farm that Greta Ann had given us, the note that had Lyla's address scribbled on it. I held it out to Stanley and his wife. "Does this help? It could be a sample of the woman's handwriting."

Stanley reached out and took the paper, the color leaching from his face even as an angry spark lit in his eyes. "Yes, it helps. I know this scrawl. It belongs to Dora Frigit."

I shook my head. "Name sounds a little familiar. Who is she?"

A muscle in his jaw twitched. "The Glitterskins inventor. The third tinker in the competition."

I squeezed Sin's hand as we walked down the Kinders' steps. "You were right."

He smiled. "Happens occasionally. But it doesn't solve anything. Just gives us one more thing to investigate. Maybe moves us closer to an answer."

"But it makes perfect sense. If Dora somehow got these other two tinkers to put up the same kind of toys, and they get disqualified from the competition, she wins by default. I mean, it's perfect."

"I agree. If it is her, I guess starting rumors about me and trying to make it seem like your cousin is after the throne are her way of distracting people from what she's up to."

"Or maybe she wasn't hoping to distract anyone but us. You know, get us off on the wrong path. Still, seems like a lot of effort to go to just to win a competition. Especially going after you. What if you'd decided to go home like you originally offered? Her distraction would have been gone pretty quickly."

"Maybe she knew you wouldn't let me go. You didn't, after all. And stirring people up is a great smoke screen. Especially if you can make them afraid. And who better to do that than a necromancer?"

We hopped into the crawler, Sin behind the wheel.

"I guess so. Something about it feels like a real reach to me. For a tinker to rely on the complicated lives of the royals to cover her deception? How would she know enough about us to even make us part of her plan?"

"You said yourself nothing stays secret in the palace."

"True." I rolled that thought over. "You know, when we were in the square waiting for the toys to be revealed, I could have sworn I heard people calling you a necromancer in the whispers that were going around, but I didn't understand how anyone would know that. That information wasn't hidden, but it wasn't published either. All I can think is that someone overheard my parents or my aunt and uncle talking about you."

Sin stared at me in that way he had that meant he was stuck on a thought. He started to slowly shake his head. "Maybe it wasn't any of your family."

"Then who?"

"Yesterday, when we were on the Segways in the hall, you said something about falling in love with a necromancer as we passed those housekeepers."

My mouth fell open. "You're right. I did. So much for taking my own advice about not saying anything in front of staff that I don't want repeated." I groaned, frustrated at myself. "I'm going to ask Mamie to give me everything she's got on Dora Frigit in the morning. In fact, if it's okay with you, I'll drop you at the paper for your interview, then go see Mamie. I want to know if Dora's got friends in the palace. Friends that would give her the kind of details she could use against us."

"I'm good with that plan. Let's keep this ball rolling."

I looked over at him. "Oh, this ball is gonna roll. But first..." I bit my lip as I smiled.

His brows rose. "What?"

"I still want chocolate cake."

"You just had hot chocolate," he teased. "Really good hot chocolate."

"That was like an appetizer. I need the main course now."

He laughed as he drove through the quiet streets. Amazing what a little info and the promise of sugar could do for our moods.

"You know, this could mean my cousin is in the clear. Or..." I tapped my fingers on my knee. "Could he be working with Dora? He's always aligned himself more with the builders than the tinkers. Although I guess that will change to the decorators when he marries Umelia."

"I guess anything's possible." He kept his eyes on the road as we went over the Meltwater River Bridge. "How can we find that out?"

"Mamie might be able to give us more info about access to the tinkers' floor. I don't know if the elevator records what badges are used, but that's a place to start."

"Can't hurt to ask, right?"

"Right."

He pulled through the palace gates and back to the south entrance. He parked, handed the keys to a valet, and we went inside.

I took his hand again and led him to the kitchens. There was no one there, which made the space feel even bigger. Everything sparkled like it was new.

He did a slow spiral, taking it all in. "This is some kitchen."

"There's a cook on call overnight too. Just in case someone gets a craving for something that isn't in the family fridge."

"The family fridge?"

I walked over to the stainless-steel double doors and opened them, showing Sin what I meant.

213

"This. The chefs prepare food that's easy to grab and go and put it in here for the family and palace staff. That way, if any of us gets hungry, we can help ourselves."

"I like that." He tipped his head toward the shelves of food in front of us. "Rather high ratio of sweet to savory, don't you think?"

I reached in and hefted out the tall, triple chocolate cake that was almost always on hand. "I think it's perfect. Grab some plates, would you?" I pointed with my elbow. "That first cabinet, middle shelf. Oh, and we need ice cream. And whipped cream. Forget plates, get those big bowls."

"What? No sprinkles?" Sin laughed and went to the cabinet I'd indicated.

We destroyed two massive slices of cake with ice cream, whipped cream, *and* sprinkles, then finally headed back upstairs.

I was happy. I was in love with a great guy, full of sugar, and we were finally making progress in the Mysterious Case of the Double Robot Chickens. Life was good.

"You think the cats missed us?" Sin asked.

I laughed. "Only if their food bowls are empty."

"Let's check." Sin unlocked his door.

Spider and Sugar were sitting there, waiting on us.

Sugar got to her feet. "Food food food."

Sin grimaced. "That is really going to take some

getting used to. I had no idea she had such a one-track mind."

Spider stood up and stretched. "Mama, Spider hungry."

I shook my head. "It's not just her."

"Hey." Sin stopped short. "He's not wearing a collar yet, and I understood that. He really does talk."

I grinned. "Told you. Maybe Sugar talking made him feel more comfortable."

"*Mama*," Spider said. "*Hungry*."

"And bossier." I scooped him up. "I'm sure you are, baby. We're going to feed you." I glanced at Sin. "I should just take him back to my place. No sense in feeding him twice, which is what will happen if he eats here."

"Okay. See you in the morning?"

"Yep." I leaned up to kiss Sin, and he met me halfway, his hands on my shoulders.

"Love you, Jayne," he whispered as we parted.

"Love you, Sinclair." I smiled at him as I hugged Spider a little closer.

"Spider loves Chicken Party."

We burst out laughing.

Life was more than good. Life was incredible.

And I was absolutely ready to say yes.

The next morning went exactly as planned. After a quick breakfast, I dropped Sin at the *Post* and went to the factory to see Mamie. She was at her desk in a twin set and matching skirt of soft blue, her strand of crystal snug at her throat. A mother-of-pearl barrette held her hair back on one side.

I'd gone more casual in jeans, a dressy tee and my leather jacket. "Morning, Mamie. You look pretty today."

"Good morning, Princess. Thank you. How are you?"

"In desperate need of information."

Mamie smiled. "You've come to the right place."

"That's what I've heard." I sat on the edge of her desk. "Is there a record kept of who's used their badge to access the tinkers' floor and when?"

She shook her head. "No, sorry."

So much for that. "Where's the constable on all this business with the Tinkers' Tourney?"

"I don't think she's anywhere. She's basically stood down after the incident with your uncle."

"I see. Well, I need her to stand up, then. I need a background check on someone and I also want them placed under surveillance."

Mamie nodded. "Then the constable's your woman. That is her job, after all."

"Good. Do you think I should go see Constable Larsen in person, or can I just send her a message?"

"A personal visit is always nice, but I'm sure you have a lot to do. Actually, I could call her in. The station is only a block away. I'm sure she'd be happy to come over here."

"That would be perfect. It'll give me time to see Uncle Kris. I assume he's in?"

"He is. What else can I do for you?"

"I'd love any info you can give me on tinker Dora Frigit. That's the woman I want surveilled. I want to know her history, who she's friends with, who her family is, all that stuff. Can you help me with that?"

Mamie sat up straighter, going into work mode. "She's the other tinker in the tourney, isn't she? The Glitterskins creator?"

"Yes, that's her. That's who I believe is behind some of this. Maybe all."

"I'll pull her file and have it for you in a few minutes, although I'm not sure how much it's going to tell you about her personal life." Mamie reached for the intercom. "You want to see your uncle now?"

"Yes, please."

She pressed the button. "Boss, your niece is here to see you."

"Send her in!"

Mamie gave me the nod.

My uncle was at his desk, reading a copy of the *Pole Post*. He set it down as I walked through the doors. "Good article here. Excellent explanation of what happened. Your father told me about the approval for more security too."

I took a seat. "Glad to hear it. The editor told me yesterday he'd be printing it today. I'll read it when I get back. Sinclair is at the *Post* right now being interviewed."

"Outstanding. That should help people get to know him."

"That's what we were thinking." I sat back. "Can I ask you about someone? One of the tinkers?"

"Of course, Jaynie. Who is it?"

"Dora Frigit. What do you know about her?"

He leaned back and steepled his fingers over his chest. "She's a good worker. Not one of the most exceptional tinkers, but very solid. Her late husband was a tinker, too, and they shared a workshop on the lab floor. I've given her some leeway since he passed because she never really seemed to recover from his death."

"That's sad."

He nodded. "I'm starting to think that's changed with her qualifying entry into the tourney. I just hope she doesn't take this nonsense as another setback."

"I don't think that's going to be the case. Mostly because I think she's behind some of this nonsense. Maybe all of it."

He pushed his glasses up onto his forehead and came forward in his chair to plant his elbows on the desk. "You have any proof of that?"

"Some." I told him about the notes and the handwriting and the chicken sent to Lyla Kinder.

Uncle Kris pulled out a snow-white hanky and mopped his face. "If that's true, then she's disqualified. Son of a nutcracker, she's more than disqualified. She's fired. Permanently on the naughty list. Exiled, even. We can't have that kind of underhanded business here."

"I'm getting Constable Larsen on it. Having Frigit surveilled. See if anything more concrete can be drummed up."

He nodded. "Good. You keep me posted. I want to know everything that's found."

I stood. "You got it."

He winked at me. "Good work, Jaynie. I knew you'd figure this nonsense out."

"Nothing's figured out yet, but progress is being made."

His smile grew. "That's my girl."

The constable seemed happy to be needed and eager to get the surveillance underway. I hoped that including her in the investigation also helped smooth things over even more than my uncle's apology and box of fudge had. My guess was there'd never actually been a need for a stakeout in the NP before, so this was a pretty big deal for her.

That worked out for me, because I knew she'd be all over it, eager to do the best possible job she could, which was exactly what I needed. I might have also hinted that there was an invite to the wedding in it for her.

Yes, I realize that technically Sin and I weren't even officially engaged, but I needed as much help as Constable Larsen could give. She probably would have been invited anyway. At least she'd have gotten a second-tier invite.

Once she left, Mamie opened her top desk drawer and pulled out a dark manila file folder about an inch thick. She laid it on the desk with a soft thud. "Frigit's file. It's as thick as it is because there's a good bit of crossover between her and her late husband. A lot of their projects were joint efforts. Can't have one without the other."

"Got it." I almost reached for it, then realized she might not let it leave the office. "Can I take that with me?"

"You can, so long as you promise on your crown not to lose or distribute any of the information contained within. This is Frigit's private personnel file. It's not exactly top secret, but it's not for willy-nilly sharing either. Usually, your uncle is the only one with access. Get my drift?"

"I do. Thank you for trusting me with this."

She smiled. "I want this tourney business solved as much as any of you. It's making Kris very unhappy." Her smile went away. "You realize how his being in an off mood could affect Christmas? I was hoping to spend New Year's in Florida with my sister. That won't happen if things melt up here. I'll be stuck doing damage control."

"Right. We can't have this affect Christmas. I promise that I understand the need to get this all squared away as soon as possible." I reached for the file.

"I know you do." Her smile returned as her

hands flattened on the paperwork. "Now swear on your crown."

"I swear on my crown that I'll keep that file safe and not share it with anyone except for Sinclair."

She gave me a look.

"What? He's helping me and as much a part of this as any of us. That's not willy-nilly sharing."

"He doesn't have clearance."

"Technically, with the badge Uncle Kris gave him, he does."

Her eyes narrowed, then her hands came off the file. "I'll allow it."

"Thanks." I grabbed the file and stuck it under my arm. I should have brought a bag or something to hide it in. "Um…"

"There are some shopping bags in the bottom drawer of the filing cabinet against the wall. Take one and put the file in it. Wouldn't do for folks to see you walking out of here with something that restricted."

Was there any wonder why she was so good at her job? "Good point, thanks. Guess I should head over to the *Post* and see how Sin's interview is going."

Mamie's gaze went icy. "Is that with August?"

"Yes. He really seems like a nice man. He had nothing to do with those nasty articles." I gave her the quick rundown of what had happened and August's explanation.

Her expression got a lot less frosty. "Well. That's nice to hear."

Shopping bag in hand, I leaned against the filing cabinet. "Why did you two divorce?"

The look she shot me said I was being a little impertinent. I didn't care. I was curious. She pursed her lips, then finally spoke. "We were too young to know what we wanted. The marriage didn't survive us figuring that out."

"You called him an old fool. He seems like an all right guy to me."

She stared at her desk for a moment. "He is. I guess you might say I never really got over him." She looked up, her smile almost believable. "Everyone has a love that got away."

I nodded, thinking about Cooper. "That's for sure. But you move past that. Or the relationship changes." Cooper's and mine sure had. We were good friends now. Maybe better than we'd ever been as a couple. And if I'd stayed with him, I'd never have met the man I was supposed to be with. Sinclair.

"I suppose," Mamie said. "But not everyone moves on." She frowned. "That's what I've heard, anyway."

I slipped the file into the bag and walked back to her desk. "You still have a thing for him, don't you?"

She adjusted her glasses and gave me a stern

look. "Speaking of love, don't you have a fiancé waiting on you?"

"Snowballs, yes." I slung the shopping bag straps over my shoulder and ran for the elevator. "See you later."

I found Sin in August's office. His secretary let me in without a hint of attitude this time. That was nice.

I peeked in. "I don't mean to interrupt."

August and Sin both stood. August smiled broadly. "No interruption. We've pretty much finished up."

I looked at Sin. He seemed happy. "How did it go?"

"Very well, I think." He turned to August. "Did you get everything you need?"

"I believe I did." He tapped the tape recorder on his desk. "I'll refer to the tape if I can't remember something, but it was a good interview. I'm excited to print it and get the truth out there."

"I can't wait to read it." I was also excited to dig into the file Mamie had given me, but I wasn't going to rush Sin out of here. "You got pictures as well?"

"We did," Sin said. "On the roof with the factory behind me and then some with the palace in the background."

"Excellent. August, are you good on security now?"

"Yes. And thank you so much for speaking to your father about that. Oddly enough, there were no attempts last night. Hopefully, whoever was adding those terrible articles decided to quit before they got caught."

I shrugged. "I wouldn't mind if they got caught."

"Nor would I, Princess, but at least it seems to be behind us now."

"For that I'm glad. Thanks again for interviewing Sinclair."

He nodded. "It was my pleasure. I'm glad I had the opportunity to get to know Mr. Crowe better. I think the citizens of the North Pole will feel the same."

Sin stuck his hand out to August. "Thank you for your time. Look forward to seeing tomorrow's paper."

"I'll be sure to send a few extra copies to the palace."

We turned to go, then a thought popped into my head. An impulse, really. I looked back at August. "Are you married, Mr. Woolsey?"

He seemed a little surprised by my question. "No, Princess."

"Neither is Mamie Wynters. At least currently. With Mamie, you just never know when that status might change."

He swallowed. "Oh? That's a curious thing to mention, I have to say."

I lifted one shoulder coyly. "Just putting that out there. In case either of you has grown up enough to take another crack at things. Have a good day."

I left before August could say anything else. I figured he was a journalist. If he wanted to know more, he could do some digging and ask some questions. That was kind of his job, after all.

Sin held it together until we were outside. "Okay, what was that all about? They've already gotten divorced. What makes you think they'd want to start something up again?"

"Just a little convo I had with Mamie in the office."

"You can't leave anything alone, can you?" He snorted, eyes bright with amusement.

I grabbed his hand. "Maybe being in love makes me think everyone should be in love."

He laughed, tugging me closer. "Even Francis?"

"Jury's out on that one."

We got into the crawler with Sin behind the wheel. He got us moving toward the palace.

He glanced at the time on the crawler's dash. "When did your dad want us to go tour that new peppermint plant?"

"Whenever we got back, but we have some other work to do first." I grabbed the shopping bag from the rear seat. "Mamie gave me Dora Frigit's personnel file. We need to go through it and look for anything that might tell us why she tried to sour the tourney."

"You going to tell your dad about that?"

"Yes. Because going to the peppermint plant would still be fun. We just need to do this first."

"Good with me." He pulled through the palace gates and took us straight to the south entrance.

From there, we went to my dad's office to fill him in on the work we needed to do. When we went in, Ezreal was at his desk.

He smiled at us. "Morning. I hear you had an interview at the *Post*, Mr. Crowe. How was it?"

"Really good, thank you."

"Excellent. They owe you." He turned his gaze to me. "Would you like to see your father?"

"I would. Is he busy?"

"Just finishing up with the Minister of Finance. Shouldn't be too much longer. Would you like something while you wait? Hot chocolate? Eggnog? Cider?"

"Cider," I piped up.

"Cider?" Sin looked at me. "I think that actually qualifies as a fruit. I'm so proud of you."

Ezreal snorted and went to the wet bar. "Shall I make that two?"

"Sure," Sin said. "Why not?"

We took seats in the waiting area next to Ezreal's desk, and he brought us the cider. "How's the investigation going? Anything new?"

"We might have a lead suspect." I tapped the shopping bag that was now on my lap.

"Excellent news. Progress is good." He went back to his desk. "If there's anything I can do, just say the word."

"I will." I sipped the cider. "The meeting with the Kinders last night is what started us on this new path. So really, you've already helped."

"This is good." Sin lifted the glass of cider. "Everything here is good. I still can't believe you don't have doughnuts."

"Isn't that odd?" Ezreal shook his head. "You'd think we would."

The door to my father's office opened, and the Minister of Finance came out, a woman named Rowena Silver. She'd been at the formal dinner, but seated closer to my uncle. "I'll be sure to get that proposed budget to you in the next few days, Your Highness."

"Very good." My father walked out behind her. "Jayne. I thought I heard your voice."

"Hi, Dad."

Minister Silver bowed as she left. "Princess Frost, Mr. Crowe."

I nodded back. "Minister."

As the door shut behind her, my father went to the wet bar and fixed himself some coffee. "You two ready to tour the peppermint plant?"

I pulled the Frigit file out of the shopping bag. "Not quite yet. We think we have a lead in the tourney situation."

My father turned, cup in hand. "Is that so? Can I help?"

I hefted the file. "If you want. There's a lot to go through."

He pointed at Ezreal. "Cancel anything I have coming up for the next hour." As Ezreal nodded, my father turned toward a different door than the one going into his office. "Let's head to the conference room, divide it up and dig in. My future son-in-law needs his name cleared."

But forty-five minutes in and we'd gotten nowhere.

Sin stared down at the stack of paperwork before him. "I hope it's not impolite of me to say this, but Dora Frigit has led a pretty boring life."

"Not impolite," my father said. "Because it's true. Even when her husband was alive, they didn't do much of note. I'm surprised she made it into the tourney."

I had to speak up. "I'm not. Glitterskins is a pretty good idea. I mean, kids love glitter, right? But it gets everywhere, which makes parents hate it. Her idea is something kids and parents can love together."

My father nodded. "I agree, it's a good product. Your uncle has actually decided it's already going into production, although that might be on hold with this new information. But if you look at all the other work she's put forward, even the work done with her husband, none of it is particularly exciting. She and her husband are what your uncle refers to as midlevels. Solid workers, good work ethic, decent ideas, but they're not about to set the place on fire. Metaphorically speaking."

Sin sat back. "There are midlevels in every profession, really."

My father's gaze returned to the paperwork in front of him. "That's for sure."

Sin stared ahead, his expression making him seem lost in thought. "And lot of people spend their whole lives, happily I might add, as midlevels."

My father glanced at him. "You're right, they do."

Sin refocused and tapped a finger on the papers in front of him. "So what made Dora suddenly step up her game?"

I leaned in. "Do you think someone gave her the Glitterskins idea?"

"Could be." Sin shrugged. "What do you think, King, uh, Your Highness?"

My father laughed softly. "Jack will do."

Sin shifted in his chair. "Okay, Jack. What do you think?"

"That you're on to something. It's out of character enough that we need to do some deeper digging. Beyond this file."

If kicking my feet up onto the table in my father's conference room wouldn't have gotten me in trouble, I would have done it. "It just so happens that I asked the constable to surveil Frigit this morning."

My father's brows lifted. "Good work, Jay. That might be just what we need to crack this thing open. Until then, however, I'm not sure there's much more we can do."

"We could tour that peppermint plant," Sin said.

A huge grin spread on my father's face. He reached over and clamped a hand on Sin's shoulder all the while keeping his eyes on me. "You should marry this one, Jay."

"Dad…"

My father released Sin and pushed to his feet. "Let's go. There are sweets to be sampled."

We took my father's crawler, which was a metallic-blue monster that made the standard ones look like tricycles. I thought Sin's eyes might fall out of his head when he saw it.

He ran his hand over the swooping lines of the vehicle. "This. Is. Amazing."

"Thank you. It was custom made for me." My dad was beaming a bit. He loved this machine.

"I can tell. It's amazing." Sin laughed. "I guess I said that."

"It's all right. It's a good word. Especially for this beast." He clicked the key fob, and the doors opened skyward, making the crawler look like a giant blue bat. "Hop in."

I climbed into the back. It wasn't even a question. "You ride up front, Sin."

"No, I couldn't. That wouldn't be—"

"Yes, you can. I've ridden up front a thousand times." I clicked on my seat belt before he could argue. Then I readjusted to sit in the middle so I could see between the seats and keep an eye on both my dad and Sin. And frankly, so I could be part of the conversation.

Sin got into the front with a smile on his face. He looked the same way I imagined I did when presented with a box of goodies from Delaney's Delectables. "The interior is so cool. It's a lot sleeker than the other crawler. I'm guessing it has a lot more options too."

"It does." My dad showed him a few things while I just shook my head, smiled, and thought about how alike my dad and Sin were. Maybe that was one of the reasons why my dad liked Sin so much. He enjoyed having another guy in the palace. Not that my uncle wasn't a guy, but he didn't live in the palace and he was busy with his own stuff.

And maybe having Sin around would be a little like having a son for my dad.

The thought that my father might look at Sin that way made me all warm inside. How sweet.

After a few more minutes, we headed off into

the tundra. The plant was a little ways out, mostly because the fumes the peppermint plants put out could be a little eye watering. Better to have some distance from town.

The crawler talk continued until the plant rose up in the distance like a giant birthday cake complete with candles, except the candles were ventilation shafts. The intense smell of mint filled the vehicle.

"Wow." Sin blinked as his eyes teared up a little. "That's strong stuff."

"That's why we put the plants out here," my father said. "Although you do get used to it after a while."

I inhaled, letting the aroma clear my head. Nothing like it in the world, frankly. Unless you've stuffed Junior Mints up your nose. Which I'm guessing you haven't. Also, don't.

My father pulled into the employee parking lot, and we headed in. "This plant has only been open for two weeks."

"Is that why you're here?" Sin asked. "To see how things are going?"

"Not really. There are inspectors for that. I just thought you guys would like to see it. Although I do like to visit the plants after they open."

"So is this a surprise visit?" Sin asked.

My father shook his head. "No, they know we're coming. No need to give anyone a heart attack."

We went in, and after all the appropriate fanfare that a royal visit entailed, we were suited up in white lab coats, paper hats, and stretchy shoe covers. We'd also been given a tour guide, Xander Sweets. He was the plant manager, and a real character.

He wore his baby-blue hair shaved short, maybe because of the paper hat his job required, but his ear tips were pierced with little silver hoops, and he had a candy cane tattooed on his neck. This was a man who loved his job.

It took us about an hour to tour the plant, try our hand at making a few candies, and sample one (or three) of everything. And there was a lot being made in that plant. My favorite were the mint meltaways, little pastel-colored mint kisses with tiny white sprinkles stuck to the bottom of them. They were sweet and minty and definitely melted in your mouth, but the sprinkles added some crunch. I loved them.

They were some of my mom's favorites too, and Xander was kind enough to send a big bag of them back for her and another one for me.

Sin had been sucking on the same cobalt and white striped wintermint candy cane for fifteen minutes. His tongue was probably blue. Meanwhile, my father was popping mint-chocolate jellybeans like they were free. Which, I guess, they were.

On the verge of being minted out, we went back to the crawler with goodies to go and headed for the palace.

I let Sin sit up front again. He and my dad were talking shop now. Production values or something. I drifted off, waking up as we pulled under the portico of the family exit.

"Grab that bag of meltaways for your mom, honey."

"Got them." I snagged the package, reminding myself to take out the ones that were for me.

Sin held the door for me. "Are we going back to the office?"

"I need to get that file and take it back to Mamie."

My father nodded. "And I have work to be done."

"Isn't there always?" Sin sighed. "I should check in with Archie. See how things are going. He was going to try out some new doughnuts while he's there. I wonder if they sold well."

"Use the snow globe in my office. We sent Archie with one, so if he's not busy, he should be able to talk to you."

"That would be great." Sin took my hand, giving me a wink. "Got enough candy there, sugar?"

I laughed. "Never."

We went into my dad's office. Ezreal was filing some paperwork. He turned as we came in. "I can tell where you folks have been. It's like a clean, menthol breeze just blew in."

Sin grinned. "Is it that apparent?"

Ezreal nodded, closed his eyes and inhaled. "Now I want meltaways." He laughed.

I pulled out my bag of candies and set them on his desk. "Here you go. All for you."

He looked surprised for a moment, then he shook his head. "I can't take these. Those are your mints."

I shrugged one shoulder. "I ate my weight in them at the plant. I'd much rather you have this bag."

He smiled. "That is very kind of you, Princess. I'm not going to refuse them twice."

I was about to hand my dad the bag since my mom's candies were all that remained in it now, when the office door opened and the constable came in.

She looked at all of us with a very serious expression. "We need to talk."

My father held his hand out. "Come into my office. Ezreal—"

"Holding your calls."

We swarmed into the inner office, not waiting to waste a minute. As soon as the door was closed, Constable Larsen spoke.

"Dora Frigit is up to something."

My father frowned. "We know. That's why Princess Frost asked you to keep tabs on her."

There was a little edge of frustration to my father's tone. He didn't like anyone playing games with him, but I didn't think that's what Constable Larsen was doing. I tried to help. "What did you find out, Constable Larsen? You've only been watching her since this morning. What have you seen?"

The constable made a face. "It's more of a hunch."

My father groaned. "Get back to us when you have solid evidence. We have all the hunches we can use."

But the constable wasn't giving up. She got points for that. "I need more help."

"You have a fairly large staff that don't do much more than direct traffic and write parking tickets." My father raised his brows. "What more help do you need?"

She stared right back at him. "I don't have access to most of the places Frigit goes. She disappears into the elevator at the factory and I'm done. I can't get into the elevator with her. That's not much of a secret tail, is it? And I certainly can't get to the tinkers' lab floor. I don't have access. So the best I can give you is partial info."

My father sighed. "You're right. We need to fix that, but I can't give you access to the tinkers' floor. And Kris won't either, not even for a situation like this."

Larsen glanced at me. "The princess and her boyfriend got access."

"That's a little different." Not much, granted, but if my uncle started allowing everyone up there, the tinkers would revolt. And that's the last thing we needed at the moment.

I held my hands up before she could argue. "We'll figure something out. Give us a few minutes to talk, please."

Larsen's mouth was a hard, thin line, but then she nodded and went back out to the waiting area.

Sin closed the door behind her. "Do you have a plan?"

"Well..." I looked at my dad. "Remember that bracelet you gave me when I first went to Nocturne Falls?"

A slow smile bent my father's mouth. "You realize I wouldn't normally approve of this kind of thing, but in this case, I think it's the perfect solution."

Sin waved his hand. "Hello, necromancer here. No clue what you two elves are talking about."

I almost laughed. He was so adorable. "A form of elf magic, actually. Most elves use a special silver bracelet to disguise their elfish looks when they leave the NP. The bracelets make us look human to other humans, but elf to other elves."

"Seriously?" Sin seemed impressed.

"Yep. They're not quite as popular now as they used to be, what with multicolored hair not really that unusual anymore, but there was a time when no winter elf ventured beyond our world without one."

My father nodded. "And when Jayne went to Nocturne Falls, I gave her a special one. It changed the way she looked to both human and elf eyes. She needed it that way because the Winter Princess is pretty recognizable."

The light in Sin's eyes showed he knew what was going on. "So she's going to disguise herself again and do the following herself. Right?"

"Right," I said. "But, Dad, I'd really like Sin with me."

"I would too. Not saying you can't protect yourself, but I'd feel better if you weren't alone. Dora might look incapable of harm, but she's a tinker, and at her skill level, boring as it is, her magic is substantial. I don't need you run through with an ice spear."

I grimaced. "Yeah, I'm not real keen on that myself."

"Okay, I have to ask," Sin said. "Is your father's desk really made of ice? Or was that glass designed to just look like ice?"

We were crouched down, taking turns peering out the mail slot of tinker Argyle Featherstone's workshop on the lab floor. We'd been here for nearly two hours, settling in right after Argyle had been summoned to my uncle's office, where he had been given the surprise gift of three days off under the guise of a new employee incentive program.

As it happened, his workshop was catty-corner from Dora's. Which made it the perfect spot to watch her from.

His mail slot smelled like those little red-hot candies. I was sure that wasn't a coincidence. Much like everything else that had been going on. Although, in Argyle's case it was easy to see he liked his sweets on the spicy side. He had a big bag of cinnamon gummy bears on his worktable. I'd never developed a taste for those things.

The only cinnamon I liked was in Mummy's giant frosted cinnamon rolls. Which I could go for now, because somehow, even after eating all that candy at the peppermint plant, I was hungry again.

I sat back for a second to answer Sin's question. My neck was getting a crick in it. "Nope. Actual ice."

"How…" Sin shook his head. "I know it's magic. I get that. But still. It's impressive."

"It's meant to be. It's a show of his power. To maintain a slab of ice in such a pristine state of frozenness is astonishing. And he does it without much more than an afterthought."

"Can you do that?"

"A piece of ice that big and that stable?" I thought about it. "I've never really attempted it. Not sure. But I'll be able to when I become queen."

"So you'll get more power when you're crowned?"

I nodded. "Comes with accepting the scepter. The ceremony is sort of your standard pomp and circumstance, but the actual transfer of power is pretty intense."

"Intense like how?"

"Hang on." I went down to a whisper. "I think I hear something."

I lifted the flap a smidge, and we both looked through.

The slight creak of the door was easier to hear now, and in a few seconds, legs went by. Female legs. Dora Frigit, to be exact.

I nodded at Sin, and he nodded back at me. We got to our feet, slipped our bracelets on and went after her. Discreetly, of course.

Our bracelets turned us into Argyle and his wife, Yula. Completely. We even had their voices.

"Hold that elevator," Sin called out.

We didn't have their mannerisms, but then, we weren't inviting Dora over to dinner, just keeping an eye on her to see what she did inside the factory. Once she left, Constable Larsen could take over.

Dora held the elevator, although she didn't look happy about it. Whatever. She could get iced for all I cared.

I smiled at her and nodded politely as I got on ahead of Sin. "How are you, Dora?"

My uncle had briefed us on the relationship between Dora and the Featherstones. They were friendly, but not buddy-buddy. That would do us just fine.

She adjusted her grip on her bag and smiled one of those polite, closed-mouth smiles that didn't reach the eyes. "Fine, and you?"

"Good, thank you. I suppose you'll be named

winner of the tourney this year, what with all that duplication mix-up business going on."

Dora's smile vanished.

Sin did his part. "Now, Yula. Dora's entry was very good."

I nodded enthusiastically and looked at her, watching her eyes. "Oh, yes, it's wonderful. Glitterskins is such a good idea."

Dora let out a breath and relaxed. "Thank you."

Of course, I couldn't leave that alone. "How did you come up with the idea?"

She tightened up again. "It just came to me."

She poked the first-floor button a second time.

"You mean like a dream?" I stared at her, all smiley and curious and innocent-like.

"Something like that." She glared at the numbers counting down the floors.

"I see. Headed home for the day?"

"Yes." Dora's tone was curt.

Sin leaned in. "We're going over to Glacier Pizza for a large pepperoni with extra cheese."

Dora did that polite smile again. "How nice for you."

He nodded. "Why don't you join us? Dinner's our treat. You're about to be the tourney winner, after all."

She hung on to the smile. "I can't, but thank you."

The elevator finally found the first floor and came to a stop. Dora stepped forward before the doors opened and was out them a half second after they parted.

Sin and I walked out casually, keeping our eyes on her.

"You really think she's going home?" he asked.

"I don't know. She seemed…"

"Squirrelly."

I nodded. "Yep." We followed behind at a leisurely pace, but we were losing her.

"It's up to the constable now?"

I took a breath. She was almost to the parking lot. "It has to be. It would look weird for the Featherstones to trail her home. Uncle Kris said they don't live near each other."

"You really want to keep following her, don't you?"

She went through the outside doors.

I grunted in disappointment. "Yes. But it's time to let the constable do her thing. I guess."

Sin snorted. "Come on, we have to get out of here before someone who really knows the Featherstones talks to us."

"Yeah, I know. Let's go call Larsen and tell her we got nothing new."

We went back to my uncle's office by express elevator and used the phone to call the constable's office. I told her Dora was headed home, and Larsen confirmed that her deputy was already trailing her, then thanked us.

I hung up, unable to contain my disappointment. "What if she's not going home? What if she's going to meet up with whoever she's in on this with?"

"Then the deputy will let us know what happens." Sin shrugged. "I know you don't like being out of the loop, but I don't see what else we can do."

Mamie was making a cup of gingerbread tea. She walked back to her desk, sending the aroma our way. It mingled with the sweet scent of the bouquet taking up the corner of her desk. Snow lilies, frost roses and crocus. Those were new. "I'm sorry the file wasn't of more help," she said.

I shrugged. "I guess it was silly of me to expect some kind of clue in there."

Mamie sipped the tea, the steam clouding her glasses for a second. "Hmm."

"What?"

She was staring at the flowers. "It just occurred to me, now that he and I are on speaking terms again, but you know who might really have the dirt on Dora?"

"Who?"

An odd look came over her face. She sipped her tea again, then set the cup in its saucer and sighed. "August Woolsey."

So that's who the flowers were from. How about that. "Why would he know?"

"He's been at the *Post* for decades. He knows

everyone and hears all sorts of things. Couldn't hurt to talk to him." She lifted one slim shoulder. "What else do you have to do while you wait on Constable Larsen?"

Sin put his hands on his hips. "She's got a point."

"I guess we're going back to the paper."

Mamie picked up the phone, smiling slightly. "I'll let him know you're on your way."

I suppressed a grin. "You do that."

August met us right inside the entrance of the *Post*. "Welcome back."

"Thank you."

He and Sin shook hands. "I understand you need some information."

"We do," Sin said.

"Let's go to the research library."

Sin nodded. "Lead the way."

"You know we're looking for anything you can tell us about Dora Frigit, right?"

"Yes," August said. "Mamie filled me in. Somewhat." He glanced at me. "I understand some things can't be revealed, so I don't know everything, just that there's an investigation going on. My lips are sealed, I promise."

"I believe you." After what we'd just been through, I counted August as one of the good guys. And I knew he wanted to stay on my good side.

We went down a level via the elevator and

exited only to be faced with a large set of locked double doors.

August pulled out a key. "All of the reporters have keys, and some of the other staff. This area is mostly kept locked as a precautionary measure against environmental influences."

He unlocked the doors and pushed them wide. They opened with a hiss of air, and the fragrance that reached us reminded me of old books. Paper and leather and bindings. Plus some age. It wasn't a bad smell. Sort of like a library on steroids. He smiled and gestured to the enormous space beyond. "Welcome to the history of the North Pole."

Sin stood silently inside while August closed the doors behind us.

I did too. Row after row of shelving filled the space. Each shelf was heavy with tall, leather-bound books. A few feet from us was a large glass case. Behind it, marking the center of the enormous room, were more glass cases. They were as tall as Sin and seemed to hold smaller books, some artifacts, and singular pieces of paper displayed on stands.

I glanced at August. "This place is huge. How have I never been here?"

He shrugged. "We were in talks with the schools to do tours here, but for some reason it never happened. Lost in the shuffle, maybe."

Sin shook his head. "Is this really the entire history of the North Pole?"

August smiled. "As much as anything can be entire, yes. The green books on the shelves contain every edition of the *Post*. The red books contain the census reports. The blue books are birth, death, and marriage records. The white books are specific to the royal family."

"And the glass cases?" I asked.

"Those contain special items such as coronation announcements, royal decrees and invitations, letters of note written to the editor, some first-edition books, rare photographs taken by staff photographers, things of that nature."

"I see." I took a quick look around. "So where would we look for information about Dora?"

"I've taken the liberty of pulling some of the census records that would mention her, as well as the books that contain the records of her birth, her marriage, and her husband's death. I'm also in the middle of a search for any past articles that mention her."

Sin's brows lifted. "That's a lot. But could you add a search for articles that mention her husband too?"

"I can," August said.

"Good thinking, Sin. And I guess while he does that, we need to start reading."

But Dora was a clean slate. A clean, boring slate. Just like with the file that Mamie had given me on her, nothing August provided led us any closer to proving her involvement in the Tinkers' Tourney mess.

And trust me, we'd looked.

My eyes were watering, and the smell of newsprint was giving me a headache. "I can't look at another page."

Sin glanced up from the census he was studying and yawned. "I have to agree with you. This is making my brain hurt."

I stretched my arm out on the table, then laid my head on it and looked at him. "Right? I know more about Dora Frigit than I ever thought possible, and yet, I've learned nothing that means anything to this case."

"Same." He sighed, leaning back in his chair to stretch. "How long have we been at this?"

I checked my watch. "Son of a nutcracker. Almost three hours."

Sin's eyes widened in shocked disbelief. "Yikes. August has been really helpful, though."

"Very." I sat up as the man himself came down one of the aisles toward us, more books in his arms.

He settled them onto the table where we were working. "I found two more articles about her husband and one about her parents, but I doubt they'll be much help."

I smiled weakly. I didn't have it in me to read one more word. "August, we're going to call it a night. You've provided us with more information than I thought possible, but none of it is helping us with our investigation."

Crestfallen, he gathered the books back into his arms. "I'm sorry, Princess Jayne. I really thought I could help..."

"You did. You're an amazing resource. I can't thank you enough for your time and effort here. The fact that it wasn't the information we needed isn't your fault. And now, it's time for all of us to go home." I got to my feet, a little stiff from sitting for so long. I smiled. "Why don't you let us help you put all of these books back?"

"Oh, no. That's not necessary." His smile

broadened. "I have interns who can do that in the morning."

Sin laughed. "Perfect. Thanks again, August. We can see ourselves out."

"And have a good night. Oh, gorgeous flowers you sent to Mamie, by the way."

August went a little pink as Sin put his hand on the small of my back. Together, we walked through the quiet space without saying another word.

When we got outside, he opened the crawler door for me, then leaned in after I was in my seat and kissed my temple. "Hungry, sweetheart? We missed dinner."

I nodded, smiling a little. A faint aurora borealis glowed in the dark sky behind him. It was another beautiful North Pole night. "I could eat."

"Good. We need a break. We need to do something fun and not related to Dora or tinkers or chickens. Where do you want to go?"

"Don't you think we should check in with my dad? See if the constable found anything?"

"Mamie knew where we were. If something had come up, she'd have tracked us down."

I blew out a discouraged breath. "Yeah, you're right."

He closed the door, walked around and got in behind the wheel. "I know you're frustrated. I am too. But we're doing everything we can."

I stared at him, a thought uncurling in my head

like a strand of ice vapor. "Maybe we aren't."

"What do you mean?"

"If there's no news from the constable, that must mean Dora went home and stayed there, right?"

"Seems like a reasonable assumption. Most people are probably in bed by now, I'm guessing. Why should she be any different?"

"Then now would be the perfect time to inspect her work space just like we did with Stanley and Terrance. I mean, why not? We looked through theirs. We should look through hers. Especially because we already know she's involved in this somehow."

I could tell by the slight bend of his mouth that he was in. He cranked the crawler's engine. "Buckle up."

He got us to the factory in a few minutes, and in a few minutes more, we were in the elevator headed to the tinkers' floor.

"The place is a lot calmer at night, huh?" He looked through the glass elevator wall at the factory floor. A smattering of elves worked diligently at their stations, crafting the toys that would brighten millions of children's lives on Christmas morning.

"The night shift is a quieter group. Smaller too. Although in another week or so, the night shift will increase to the same numbers as the day shift. Christmas production schedule."

He kept watching. "This place is fascinating."

The elevator stopped at the tinkers' floor, our badges getting us access once again. "I'm glad you think so."

We stepped out, and I groaned as I realized I'd forgotten a very important detail. "Snowballs. I can't remember the number of her workshop. I know we were just up here, but I was so fixated on watching that the number slipped my mind."

"Forty-six," Sin said. He was grinning like he was rather pleased with himself. And he was right to be.

"You have a better memory than I do."

He laughed softly. "Not really. It was in an article I read about her husband."

"I guess August really did help us. And good on you for paying attention." I kissed him. He deserved it. And so did I. "Let's go."

The inside of Dora's lab was nothing like Terrance's or Stanley's work spaces. It was neat, but not obsessively so. There were no labels on things, and there were a few stacks of papers. Small ones. It didn't have the energy of either of their spaces either.

It seemed rather...sedate. A lot like the life she lived.

The only thing that really stood out was the framed photo of her husband, Earl Frigit. He was a kind-faced man with a large nose and a slightly receding hairline. There was warmth in his eyes, and I wondered if he'd been looking at Dora when the photo had been taken.

A small spotlight shone on the photo, and the frame was draped in black crepe. A shelf had been installed under it and on that shelf were a few candles, another smaller photo of Dora and Earl together in front of a fireplace, and a single red silk rose.

It was sad and sweet and made me hurt for Dora. "She's not over him."

Sin shook his head. "She might never be. He's been gone for nearly six years."

"They looked so happy in their wedding picture in the *Post*." It was odd to stand in Dora's space knowing so much about her and yet not really knowing her at all. I suddenly wanted to be out of there as quickly as I could. "Okay, let's do this and then go eat."

"You got it."

I went to the cabinet to search like I had in Terrance's and Stanley's, while Sin did the shelves. I opened the doors, not sure what to expect. And found a red velvet box. "Hey, look. Another memo box."

Sin came over to stand beside me. "I realize all the tinkers use them, but it's interesting that she's got one just like Stanley did."

I picked it up and gave it a gentle shake. "There's something in it too."

"Work your magic and pick that lock."

"I don't have to." I opened the lid. "It's not locked."

Inside was a crisp sheet of folded white paper. Not the cream-colored stuff the tinkers used. "Interesting."

I unfolded it so Sin could see it too. It took only a few lines of reading to know we'd found something worthwhile.

My dearest Dora,

I hope you are not suffering too much in the wake of my demise. I miss you terribly, sweetheart, but know that we will be together again someday. Until then, I want only the best for you, which is why I am sending you this note and this idea.

The idea is for a machine that produces adhesive glitter sheets. Just like the sticker machine we created the year before I died, except with glitter. I think it'll be a big hit. And it should win you a place in the tourney.

Be well, my love.

Earl

We stared at the paper for a few seconds longer.

Then Sin cleared his throat. "That's not weird at all."

"Babe. That is super weird."

"I was being sarcastic."

I snorted. "I know."

We went back to staring at the paper.

I shook my head. "How does this happen? When did this happen? He's been gone for almost six years. He couldn't have just sent this, but she only entered the Glitterskins in this year's competition. Or did it take her that long to produce a working prototype? I have so many questions."

"Me too. And the only one who can give us answers is Dora. We need to talk to her. The sooner the better."

"Actually, I think we should talk to Mamie. Ask her about the paper this note is written on, just like we did with the others. Get a little info, then go talk to Dora."

"Solid plan. Do you know where Mamie lives?"

"I do." My stomach growled. Loudly. Like I'd swallowed a yeti.

Sin chuckled. "Okay, listen, it's late. You're hungry. This can wait until the morning. No one's going anywhere, anyway, right? Let's get you something to eat. What's still open at this hour?"

I was hungry. Starving, really. And he was right that no one, Dora or otherwise, was going anywhere. "The cafeteria is."

"Perfect." He smiled. "Just one request. Can we take the slide?"

I laughed. "Yes. We just have to go down one floor for the nearest one. But what are we going to do with this letter? We can't leave it here if we want Mamie to look at the paper."

"I'll put it in my jacket pocket."

I folded it in half again and gave it over.

He tucked it away and took my hand. "Lead the way."

We took the elevator to the floor below, then the slide to the cafeteria. It had been a long time since my backside had been on one of those, and I'd forgotten how fun it was. Especially from so many floors up.

Sin was still laughing as we walked into the cafeteria. "I really have to do that again before we go home."

I giggled a little. "Your hair is all messed up from the wind."

He finger-combed it back into place. "Better?"

"Gorgeous as always."

He snaked his arm around my waist, smiling and giving me a quick peck on the cheek. "Let's see what's on the menu."

We glanced at the specials board and I read them off. "Stuffed pork chops, fish and chips, and pot roast. Plus navy bean is the soup of the day."

"Fish and chips."

I nodded. "Same. Plus a big slice of that chocolate peanut butter pie."

"I'm going with the caramelized pear cobbler with ginger ice cream."

"Can I have a bite?"

"I'd be worried if you didn't want one."

We got in line, got our food, talked to a few folks, but were left alone to eat. Some of that might have been that there weren't many people in there. Some of it might have been that we sat in my uncle's booth, next to each other. I had no doubt we were giving off a "privacy please" vibe.

For the first few minutes, we were quiet. Too busy eating. But as the edge of our hunger wore off, the conversation started back up.

"Something's just occurred to me," Sin said.

"What's that?" I dipped a french fry in tartar sauce.

"This note from beyond the grave...you don't think it's part of some elaborate scheme to blame me again, do you? I mean, Earl's dead and..." He shrugged.

"The death angle. Right." I thought about that. "I don't think so. At least, I hope not. We'll know more soon enough."

"Do you think Earl really could have arranged to send her a note after he died?"

"Sure. From what I learned tonight, he had a rare strain of hypothermia that causes a winter elf not to be able to control their body temperature. It's not always terminal, but he could have written that and left it with a friend to send in case he didn't make it."

"You still don't sound convinced."

"That note is so specific. It feels obvious. Like someone planted that note to give her that idea. They wanted her in the competition."

"Why?"

"Could be a couple of reasons. Maybe a friend knew how down she was and wanted to give her something else to focus on." I ate another fry. "Maybe they thought a note from Earl would cheer her up. Especially one with a new toy idea in it."

Sin nodded. "Or maybe someone really wanted her in the competition."

"That too." I reached for my dessert. "We really need to talk to Dora first thing in the morning."

Sin's fork edged closer to my pie. "You still want to see Mamie about the paper the note is written on?"

"Yes. Mamie, then Dora." I gave him a stern look as his fork breached the edge of my plate. "I thought you were all about that pear cobbler?"

"I am." He wiggled his brows. "Right after I have a bite of your pie, Princess."

I slept hard and woke up with Spider sitting on me. I knew what he wanted. I reached up and ran my fingers through his soft fur. "Morning, Spider boy."

He pushed his head into my hand for more scratches, but didn't break eye contact. "Mama sleeps too long. Spider hungry."

I looked at the clock. "It's seven fifteen. That's not sleeping too long. Noon. Noon is too long. This is an indecent hour."

"Spider hungry."

"So noted." I flipped the covers back anyway, making him move in the process.

"Mama cranky."

I snorted as I sat on the edge of the bed. "I'm not cranky. Just not awake. And not happy about not figuring things out faster, but hopefully we'll get some answers today." Assuming Dora didn't clam up and play dumb.

He came to sit next to me. "What's things?"

"Just some stuff Mr. Sinclair and I are working on. Nothing you have to worry about." I picked him up and cradled him like a baby, nuzzling my nose into his furry cheek.

He pressed his nose to my cheek in response. It was wet and a little cold. "Spider loves Mama."

"I love you too, baby cat."

He purred in my ear. "Mama feed Spider?"

Such a manipulator.

"It's my every desire." I carried him out to the kitchen and put him down on the floor so I could get him a can of Chicken Party. "You want to hang out with Sugar today?"

He sat upright, tucking his tail around his feet. "Spider likes Sugar."

"I know you do. Do you like that Sugar can talk now?"

He stared at me like I was suffering from a mental malfunction. "Sugar always talks."

I considered that. "I guess you didn't need her to speak English to understand her, did you?"

I put his food down, grabbed a Dr Pepper out of the fridge and headed for a hot shower. I would have rather gone back to bed, but there was too much to do today. And truth be told, I was really curious about what Dora had to say.

This note from beyond the grave was strange stuff.

I got myself ready in about half an hour, did my hair, makeup, and got dressed (black leggings, big sweater, tall boots) and went across the hall to Sinclair's.

He answered the door in jeans, a black sweater with a navy stripe across the chest, and bare feet. He was towel-drying his damp hair, and the spicy-woodsy cologne he had on made me a little warm inside.

Yum. But I digress. "Morning. You want to grab some breakfast in the dining room then head over to see Mamie?"

"Morning, beautiful. Sounds like a plan. I'll be ready in ten."

"How about if I bring Spider over while you finish getting ready?"

"Good. Sugar will like that."

"Okay, back in a few with the boy."

We got Spider and Sugar set up for the day, then went to breakfast. My father, who was an early riser, had already eaten, but my mom was still in the dining room.

Sin greeted her as we walked in. "Good morning, Klara."

She smiled at us. "Well, hello there." She patted the folded paper next to her plate. "I read your interview this morning. Very nice. I think it will help a lot. Although, I have to confess, I feel like I've barely seen you two since you've been here."

"I know. I'm sorry." I kissed her cheek, then took the seat across from her. I was happy to hear the interview had turned out so well, but that wasn't going to help us figure out who was behind this tourney fiasco. A footman filled my cup with coffee. "We've been so caught up in this tourney business."

Concern darkened her eyes. "How's that going?"

Sin sat next to me, the footman pouring for him as well. "We're going to talk to—"

"Um, Sin?" I interrupted.

"Yes?"

"Can you hand me the cream?" I shifted my eyes at the footman, hoping Sin got my drift. I wasn't sure how to tell him I didn't think we should discuss the particulars when we weren't alone. I didn't know the two footmen who were waiting on us this morning, and at this point, I didn't want word spreading that we had a potential suspect.

Dora might get wind and disappear. I didn't think it was likely, but then, I'd never seen two nearly identical toys show up in the tourney either.

"Sure." He passed me the little pitcher. "As I was saying, we're going to talk to—"

My mother understood. She clucked her tongue. "Timpson, get a fresh pot of coffee made, will you?"

The footman bowed. "Yes, Lady Frost." He disappeared.

She glanced at the second footman standing by the serving board. "Springle, I'd like some elderberry jam for my toast."

"Yes, Lady Frost." With a bow, he too, disappeared.

My mother leaned forward. "Now go on, Sinclair."

I knew from his slight smile and a shake of his head that he understood what she'd done. "Sorry I didn't pick up on that sooner."

"It's fine," my mother said. "And you'll get it."

"I hope so." He continued. "We're talking to Dora Frigit this morning. There's been a development."

"She's the other tinker in the competition, isn't she?"

"Yes," he answered.

"And you think she's up to something?"

I shrugged. "There's some hinky stuff going on, I can tell you that much."

Timpson returned with the coffee. He poured fresh cups for all of us and then stood by to take our order.

"French toast, bacon and a side of fruit," I requested.

Sin glanced at me. "Is there a menu?"

"Just ask for whatever you want. The cooks can make anything."

My mother smiled. "They're very good, Sinclair. I assure you. Absolute wizards in the kitchen."

"I believe you," he said. He glanced at her empty plate. "What did you have, Klara?"

"A garden omelet. With a side of toast that I'll be eating shortly." Just then, Springle returned with her elderberry jam. She picked up her knife. "I do love my jam."

He looked up at Timpson. "Blueberry pancakes with bacon, then. And a glass of orange juice."

"Very good, sir." Timpson went off to the kitchen.

Sin laughed softly. "I could get used to this."

My mom stayed while we ate. She had more toast and jam and another cup of coffee, but mostly entertained Sinclair with stories about me as a child. It was a little embarrassing, but let's be honest, I haven't changed all that much.

She and Sin had a great time, and even I laughed a little. No wonder my parents never had a second child.

After breakfast, Sin and I went straight to the factory. It was a little early, but Mamie came in a half hour before my uncle to get everything ready for him.

She was in his office, putting paperwork on his desk when we walked in. "Hi, Mamie."

"Good morning, Princess, Mr. Crowe. How did it go at the paper last night?"

Sinclair reached into his jacket pocket and pulled out the letter we'd found. "Not as well as we'd hoped, but we had an interesting evening anyway."

"Oh? Did the constable find something?"

I shook my head. "We haven't heard anything new from her in a while. I guess there's been nothing to report."

"Then what made the evening interesting?" She laughed softly. "Or shouldn't I ask?"

"We did a little investigating on our own." I looked at Sin.

He put the folded letter on her desk. "What can you tell us about this paper?"

She put her hand on it, then looked at us. "Would you prefer I not read it?"

"No," I said. "You can read it. It's a note we found in a memo box in Dora's workshop. It's from Earl."

Mamie nodded, picked up the paper and unfolded it. A few moments later, her eyes widened. "You didn't say it was from Earl *recently*."

"Hmm. I guess I didn't. Sorry about that. But we really don't know when he sent it, just that he was already...you know."

"Yes." She narrowed her eyes at me. "Strange."

"Agreed."

Just like she had with the previous note, she held the paper up to her desk lamp. I realized we could have checked for a watermark. I chalked it up to the late hour and the amount of time we'd already spent in the research room.

Her brows furrowed as she stared at it. "That's odd."

"What?" Sin asked.

"This paper…you got this out of a memo box in Dora's work space?"

"Yes. The box was in her cabinet, unlocked."

Mamie frowned. "I don't understand this."

I wasn't sure what to think. "Understand what?"

She hesitated. "There has to be an explanation." Her gaze seemed almost apologetic. She moved the paper so Sin and I could see it better and pointed to a small watermark near the corner. "You see that?"

I nodded. "Another watermark. Which we should have noticed, but were too tired to even think about. Looks like…" I peered closer.

"Half of a snowflake," Sin said. "Whose mark is that?"

Mamie's jaw tightened for a moment. "He can't be involved in this. He can't be. There has to be an explanation. He wouldn't—"

I interrupted. "Mamie, whose watermark is it?"

She exhaled a ragged breath. "Ezreal's."

A moment of light-headedness swept through me. "Are you sure?"

She nodded.

Sin cupped my elbow. I leaned into him. "That can't be. Maybe...maybe Earl just had a piece of his stationery. Maybe Earl had Ezreal send the note for him. Maybe..." I needed to sit down. "There's an explanation. I know there is."

"Of course there is," Sin said. "And we're going to talk to Ezreal and ask him. Right now. Come on, let's go back to the palace."

"But Dora—"

Mamie made a dismissive noise. "Dora isn't going anywhere. Talk to Ezreal. You'll feel better."

Or worse, I supposed. But he couldn't be a part of this. He couldn't be. He was one of the good ones. One of the great ones. My father trusted him. I trusted him. We all did. I nodded weakly. "Okay. Let's do that."

Sin took the note back from Mamie and returned it to his pocket. "Thank you for your help."

She sighed. "I'm sorry I didn't have something different to tell you."

"The truth is always best." He took my hand in his.

Somehow, we got from Mamie's desk to the crawler, but I didn't remember riding down in the elevator or walking outside. I was numb and heartbroken and sick to my stomach.

Sin got the machine moving back toward the palace grounds. "Ezreal's not involved in this."

I stared blankly ahead. "What makes you so sure?"

"Just my judge of his character. This isn't something he would do. Is it? You know him. Would he ever be involved in something shady? Something that would create chaos for you and your family?"

"No."

"Is his stationery readily available? Could someone have swiped a piece to make him look bad?"

"I don't know if it's that accessible. But he could have enemies. We already know there were those unhappy with his appointment."

"Then it's very possible he had nothing to do with this."

"You're absolutely right." I was angry that I'd reacted so badly, but then, this whole thing was such a mess, who wouldn't have reacted that way? "Ezreal is a good man. He's not behind this. Why would he be? If a Frost isn't on the throne, he could very well be out of a job. But he might be able to help us figure out who is behind this."

"I'm sure he'll do everything in his power."

I turned to watch as we passed through the palace gates. I hoped so. Because too many good people were getting caught up in this. And that made me wonder if someone wasn't trying to throw all of the NP in chaos.

We'd never been through this kind of turmoil before. Not that I could recall, and much of my education had been focused on our history.

Was someone trying to bring down my father's monarchy? Or was someone trying to make sure no Frost ever took the throne again?

Regardless of the goal of all this, things were going to come to a head in a big way very soon. I could feel it in my bones.

I strode through the entrance of my father's office and into Ezreal's space with as much confidence and optimism as I could.

"Good morning, Princess." Ezreal got to his feet. "How are you?"

I smiled and meant it. "I've been better. I need your help."

Trouble clouded his eyes. "Of course, what's wrong? What can I do? Just name it."

Sin took the letter out again, but this time he handed it to me. "We found this letter in Dora Frigit's workshop."

I gave it to Ezreal.

He unfolded it and read it, then looked at me again. "How odd. A letter from her dead husband. I'm not sure what you want me to do with this. But I'm happy to do it."

My chest constricted. "Look again. At the watermark."

He held the letter up to the light. A soft, almost unintelligible curse slipped from his lips. He cleared his throat. "My apologies for the coarse language, Princess. I didn't expect to see my own watermark there. I suppose you think I wrote this?"

"No, Ezreal. I don't. I know you better than that. But we would like any help you can give us in figuring out who might have written it. Or at least who could have gotten ahold of this paper."

He nodded and swallowed. "Thank you for not thinking I did it." His voice was husky with emotion. "But I'm sorry to say I don't have a clue who would have."

I was afraid of that. "They used your paper and that makes me think they meant to involve you. That it was no accident."

"Do you have any enemies?" Sin asked.

Ezreal choked out a laugh. "I have a few. Mostly a couple old opponents who didn't take losing well." He shook his head. "But they wouldn't have access to my personal stationery."

"Who would?" I asked.

"Most people who work in the palace, really." Ezreal glanced at the door. "Anyone can come in here. You know your father's policy. Anyone who wants to see him, can."

I nodded. "But that doesn't mean they could walk out with some of your stationery."

Ezreal made an unhappy face. "I suppose they could if they were sly about it. I get up from my desk a lot in the course of a day. I leave the office a lot too. There are plenty of opportunities."

He was right. Which sucked. "That's not helping us narrow this down."

Sin leaned against a bank of filing cabinets. "We need to consider those who work in the plant that makes the paper too." He glanced at me. "I'm assuming all the kingdom's paper is produced in the same place, which means they'd have access to the tinkers' paper. And maybe access to the *Post*, if there was a delivery situation."

"Could be," I said. "We'll have the constable look into that. But this feels more personal to me."

Ezreal nodded. "Whoever it is, they're making this about the royal family." His gaze shifted to Sin. "About those close to them."

"I agree," Sin said. "I was just trying to offer another possibility, but even as I spoke the words, I was thinking the same thing. This is personal. Someone has an ax to grind. An end goal."

I sighed. "So, Ezreal, who has the easiest access to your personal stationery? I'm talking about those who could walk in and help themselves when you aren't here."

He shook his head slowly. "You're talking

afterhours, then. There aren't as many who have that kind of access to this office. That would be housekeeping and a small handful of others. But do you really think it's someone in the palace? That's...shocking."

"I think it's more likely that someone in the palace inadvertently supplied the paper to someone else, not knowing what it was going to be used for. Maybe someone took some home as a lark, and a friend found it. Do you take the paper home, Ezreal?"

"Sometimes. But it usually already has something written on it."

"Could someone have taken used paper and bleached it to reuse it? I know that happens in counterfeiting money sometimes." Sin shrugged. "Anything is possible."

I rubbed the bridge of my nose. "This isn't getting us anywhere. It's just opening up more questions."

"Princess," Ezreal said softly. "I will make a list for you of everyone who has the ability to get into this office unaccompanied. Everyone. And I will have that list to you by the end of the day."

"Thank you. I know you already have plenty to do."

"This is important. I would be happy to talk to the constable as well and let her know to process all the employees at the paper plant."

"That would be great." I would take the help, especially if it meant including Ezreal in the loop. "If she has anything new to tell us, make sure she speaks to my father as well."

"I will. Would you like to see your father while you're here?"

"Not yet. I'd rather have more information to share with him, so we'll be back later today. Sin and I have one more person to talk to. Thank you, Ezreal."

"It's my honor to serve, Princess."

I smiled. He was a good man. He was *not* involved in this. I'd stake my crown on it. "Keep this matter between us for now, will you?"

"As you wish."

Sin and I left. He took my hand. "You okay?"

"I am. Better for having talked to Ez. Now let's go see what Dora has to say."

Back at the factory, Mamie confirmed that Dora was in the building and most likely in her workshop.

I had Mamie summon her to my uncle's office. And although his office was enormous, I'd decided to use the small, more private conference room he kept. He never used it anyway, and meeting in Santa's office would be too much of a distraction for Dora, I imagined.

Mamie brought us coffee while we waited. She was exceptionally cheerful.

I had to ask. "What's going on? You're very smiley."

Her lips pursed in a playful way. "I should be cross with you, but I'm not."

I put a hand to my chest. "Cross with me? Why?"

Light sparkled in her eyes. "I know you said something to August. That's why he sent the flowers. But I forgive you. Especially since we're going to dinner this evening."

Sin snorted and shook his head. "She can't leave anything alone."

"It's a blessing and a curse." I smiled. "I'm glad. True love deserves a second chance."

The elevator opened, and Dora walked into the reception area. "Hello?"

"I'll bring her in," Mamie said.

A moment later, Dora joined us in the conference room. Curiosity covered her face. She made a little curtsey before sitting. "Princess Frost. I didn't expect to see you here. Is this about the tourney?"

"It is," I said. "But first, would you like something to drink? Coffee? Tea?" I wanted her as comfortable as possible.

"No, I'm fine. Thank you."

Mamie was waiting by the door. I gave her a nod. She closed the door as she left, giving us privacy.

I stretched my hands out on the table. "We have some questions for you, Mrs. Frigit. First things first, though. Do you know who's sitting next to me?"

She looked at Sin and nodded. "Mr. Crowe. Your beau."

There was no change in her expression, no sign of animosity. "Correct. There have been a lot of rumors going around about him, and some stories in the paper lately—"

"I read the interview this morning." She smiled. "That was very nice. I hope you and the Princess are very happy together."

"Thank you," Sin said. He shot me a look.

This wasn't what either of us had expected, but then again, she could be very good at hiding her true feelings.

I pulled out the slip of paper that had Lyla Kinder's address written on it and slid it across the table to her. "Did you write this?"

She picked it up. "No, but…it looks like my handwriting. A lot like it. But I don't remember writing this." She blinked a few times. "I know I'm getting older, but I like to think all my faculties are still in working order."

"You're positive you didn't write it?"

She studied the note a few seconds longer. "Yes, Your Grace. I did not write that. But I do know who Lyla Kinder is. Stanley Kinder's granddaughter, I believe. Although don't ask me which one. He's got a few. I met them all at the Tinkers' Picnic this summer."

Her thumb brushed the edge of the paper. "Earl and I weren't as successful at having kids. But my sister's boys come see me now and then. Being an aunt is good too."

She looked up at us, her smile thin and her eyes sad.

None of this was going how I thought it was going to. Still, I pushed on. "Did you send Lyla a stuffed chicken from the Sweet Acres Farm in March?"

Dora frowned. "What? I don't understand. Why would I send her a chicken? I only met the child once, and I can't even remember which one she was."

Sin crossed his arms and leaned back in his chair. "A woman fitting your description went to the Sweet Acres Farm store and sent Lyla Kinder a stuffed chicken along with a sealed note telling the little girl she'd won it in a contest. The woman gave that slip of paper to the clerk at the register for Lyla's address."

Dora shook her head, still looking very confused. "It wasn't me."

"March fourth," I said. "If you weren't at Sweet Acres Farm, where were you?"

"March fourth," she repeated. She went silent then, frowning a bit like she was trying to remember. Suddenly, the frown disappeared. "March fourth I was with my sister, Cindy. I know it was March fourth because my wedding anniversary is the third of March and Cindy always takes me out so I don't have to spend it alone, but her car had a flat tire on the third."

"Why didn't you take your car?" I asked.

"Because I don't have a car. I go most places on skis or skates. Earl was the only driver in our family."

Sin glanced at me before giving Dora his attention again. "What did you do that day?"

"We had lunch at the Snow Shoe Café, then went to see a movie. It started at one thirty. Afterward we had ice cream and did a little shopping. I bought some yarn, which I've since turned into a baby blanket for one of my neighbors' children. Anyway, Cindy and I were together almost the whole day. You can ask her."

All of that would be easily provable. People would have seen them. Shopkeepers would have sales records. And her sister, no doubt, would vouch for her.

Sin uncrossed his arms and looked at me. "There's no way she could have gone up to Sweet Acres and back and still done all of that. Not on skis or skates, especially."

"No," I said. "Which means whoever that was up at Sweet Acres, it wasn't her."

Dora shook her head so hard her curls shivered. "It wasn't me, I swear it."

We already knew she didn't have any other siblings. Her file had covered that. I had another question for her. "Why do you think the other two contestants ended up with similar toys? How do you think that happened?"

"I have no idea."

Sin took a deep breath. "You have to understand why we might think you had something to do with that, seeing as how you stand to benefit if the other two tinkers are disqualified in this year's tourney."

She swallowed. "I do understand that. But all I wanted to do was make Earl proud. I'm not sure I ever did that while he was alive."

Sin glanced at me. "The letter?"

I nodded.

He took it out of his jacket pocket, unfolded it, and placed it on the table between her and us. "What can you tell us about this?"

Her expression darkened. "You went into my workshop."

"We have that right," I said.

She nodded stiffly. "I know that. But that letter is personal. That's from my Earl."

"You really believe he sent you this letter after he passed?"

She didn't answer right away. "I believe he

arranged for that letter to be sent. There's no crime in that."

"No, there isn't." So far anyway. The methods used to source the paper had yet to be determined. "How do you think he arranged to do that?"

She opened her mouth, but nothing came out for a second. "He...had a friend do it, I guess."

"Which friend?" Sin asked. "One of the other tinkers?"

"I don't know." She worried the wedding band on her finger. The shine was long gone from it, dulled from years of wear. "It had to be, I suppose. You already know it came in a memo box."

I nodded. "Do you know the origin of that paper?"

She glanced at the letter. "I never thought about it. Why?"

"Because the watermark on this paper indicates that it's from the personal stock of Ezreal Zur'dar, my father's office manager."

Her expression stayed blank for a half second, then her eyes widened. "How would Earl get paper from the king's office manager?"

I raised my brows. "That's what we'd like to know."

I let her sit with that question for a bit.

After a minute, she shook her head, shifting in her chair. "He couldn't. No way I can figure out."

I hoped she'd get there on her own. "Then what do you suppose that means?"

More thinking. "That...he didn't send that letter? But it's his handwriting."

Sin pushed the letter closer to her. "Are you sure? We haven't done a comparison yet. But we will." He shot me a look.

I nodded. We definitely needed to do that.

She picked up the letter and studied it. "I've read these words a thousand times. Never occurred to me it might not be from Earl. Looks like his handwriting. But now that you bring it up..."

"Yes?"

Her lower lip trembled. "Maybe...maybe it's not."

With Dora on her way home and no longer on our suspect list, Sin and I had to come up with a new game plan.

My frustration levels were rising. "I don't know what's going on. Every time we think we've got a lead, it dries up. If Dora wasn't at Sweet Acres, then who was? Because someone *was* there. Someone who looked like her."

"Good question." Sin paced in front of Mamie's desk. "If we could answer that, we'd probably figure this whole thing out."

He suddenly stopped pacing. "Could they have used one of those fancy magic bracelets that can make someone look exactly like someone else?"

"No, only my father has access to those."

The phone on Mamie's desk rang. She answered it while Sin and I moved to the other side of the room to continue our discussion.

He raked a hand through his hair. "Jayne, I'm starting to think this case can't be solved. Whoever is behind this knew exactly how to work all the angles and cover their tracks."

"I know. It feels like we're dealing with someone with a lot of inside access. Someone high up. I don't think it's my cousin, but I honestly have no idea anymore."

"You should talk to the constable. Tell her to ramp things up. Maybe an increase in police presence around town will shake up our culprit."

"That's not a bad—"

"Mr. Crowe?" Mamie held her hand over the receiver. "Sorry to interrupt, Princess."

He turned. "Yes?"

"Gregory is calling to say an urgent message has been left for you from Archie and that you're to reach him through the snow globe at your earliest convenience."

"Thank you." Sin groaned. "I never did call him. I hope the shop's okay. I'd better go deal with that."

"Absolutely. Take the crawler, call him back, then meet me at the station. It's one block south from here in a red brick building. You can't miss it. By the time you get there, I'll probably be done and we can go grab a bite to eat."

"You sure you're okay by yourself?" He laughed. "Silly of me to ask. I know you are, but I hate leaving you alone to handle all this."

"I'll be fine."

"You'll be better than that. You'll probably solve the whole thing while I'm gone." He pulled me in and gave me a quick kiss.

"I doubt that." I smooched him back, making Mamie duck her head and smile.

He glanced back at the conference room. "Don't forget the letter. We need to compare the handwriting on that and see if we can figure out who really wrote it."

"I'm giving that to the constable to do. It's her area."

"Perfect. See you in a bit. Love you."

"Love you too."

With a squeeze of my hand, he went for the elevator. The doors opened as soon as he pushed the button. He waved as they closed. I waved back.

I missed him already. Yes, I was that woman.

With a happy sigh, I grabbed the letter and stuck it in my purse. "Mamie, do you have any idea who could be behind this? Who might want to cause such chaos in the NP? You know this town and its people better than most."

She shook her head. "I wish I had an idea, but I can't think of anyone with such a big ax to grind."

"Me either. And I guess that's a good thing, but at the moment, it doesn't feel that way." I took a breath, my head full with all that was going on.

"All right, I'm off to see the constable. Would you call ahead and tell her I'm on my way?"

"Will do." She was smiling broadly as she picked up the phone.

I hesitated before calling the elevator. "What?"

"Just thinking about how that man is completely smitten with you."

"He is, isn't he? But it's mutual. Believe me." With a smile, I tapped the button to call the lift.

She nodded. "I can tell. You're going to make a wonderful queen and consort."

"Thanks, Mamie. You know, I wasn't sure what he was going to think of life here, but despite everything that's happened, he's been my rock. He's hung in there and stayed strong. I cannot wait to marry him."

"And I can't wait to dance at your wedding. Possibly with August."

"Sounds like a plan." I laughed as the doors opened and I got on.

Twenty minutes later, I'd finished up with the constable, who was all over the handwriting analysis, and was standing in the vestibule keeping an eye out for Sin to pull up in the crawler. The smallest of flakes had begun to fall when I'd walked into the station. They were coming down in earnest now, making me glad that my ride was on the way.

But the minutes kept rolling by, the snow kept falling, and there had yet to be any sign of him.

When I'd been there forty-five minutes, I figured Archie's issue had been something much more serious than I'd imagined.

It wasn't a big deal. The constable had one of her deputies take me to the palace. The snow meant it took an extra five minutes, but that was just life in the NP. I went straight to my dad's office to see what was going on.

"Hi, Ezreal, is Sin still here?"

Ezreal got up. "No, Princess. And I'm not sure what you mean by still. I haven't seen him since you were both here earlier."

I frowned. "He came back here to use the snow globe to call his shop. We got a message at Uncle Kris's that Gregory said Archie had called and it was urgent."

Ezreal shook his head. "Maybe Gregory arranged for a snow globe in Mr. Crowe's apartment?"

Of course. "You're right. I didn't think of that. Thanks. Sorry to bother you."

He smiled. "You could never be a bother, Princess. You know that. I have that list for you of everyone with access to this office." He handed me a file with a single sheet of paper in it. "Anything new on the case?"

I sighed as I took the file. I tucked it under my arm. "No, nothing yet. Dora wasn't the hot lead we thought she was. I guess I could tell my dad about that."

"He's not here either. He left about ten minutes ago to meet your uncle at the builders' headquarters to approve the finalized plans for your aunt Martha's new fudge factory."

"Just as well. My news isn't good news." I'd been hoping the next time I spoke to my dad I'd be able to tell him Sin and I had cracked the case.

"What happened? If you don't mind me asking?"

"Well, basically there was no way Dora could have been at Sweet Acres on the day the stuffed chicken was sent to Lyla Kinder. I don't know who was, but Dora has a solid alibi. She doesn't even drive."

"What day was that?"

"March fourth."

His eyes narrowed. "And yet the woman at the farm gave you a description that fit Dora and the handwriting on the note matched hers?"

"Yes to both. How that happened is just one more thing we've yet to figure out." I sighed. "If you think of anything, let me know. I'm going to Sin's apartment to see if there's anything I can do to help with whatever's going on at the shop."

"I will. And if I can help with Mr. Crowe's situation, I'm here."

"Thank you." I left and went straight to Sin's. I knocked, but then realized if he was on the snow globe in the midst of a big discussion, he might be too tied up to answer. I had two options. Use my magic to go under the door via the Santa Slide or magic up some ice picks and let myself in.

Since the Santa Slide left me a little woozy, and seeing me suddenly appear in his apartment might freak Sin out, I went with picking the lock.

"Sin?" I walked through the living room and into the bedroom area, but there was no sign or sounds of him. Weird.

Spider and Sugar came running out of the closet. "Mama Mama Mama—"

"Spider, I can't feed you right now." Could Sin be in my apartment? But how would he get in?

Sugar pawed at my leg. "Lady lady lady—"

"You guys need to chill. There's dry food in your bowl." The cats could wait a cool minute. I had to find Sin. With no other immediate place to look, I went across the hall and checked my own living quarters.

Nothing.

Except a note on the coffee table. It was standing upright, tented. There was a J on the front of the ice-blue card stock, because it was my personal stationery. I smiled. Sin must have come in here and taken it out of my desk to leave me a message.

Had I left my door open? No, I'd just unlocked it. Gregory must have helped him. That was sweet.

I put the file from Ezreal on the kitchen counter, then went over and picked up the note to see what he had to say.

My dearest Jayne,

As much as I love you, life in the North Pole is far more complicated than I'd anticipated. I am sorry, but it's not for me. I regret informing you this way, but I felt a clean break was best. I am returning to Nocturne Falls. I wish you all the best and hope that we can remain civil.

Please bring Sugar with you.

With great affection,

Sinclair

I dropped onto the couch, trembling slightly. I reread the note. Then reread it again.

There was no way Sin had left me. No. Freezing. Way.

As the initial gut-punch wore off, I got angry. Something was incredibly shady about this. I needed to talk to someone with a pulse in the palace. I stormed toward the door and yanked it open to stand in the hall. "*Steward Gregory!* I need you. *Now.*"

My voice echoed through the corridors. Of course, that didn't mean he'd heard me. He could be in any part of the palace.

A housekeeper popped out of a room a few

doors away. "Your Highness, would you like me to fetch him for you?"

"Yes. Immediately."

With a nod and a curtsey, she took off on the Segway parked nearby.

I went back inside, leaving the door open. I walked in a small circle, too busy thinking to pay attention to what my feet were doing.

At last a clear thought made it through. If Sin had really left, his things would be gone. I went back to his apartment and looked.

His closet was empty.

That struck me hard. Maybe…maybe he really had gone. I sat on his bed. The apartment still smelled of him. I wanted to cry. Instead, I swallowed that urge down and got back on my feet.

The cats were milling about, tails swishing, but they must have sensed my mood because they were steering clear.

I let the anger wash over me, stripping all other emotion out. It was cleansing in a way, but the one emotion that it couldn't remove was love. I loved Sin. And I knew without a doubt that he loved me.

That calmed me down a little.

Sugar rubbed against my shins. "Lady lady lady."

Sin also loved his cat. There was no way he'd leave me with just a note, just like there was no way he'd leave Sugar with nothing more than an offhand request that I bring her home.

I gathered the air in my lungs and hollered again. "*Gregory.*"

He appeared in the doorway. "Yes, m'lady? Apologies for my delay. What can I do for you?"

"Where is Sinclair?"

His brow furrowed and he shook his head. "I don't understand the question, Princess. I thought he was with you."

"When he came back to make the call to his shop, where did he go after that? Did you bring him a snow globe here to use?"

Gregory's brows lifted ever so slightly. "I wasn't aware he'd returned to the palace."

Ice sluiced down my spine and a sob stuck in my throat. "He never came back?"

Concern filled Gregory's eyes. "Not that I am aware of. Did you drop him off?"

"No, I told him to bring the crawler back then come pick me up when he was done with his call to Archie. You did call him at my uncle's office, didn't you?"

"Yes, I did."

I pressed my hand to my head. If he hadn't come back, how could he have left a note? I couldn't process everything that was happening.

All I could think about was that Sin might be hurt. Or worse. He wasn't used to all this snow.

And he liked to drive that crawler fast. "Please don't let him have had an accident."

Gregory snapped to attention. "I will go to the south exit and talk to the transportation office immediately. I'll get a search party sent out. In fact, I'll personally go with them. We'll find him, Your Highness."

I nodded, feeling sick. "Thank you."

Gregory nodded and disappeared, the soft whir of his Segway the only sound.

I went back to my apartment, but as I stood there alone, I could feel my mental state on the verge of cracking. I couldn't handle Sin being gone. I needed him in my life. I loved him.

I wanted to marry him. To be with him for the rest of my life. Wherever that was, here or in Nocturne Falls. Location didn't matter. Just that we were together.

None of this was right. He wouldn't do this to me. He loved me too much. This wasn't his style.

That note wasn't his style either. Not only wasn't he the kind to do something like that, but that note sounded way too stiff and formal.

Someone had done this to him. The same someone who'd been playing us all along.

I had to go back to his apartment and look for anything I might have missed. And hope in the process my head settled down enough for me to make sense of everything. The jumbled mess in there wasn't doing me any good.

I stepped into the hall and a familiar voice called out to me.

"Princess, I found something." Ezreal jogged toward me.

I shook my head as my hand touched Sin's door. "I don't care about the investigation right now. Sin is missing."

He stopped short, a horrified expression overtaking his face. "What?"

I nodded and pushed the door open. "Finding him is all I care about."

"Let me help."

"Start from the beginning," Ezreal said as he followed me into Sin's apartment.

"I got a note from him saying he left, but that's not his style. He didn't write it. I know he didn't." I started opening kitchen drawers. I don't know why. Searching everything just seemed like the thing to do. "And then Gregory said Sin never returned in the crawler."

I pulled out pots and pans, moving with an urgency I couldn't control. "If he never returned, how could he have left the note?" I was going to cry. Or scream. I could feel it coming. "Nothing makes sense. I have to find him. I have to—"

A sob bubbled up, choking off my ability to speak. I leaned against the fridge, closed my eyes, and let the fear and anxiety hit me.

Strong arms pulled me close. "Princess, we'll

find him. He wouldn't have left you with a note. He loves you."

I nodded and sobbed against Ezreal's shoulder. Not very queenly, but my world was collapsing. "I love him too."

"Of course you do." Ezreal took me by the shoulders and held me at arm's length. "Show me the note."

I took one long sniff, pulled myself together and squeaked out, "Okay."

I led him back to my apartment and pointed to the wretched thing.

He read it, shaking his head. "Doesn't sound like Mr. Crowe."

"No, it doesn't." My anger was returning. That was good. I functioned better angry than sobbing.

Spider and Sugar raced through the door to stand in front of me. I knew they wanted food, but Sin came first. "Not now, guys."

Spider bit me on the leg.

"Ow." I glared at him. "That is not cool. I know you're hungry, but—"

"Mama Mama Mama. Bad man came in. The bad man made Sin leave. Spider and Sugar hide in the closet."

Ezreal's brows went up. "Your cat can talk?"

"Yeah, long story." I crouched down. "What bad man, Spider?"

"Bad man."

So descriptive. "What did the bad man look like?"

Spider licked his foot before answering. "Bad man have blue hair."

Pretty much everyone in the NP had blue hair, unless they'd gone gray already. "How did the bad man make Sin leave?"

"Cold," Spider said. "Bad man made Sin cold. Chicken Party now?"

Someone had used their power against Sin. I kissed Spider's head. "Yes, Chicken Party now. Is that what you were trying to tell me before? I'm sorry I didn't listen to you."

I glanced at Ezreal as I got to my feet. "That confirms that Sin didn't leave on his own."

Ezreal nodded, but he was watching the cats. He still seemed a bit flabbergasted by Spider's vocal talents. "Uh huh."

I opened a can of Chicken Party and divided it into two bowls, then put them on the floor for the cats. "We also know a winter elf took Sin. If he had blue hair and used cold to get him to go with him, there's no other explanation. Not that it narrows down the suspect pool much."

Ezreal snapped out of it. "Well, someone in the palace had to see Mr. Crowe with whoever it was. We'll call the staff together. We need Steward Gregory."

"He's already gone to transportation. After he told me Sin never came back with the crawler, he said he was going to transportation to get a search party to find him. He said he was going with them to look too."

"Okay." Ezreal thought a second. "If Mr. Crowe never came back in the crawler, he could have been picked up by the kidnapper somewhere in town, then brought back here and forced to leave you that note. They'd have to have gotten through the gates, which implies someone the guards are familiar with. But they might have hidden Mr. Crowe to keep him from alerting the guards to his situation. Maybe put him in something that wasn't suspicious."

"Like the back of a truck. Someone in receiving could have seen something."

Ezreal nodded. "We need more help. Your parents, your aunt and uncle, we need everyone. Whoever took him can't have gone far."

"They might not have needed to get far if their goal was to…" I couldn't bring myself to say the words. I grabbed the kitchen counter to keep myself from collapsing. The thought that someone might be trying to permanently take Sin from me was more than I could take.

"Don't think that, Princess. Mr. Crowe is a fighter and a necromancer. He won't let himself be taken from you without a lot of noise and struggle and the exhaustive use of his powers. We're going to find him."

"Right," I whispered, staring at the counter. "I hope so."

"Princess, look at me."

I raised my head and made eye contact.

Ezreal seemed to radiate confidence. I wondered if that's what he looked like going into the ring. "Mr. Crowe is going to be okay. We're not going to let anything happen to him, are we?"

"No."

"And no one would dare hurt him, because that would mean they'd be hunted for the rest of their lives. No one goes against the Winter Throne and comes out a winner, do they?"

I straightened. "No."

He nodded. "You are Jayne Frost, daughter of the Winter King. Heir to the Winter Throne. Owner of a talking cat. You are one of the most powerful women to have ever been born in this kingdom. Your magic is second to no one's but your father's. Only a fool would want you as an enemy."

I smiled. I knew what he was doing. And it was working. "Thank you, Ezreal."

He smiled back. "You're welcome, Princess. Now let's go find your fiancé."

"We need to figure out who the bad man was. If someone was in Sin's apartment—" I whipped around and looked at Spider, who was now sitting on the windowsill in the living room. "Spider, did the man who took Sinclair come into the apartment with Sinclair? Or did the bad man come in by himself?"

Spider looked at me, head tilted. "Himself."

I glanced back at Ezreal. "That narrows it down a little. Only someone with a key could have come in on his own. Sin's door was locked when I got here."

Ezreal shifted his gaze across the hall at the open door. "Did you have a key?"

"No, I—snowballs. I guess they could have picked the lock like I did."

"True. But it's a start."

A new thought occurred to me. "What were you coming to tell me?"

"That I found something that might be important, but I don't think it matters now."

"Tell me." I was grasping, but anything could be significant right now. "There's no way Sin's disappearance and the mess with the Tinkers' Tourney is unrelated."

"Agreed. I went back through my daily log, and on March second, one of your father's magic bracelets went missing."

"Like the ones he gave Sin and me to change our appearance?"

"Yes. I found the bracelet on March fifth. It was under a stack of papers on my desk. I assumed it had just been misplaced, which isn't something I or your father would ever really do, but it was the most logical explanation. Now, after what you told me—"

"Someone took it and used it to impersonate Dora Frigit at Sweet Acres."

He nodded. "I think so."

I grabbed the file he'd given me and opened it to read the list of names. Beside each person, he'd put their occupation. "These people that have access to my father's office. Which of them do you trust the least? Or think might be capable of something like this?"

He read over my shoulder. "I'm not really sure. The two housekeepers are some of the newest hires. I don't know them as well." He pointed to another name. A maintenance man. "Junger Glace. He was upset that his son didn't get hired as a Zamboni driver."

"That seems like a thin reason to cause a problem of this scale."

"Agreed." He frowned. "We need to ask Gregory. He knows everyone who works in the palace. He could look at this list and tell us immediately who we should be going after."

"Then we're leaving for transportation right now. If there's a crawler left, we'll go after them."

Ezreal hesitated. "Maybe you should go there and I should gather your family."

I closed the file. "No, please come with me. I don't want to be alone right now."

He smiled. "Let's go."

We ran to the south exit. Perhaps not the most royal behavior on my part, but I wasn't interested in being royal while Sin was in trouble.

I expected the place to be deserted, but two valets were standing by the transportation office shooting the breeze. The snow was coming down in fat, wet flakes now. The younger valet hurried over when I came through the door, the other snapped out of his relaxed slouch to stand straighter.

The younger valet bowed. "Would you like a crawler, Princess?"

"I want to know how the search is going."

He started to scratch his head, realized who he was standing in front of, and stopped. "The search for what, Your Highness?"

I'd never throttled a member of the palace staff, but I was thinking about it. "The search for my boyfriend, Sinclair Crowe."

Apparently, my tone was a little more strident than I'd intended as the young man's eyes widened. "I—I'm very sorry. I did not know he was missing, Your Highness."

"What are you talking about? Gregory came down here to organize the search. Did you just come on duty? Doesn't anyone—"

Ezreal put his hand on my arm. "Princess, if I may."

I nodded and tried to breathe.

Ezreal waved the other valet over. "What time did your shift start?"

The older man hustled toward us. "I've been here since midmorning."

"Then you tell us," Ezreal said. "How's the search going? Has there been any news?"

He looked at the other valet before answering. "What search?"

My hands clenched, and the air around me crackled like thin ice giving way. "What in the bloody Christmas is going on?"

Both valets retreated a few inches.

Ezreal stepped toward them, narrowing the gap. "Are you telling me there's no search happening right now? What happened when Steward Gregory came down here?"

The valets looked at each other again, perhaps deciding which one was going to answer. The older one cleared his throat. "I'm sorry, but Steward Gregory hasn't been here today. There's no search of any kind going on that I'm aware of."

Shards of ice pricked my heart. I was on the verge of going full-blown blizzard. I found my voice and decided to confirm what Spider had told me. "Did Mr. Crowe return in the crawler earlier today?"

Both valets nodded, but again the older one spoke. "Yes, Your Highness. He returned about two hours ago."

So Sin *had* come back. Gregory knew everything that went on in the palace. How did he not know that?

Because Gregory was a liar.

The gut-punch feeling returned, turning my knees to liquid. I reached for Ezreal. He caught my arm and held me up. "Ezreal..."

He nodded. "I know, Princess." He held my arm tightly to his side, turned me around and marched me back into the palace.

I was livid and trembling, and snow had begun falling around us, which wouldn't have been odd except we were inside. "Gregory did this, didn't he?"

Ezreal nodded. "It seems that way. He's at least involved."

"Gregory. *Gregory.* That lying piece of garbage. We trusted him. For years. It has to be him. He has the access, he has the connections, and he knew the moment Sin and I were planning on coming to the North Pole."

"He must have worked very hard to set this all up. He wanted to discredit Mr. Crowe. But why?"

"We'll figure that out when we find him. If I let him live long enough." I sucked in a breath, suddenly unable to get enough air in my lungs with the weight of betrayal pressing down on me. "Sin." It was the only word I could manage.

Ezreal held on to me. "We're going to find Mr. Crowe. We know where Gregory lives. His apartment isn't exactly hard to find in the staff wing."

I shook my head. The snow came down harder. Big, blinding clumps. "He won't be there. He's too smart for that. He's already outsmarted us every step of the way. He knew we wouldn't suspect him until it was too late."

"Good thing it's not too late," Ezreal said.

I stared at him. "How do you know? How are we going to find him?"

A glint came into Ezreal's eyes. It was as sharp and bright as a newly honed blade. "I believe I can help with that."

I thought I knew a lot about Ezreal. About his past and what he'd done before coming to work for my father. And I did. It was his ice troll side that had always remained a bit of a mystery to me.

Sure, I knew a little about them, but not that they were exceptional trackers thanks to a sense of smell that rivaled the ones my shifter friends in Nocturne Falls had. Of course, there wasn't much call for Ezreal to do any tracking as the king's office manager.

Until now.

We made a quick trip to my dad's office, where Ezreal grabbed something from his desk, then we went straight to Gregory's apartment.

At the door, Ezreal produced a key that opened the lock.

"You have a key to the steward's apartment?"

He shook his head as he turned the knob. "Not

just his apartment. It's a master key. Opens all the suites, rooms, and apartments. No one but your parents and I know it exists. And now you, obviously."

"Well, I'm glad it does."

"Me too. I'd hate to have to break this door down and cost the palace the repair." He pushed the door wide and we went in. I'd never been in Gregory's apartment. It was smaller than mine, obviously, but not by much and still very luxurious and well appointed. Probably twice the size of Ezreal's, but then, the man held the highest position in the palace, after all, and had been here for decades.

Knowing what I knew about him now made being in his personal space a very uncomfortable feeling. My skin itched. "What do you need to track him?"

"Not much. Just give me a minute to stand here and imprint on his scent."

"Go for it." While Ezreal did his thing, I wandered around, opening cabinets, looking in drawers, and generally trying to find something that would give us an idea where he'd taken Sin. I didn't find anything interesting until I peeked into his walk-in closet.

The back wall was blank.

"How odd." No shelves, no hooks, no racks of hanging clothes. Just a blank wall in a space that otherwise utilized every inch for organization.

I flipped the light on and immediately understood why. There was a sheet covering the wall. It was hung on a slim curtain rod and, with the light off, looked very much like a regular painted wall.

I pulled the sheet back. It took a moment for my brain to register what my eyes were seeing. "Ezreal, come in here."

He was at the door a few moments later. The same curse he'd used before slipped out again. "He really has been planning this for months."

The wall beneath the curtain was covered with notes, photos of me, Sinclair, and the three tinkers. Timelines that included our trip up here, Lyla's visit to Sweet Acres, and the Tinkers' Tourney. There were clippings of the biased articles from the *Post*.

Next to one of them, a single white feather was tacked up. On a small hook beside that was what had to be a copy of my father's ID badge. There was even a photo of Sin and me with Sin's face crossed out with a black X.

Everything was here. From how he'd set up men in the crowd at the toy reveal to cast suspicion on Sin to how he'd influenced Stanley and Terrance to make identical toys with the ultimate goal of blaming Sinclair's influence as evil. There was even a duplicate ballot that the tinkers themselves used to nominate each other for the tourney.

Gregory's hands had been in all of it. The whole thing was a road map for the horrible, desperate attempt he'd made to smear Sin's good name.

I was breathing in deep, measured breaths as I processed the nightmare in front of me. "He's got everything he needs to set this whole thing up, but why? Why would he want to get rid of Sin? What has he ever done to Gregory?"

Ezreal tapped a key hanging farther down. "Including a copy of the master key that no one else was supposed to know about." He shook his head. "I should have seen it."

I looked at him. "How could you have?"

His gaze went dark with memory. "When your father hired me, there were some who were very outspoken about what a bad decision that was."

"Because they didn't think a former fighter belonged in such a delicate position."

He snorted softly. "That was the story your father and I put forward to diffuse the harder truth."

"Which was what?"

"That I was half ice troll." His gaze returned to the wall and all its damning evidence. "Gregory was one of the loudest opponents, but your father told him in unequivocal terms to get over it."

"But you didn't call him out as one of your enemies when Sin asked you."

"You're right, I didn't. Because I wanted to

believe that was all in the past. But this wall, and his actions, prove otherwise."

"That's why he used your personal stationery. He wanted to snare you in all this too."

Ezreal nodded. "Taking me down would have just been a feather in his cap."

"Just like preventing Sin from becoming consort would be the crown jewel." I couldn't believe someone I'd trusted for so long had betrayed me and my family in such a horrific way. "He must hate Sinclair. Sin doesn't have an ounce of elf in him."

The steely, honed look I'd seen before returned to Ezreal's eyes. "I've got all I need. Let's bring Mr. Crowe home."

"There's one more thing I need to do." I turned and marched back through the apartment and into the hall.

As soon as Ezreal was beside me, I pulled the door shut. He dug the key from his pocket.

But I stopped him. "You don't need to lock it. I'm going to do something better."

I raised my hands. "I'm going to seal it shut so that no one can get in to remove anything until I'm ready for that to happen. For all we know, he could still have an accomplice in the palace. I want all this evidence preserved."

I called up my magic and sealed the door top to bottom in a thick layer of impenetrable ice. It gleamed glacial blue in the palace lighting. Cold radiated off of it and spilled over us as I dropped my hands. In my current aggravated state, holding this kind of magic didn't even register. It was an afterthought. As easy as breathing. "That should do it."

"I'll say." Ezreal let out a little laugh. "That should also remind anyone who sees it that you are most definitely your father's daughter."

"Gregory's about to find that out for himself in a very personal way. Which direction?"

Ezreal's nostrils flared as he inhaled. He turned his head, sniffing both sides of the corridor.

Suddenly, doubt filled me. "How can you tell anything in here? This whole place must reek of him. Gregory's haunted these halls since before I was born."

Ezreal's eyes suddenly shifted from his normal gray to a deep, crystalline blue. I'd seen that happen a few times before when his emotions had been high. "I only needed Gregory's smell as a baseline. It's Mr. Crowe's scent I'm tracking. I wanted to make sure he hadn't been here. And he hasn't. But I can find him now. They may not have left the palace."

"Makes sense. Getting Sin out of here would be hard to accomplish. Even for Gregory."

"Follow me." Ezreal stopped short and grimaced. "I didn't mean to command you, Princess."

"Command away. Now isn't the time for protocol. Let's go. I'm right behind you."

Ezreal took off back the way we came. We ended up in the freight elevator. His nostrils flared again. "They were in here, but I can't know which floor until I smell it."

"Then we'll check every floor." I ran my hand down the panel, lighting up every button.

The elevator moved too slowly for my mood. At each floor, Ezreal got out, sniffed, and got back in, shaking his head.

Until we got to the sub-basement. I'd never been to this floor. It was several stories deep within the permafrost, and as a child, I'd been forbidden to come down here. Not like I'd wanted to. Not after one of my cousins had come down here on a dare and run into a trio of hibernating yetis.

He'd escaped with a couple of deep scratches and the lingering stink of hot garbage that had taken many baths with peppermint soap to get rid of.

They hadn't really meant to hurt him, I'd found out later. They'd merely held him down and tried to lick the jam off him. He was a messy eater.

And since as a child, I always had candy in my pockets, I was convinced they'd hunt me down if I ever came near here. That was enough to keep me from even thinking about exploring this level.

Sure, the yetis had been shooed out by one of the groundskeepers trained for that sort of thing.

And that had been years ago.

But as the doors opened onto the dark, dank, freezing space, I fully expected to be attacked by small, toothy balls of fur that stank of rancid fish and sun-warmed diapers.

Ezreal nodded, his voice a whisper. "They were here."

I stilled. "Yetis?" I whispered back.

"What? No. Gregory and Mr. Crowe." He put his hand against the door to keep it from closing.

"Oh, right." That bucked my courage up. "Wait, what do you mean *were*?"

He shook his head. "The scent trail stops here."

I wanted to throw up. "We have to find them. If the trail stops here, where did they go?"

"There's only one explanation. They doubled back. Gregory did this to throw us off. They must have left the palace after all." He closed his eyes for a moment. "I've failed you. I'm sorry."

"You haven't failed me yet. If the valets haven't seen Gregory, that means he took Sin out a different way. Probably by the staff entrance. Aren't there crawlers there?"

Ezreal picked his head up. "There are. And unlike the family entrances, there's no one monitoring the staff entrance."

He got back into the elevator and jabbed the button for the main floor. "Can Mr. Crowe stand the cold?"

I nodded, thinking back to when we'd been frozen in place at Elenora Ellingham's Black and Orange Ball by Lark and her crew of thieves. A caper that had resulted in Lark's magic being stripped through an intense saltwater treatment program. Salt water being the winter elf's kryptonite. "He can better than most. Being a necromancer gives him an edge there."

"Good. He's going to need that edge. Because I'm pretty sure Gregory's taken him where he thought no one would go looking."

I had a feeling I knew exactly where Ezreal was talking about. But at the same time, I didn't want it to be true. "The polar forest."

He nodded. "Yeti country."

One of the best and worst things about living in a land where snow perpetually covers the ground is that it's impossible not to leave tracks.

That didn't mean it was easy to find the route Gregory had taken. For one thing, the polar forest surrounded us on three sides. Any direction out of town and away from the palace except for east, which would take you to a glacier, would lead you to the polar forest eventually.

For another thing, the staff entrance was well-used. All of the staff and some deliveries came through there, so the ground might have been covered in snow, but it was packed down, and where it wasn't, the tracks went in every direction.

Many sets of crawler tracks ventured far enough out to indicate they'd gone toward the forest. It was a popular place to hike and picnic. Or rather, the edges were since the yetis rarely ventured out that far. They generally preferred the deepest parts of the forest.

We preferred them to stay there too.

Some of the braver cooks often went deeper in to forage for specific delicacies, like the wintermint my mother so dearly loved and seasonal edibles like brisk berries and buttercaps, a mushroom that appeared after a particularly dry snowfall.

But the third thing about living in a winter wonderland was that it snowed a lot, and not always because my father had decided it should. Today, for example. The snow that had been coming down since early morning had rendered most of the tracks nearly invisible.

So which way to go when we were basically surrounded by snow fields and forest?

Ezreal deduced north. That part of the forest was the least visited, as it was very dense and also one of the coldest areas. Ezreal believed Gregory would use that cold as another tool against Sinclair and that he'd count on the density to hide him and his captive.

Fortunately, we had a tool of our own. Ezreal's incredible ability to sniff out scents. He was as good as Birdie. Maybe even better. We rode with the crawler's windows down, allowing the air to pass over us. We weren't even at the tree line when he lifted his head and seemed to catch a scent.

He steered the crawler slightly right and slowed down. "They're here."

I was overjoyed, but the look on his face was odd. Not happy, as I'd have thought it would be, but concerned. I sniffed the air for myself to see if I could make sense of his expression.

It would have hit me a second later, I'm sure. Yetis. The stink was faint but very present. That was not good. "Ezreal, I'm worried. And I can tell you are too. I see it on your face."

He frowned as he parked the crawler. "I don't like what I'm smelling."

"I know. Me either. Yetis. But they should be deeper in than what Gregory has gone. Right? At least if he's smart, he won't have gone that far."

"If he was smart, he never would have started any of this."

"True, but he's been smart enough to keep us guessing for a long time, so who knows what he's capable of? Or how lost in his own misconceptions he is." I was worried about that. Gregory might have gone into some kind of delusional state where he thought he was actually going to get away with this. That could make him more dangerous and unpredictable than he already was.

Ezreal parked the crawler and grabbed a bag out of the back seat. It was an emergency pack and he'd made sure it was in the crawler before we'd left. "We have to go on foot from here. The trees are too thick."

"But you have the trail, right?"

"I do." He slung the bag across his body.

"Then let's run."

"That won't be possible. It's too thick here."

"Then let's move at the fastest pace possible. I don't want to waste another second." Or make ourselves any more vulnerable to the yetis than we already would be. Getting attacked wasn't going to help rescue Sin.

"We'll go as quickly as the terrain allows. And the plan for when we get there?" He opened his door.

I opened mine too. "I'm going to hit Gregory with as much ice as I can, which should hold him long enough for you to subdue him, but beyond that, I'm going to Sin's aid immediately."

"Then that's our plan. How we actually make the approach can be determined once we find him."

"Works for me."

"Let me get my bearings on the scent line, and we'll head in."

We got out and stood for a second at the forest's edge while Ezreal breathed the trail in one more time. The wall of trees in front of us ascended into the clouds, their tops disappearing into the snow-laden sky. The deeper I looked into the woods, the darker it got. Very little sun penetrated the depths of this forest.

A rough trek lay ahead of us.

I glanced at Ezreal, glad this warrior of a man was on my side. I would do anything for Sin, but that didn't mean I wasn't afraid. "Ezreal? You're authorized to use whatever force necessary. You understand me?"

His gaze was dead serious. "I do, Princess."

"Then lead the way."

He went in first, and I followed as closely behind as I could. The polar forest was a unique place. Most of the trees were centuries old and twice as thick around as a crawler was wide. I've never seen the redwoods or sequoias in person, but I'd been told those trees were the lesser descendants of the polar pines.

There was no running through this part of the forest. I'd been foolish to think that was possible. The trees were almost trunk to trunk in some places, the pines like soldiers standing at attention. Some of them had grown so close together there was no fitting between them, creating an obstacle we had to go around. A little light filtered through here and there, but it was as if a perpetual twilight existed in this place.

Where the pines allowed some room, small scrub brush took over.

We made time where we could, but it felt like a snail's pace. A very loud snail. In the polar forest, the stillness almost hurt your ears. There *was* some sound, the crack of an iced branch, the whistle of wind, the scurry of an alpine squirrel. But for the most part, the snow absorbed everything, leaving behind a quiet that was a little unsettling.

Any noise we made seemed as if it had been broadcast through a megaphone. I cringed at each snap of a twig or crunch of iced-over snow.

Occasionally, Ezreal adjusted our course according to the scent line he was following, but for the most part, we trudged on without a word. Driven by our purpose. Curls of vapor spun out of our mouths, our breathing heavier the deeper in we got. The air was crisp and clear and scented with pine.

Finally, the forest began to open up a little. Not much, but enough that we could quicken our pace.

Then he stopped abruptly and raised his hand. He pointed to me, then tapped his ear.

I listened. And heard the faint ravings of a man gone mad.

"Gregory," I mouthed.

Ezreal nodded. He made more hand motions, indicating we should split up and go in separately. It was a good plan. It would create more confusion and throw Gregory off.

After all, we were assuming he was alone with Sin, but we couldn't know that for sure.

A few more nods and gestures and whispered words, and we went in opposite directions to circle around. Ezreal had told me to wait until I heard his call. The trolls had a deep guttural woof, and I expected that's what I'd hear.

Not rushing directly to Sin was killing me, but I knew this was a good plan. I went as quietly through the snow and trees as I could, finally finding a spot that allowed me to at last lay eyes on Sinclair.

Gregory's rantings came through in bits and pieces, all about how no foreign influence should taint the throne.

But it was the sight of Sinclair that caused my heart to clench. He was bound to a massive pine by bands of ice at his chest, thighs, and ankles. His head lolled to one side, eyes closed. I wasn't sure he was conscious.

Or alive.

Without thinking, an ice dagger appeared in my hand. That was an emotional response, my anger and magic melding. A dagger was pointless. It wouldn't free Sin, and it wasn't the right weapon to use against Gregory.

That dirty double-crosser. He was pacing in the small clearing, muttering to himself and waving one hand in the air. His other arm hung limply at his side, his hand black. Sin's death mark. It had to be.

Occasionally, Gregory charged at Sin, only to stop and burble on again about how unseemly it was that a merchant of death should take the throne.

Gregory, it seemed, had truly gone over the edge. Far, far over.

I dropped the dagger and crouched, my vision red with rage and the desire to free Sin, but I held back, waiting, waiting...

A throaty, feral howl shook the forest.

Gregory spun toward the sound.

I leaped forward, the power of my anger moving me with new speed. I thrust a wave of magic at Gregory's back, knocking him into another massive pine with a punch of ice.

At the same time, Ezreal dropped from the branches above and caught Gregory as he ricocheted off the tree. Good. Gregory was his to deal with now.

I ran to Sin and put my hands on his face. His skin was icy, and his lashes were white with frost. A pit opened in my stomach. "Sin, Sin, are you okay?"

No answer.

"Please, Sin, talk to me. Say something."

Then a small groan.

"Hang on, sweetheart." I reluctantly took my hands from him and planted them on the ice. Immediately, I started absorbing the cold, pulling it into my body to melt the ice and free him.

I shivered for more than one reason. Sin would never want to live here now, would he? And who could blame him? But that was fine. As I began to shake with the cold, I knew I'd do anything to be with him, including abdicate.

My cousin could have the throne.

All I wanted was Sin.

The ice melted, and Sin fell forward into my arms, but I was weak with cold and we toppled into the snow together.

I pushed him off me, rolling him over so I could get to my knees. I smacked his cheeks lightly, trying to bring him around.

As I did that, I realized I'd completely (and understandably) ignored what was going on with Ezreal and Gregory. I glanced up. Ezreal had Gregory subdued and tied up with plastic bands.

The zip ties must have been in the bag he'd grabbed from the crawler.

Ezreal rushed to my side. "How's he doing?"

"Frozen. Not much response."

"I'll start a fire." He pulled a kit from the bag and set to work getting a pile of dry branches gathered in a flattened area of snow.

"Can't we just get him back to the crawler?"

A few sparks from the lighter and flames shot up from the kindling. He shook his head. "You know what a trek it was getting here. He won't make the trip back unless he can walk on his own."

"You're asking a lot."

"No," Sin whispered. "I can do it."

"Sin." I sucked in a breath, overjoyed to hear his voice. I kissed his frozen mouth. "We're going to warm you up by the fire."

I pulled him closer as Ezreal went to gather more wood.

Sin began to shiver. It was a good sign. He was getting the feeling back in his body. Pain would come next. Pins and needles that felt like spikes and daggers.

I held his hands in mine. The fire was warming me up too, leaching out the cold I'd willingly absorbed. I gently massaged his palms and fingers to help the blood circulate.

He groaned again.

"I know," I whispered. "It hurts."

He nodded a little. "Thank you."

Ezreal returned with more wood.

I shook my head. "I'm so sorry."

Sin smiled. "I love you."

Ezreal added the wood to the fire, crouching down next to us. "Princess?"

I looked up. "Yes?"

"We have two small problems."

"What are they?" Sin had survived. I could handle anything now.

"Night is coming fast." Ezreal glanced over his shoulder. "And so are the yetis."

I looked into the woods behind him, but didn't see anything. Yet. "Great."

"The fire will draw them. They'll be afraid of it, but it's still going to get their attention."

I nodded. "Understood. We need to move, then."

"We do." He looked at Sin. "Mr. Crowe, how are you feeling?"

He was still lying down, but managed to shrug. "Better every second."

"Do you think you can walk?"

He slowly pushed himself to a seated position. "Yes."

His lips were still a little blue.

I frowned. "What about Gregory?"

Ezreal pushed to his feet. "I'll handle him. He seems to have lost the use of one arm. His hand is black."

326

I stood as well. "I saw that." I looked at Sin. "You did that, didn't you?"

He got to his knees. "I did. Just defending myself."

"Good job. I'm sorry you even had to—"

"He tried to kill me." Gregory snarled. "Would have too, if I hadn't—"

"You're lucky he didn't," I snapped back. Then I glanced at Sin again. He was still sitting up and seemed a little more stable. "I guess we might need to explain your death touch now."

He slowly rubbed his hands together. "Yeah, I'm sure you're right. There will be questions. And without answers, more rumors will start. Maybe August will let me post something in the paper."

"I'm sure he will. But we can worry about that later." Sin was finally standing. He didn't wobble, which I was thankful for. "You seem like you're doing better. The fire really helped, huh?"

"It did," Sin said. "Thank you, Ezreal."

Ezreal nodded. "You're very welcome, Mr. Crowe. Now I suggest we get moving."

He hoisted Gregory to his feet. "Follow me. Stay as close as you can."

Gregory had gone pretty quiet at the mention of yetis. Apparently, his crazy didn't extend so far as to think he could handle a pack of them on his own.

But he had to know what awaited him back at the palace. His actions would not go unpunished.

Ezreal pushed through the brush, and we found our trail again. I looped Sin's arm over my shoulders to help support him. He didn't complain. We pushed on as fast as we could. Darkness was settling fast, erasing what little light there was.

A faint, and thankfully distant, scrabbling carried through the forest from behind us.

My pulse increased. I knew it was yetis. I knew they were coming for us. And I knew there was a lot of forest left between us and the crawler.

The wind picked up as night came, whistling past us. Carrying our scent to the yetis. But at least it wasn't carrying their stench to us. If there was any silver lining, that was it.

"Are we going to make it?" Sin asked softly. He was leaning into me more than he had at the start.

"Of course," I answered. "We're almost there."

We weren't. But what else could I tell him? It was a lie of kindness. And my desperate attempt to keep him moving.

I swallowed, trying to keep my fear at bay. But yetis were fast, really fast. The only reason they weren't nipping at our heels yet was because they weren't ready. Maybe they wanted to circle around us more. Who knew the mind of a yeti?

The attack would come at any moment. My heart was about to break through my rib cage. I tried to breathe normally and failed. Panic was seeping through me faster than the cold. And the cold I could handle. The panic…not so much. "I never thought I'd want to see a wendigo so badly as I do right now."

Ezreal snorted, then slowed as he turned to look at me. "That's a phenomenal idea."

"It is?" We slowed, too.

He came to a stop and stared into the forest beyond us, nodding. "Keep going toward the crawler."

Sin and I stood beside him. "We're not leaving you here."

"Or me," Gregory snarled. "You're not leaving me."

Ezreal cut his eyes at the man. "Another good idea. But we'll save that for plan B." He went back to staring into the trees. "Go ahead, Princess. Get to the crawler. I won't be far behind."

"Promise?"

"Promise."

I got Sin and I moving forward again, passing Ezreal and Gregory in a few quick steps. The path we'd made coming in was getting harder and harder to pick out in the dying light.

Gregory started to mumble about not being left behind again, but a piercing, brittle scream broke through all other sounds.

It was so sharp and sudden, it almost knocked us to the ground. I caught us at the last second, my heart in my throat now.

"What was that?" Sin twisted to look back.

"Wendigo," I managed despite the fear clogging my airways. Then the understanding of what Ezreal had done hit me. "Well, Ezreal's best impersonation of one."

"For real?"

Sin and I kept going forward. My pulse was tapering down toward normal. "Yes. Ice trolls are great mimics. No doubt the yetis are hightailing it in the other direction by now. The wendigo is their only real nature predator."

He nodded. "I remember you mentioned that when Nocturne Falls had that unfortunate yeti infestation." Then he lifted his head and inhaled. "There does seem to be less stink in the air."

"Always a good thing. Now save your breath, we still have a ways to go."

I didn't know how much longer it took us. Could have been ten minutes, could have been an hour. Trudging through the snow and brush and dense forest made every new step very much like the last, but finally we broke through the tree line.

I helped Sin into the back seat of the crawler where he could lie down, then I got the engine started so I could crank the heat on. Our vehicles were very good at warming up, and every seat had a heater built in and several vents to ensure the person at that seat had the proper temperature. He'd be warm in no time.

The crawler also had exterior lights, so I turned those on to help guide Ezreal in. He probably didn't need them, but it couldn't hurt, and I didn't want Gregory taking advantage of the dark to try to escape.

Hunting him down in this inky blackness would not be fun. The stars were brilliant and plentiful, but not enough to see by. Thankfully, the snow had stopped.

A few minutes later, Ezreal walked out of the forest with Gregory in tow. Mostly dragging him. I jumped out of the crawler and went to help. This was a multi-use crawler. It had a cargo hold in the back, which was probably used to haul supplies back from the market. But it's where Gregory would be riding now.

He'd earned it. And I was not about to make Sin share air space with the crazy who'd tried to kill him.

Yes, I was still angry. I probably would be for a long time to come. Gregory's selfish, reckless actions had ruined everything. I never wanted to see his face again, and planned on doing everything in my power, which was considerable, to make sure that happened.

I grabbed Gregory's dead arm and helped pull him forward. "That wendigo call was amazing, Ezreal."

He smiled. "It was your idea."

"No, it wasn't. It was my random statement. You had the idea. You saved us."

I couldn't tell if he was blushing or wind-burned. He shrugged. "Let's call it a team effort."

"I like that a lot. How about some more team effort getting Gregory into the cargo hold?"

Gregory spat at us. "How dare you? I'm the house steward. I will not ride in a cargo hold."

I leaned in toward him. "You *were* the house steward. Now you're a prisoner of the realm and will be treated as such. Letting you ride in the hold is a kindness you don't deserve, so if you'd prefer to be strapped to the roof, that can happen just as easily."

"Princess." He blinked at me like he was dismayed at *my* behavior.

The living nerve. I almost laughed at him. Almost. "Don't."

Ezreal popped the hatch on the crawler and stood there waiting. "What's it going to be?"

Gregory scowled and muttered some more, but limped his way to the hold.

Ezreal shut it, smirking. "What a piece of work."

"I'll say."

"You all right, Princess? That was a lot of effort back there. And you're still holding the ice sealing his door shut. You must be wearing a little thin."

I shook my head. "Getting Sinclair back has erased a lot of my tiredness."

"Glad to hear it." He tested the latch on the hold, double-checking it was locked. "What do you say we head home?"

"I say that's all I want to do."

He drove, and I sat in front since Sinclair was lying down, but within twenty minutes he was sitting up and seemed very much himself again.

I was twisted in the seat to see him better. "Don't overdo it. The cold can really take it out of you."

"As I found out. But I promise I feel all right. Nothing a good night's sleep wouldn't help." He touched Ezreal's shoulder. "Thank you for your part in this. I owe you my life."

"Sir, I don't think—"

"I do, Ezreal. Jayne was smart to get you involved. Doing this by herself would have been a monumental task. Your help was invaluable."

I nodded. "He's right. Your help was key. Getting Gregory and Sin back to the crawler was a two-person job. I really needed you for that."

Sin smiled. "And your wendigo imitation is the best I've ever heard. It's also the *only* one I've ever heard. And the only one I hope to hear."

We all laughed for a second, but Sin turned serious a moment later. "What's going to happen to Gregory?"

Ezreal stayed quiet, letting me answer. In part because he had to know how much of a role I would play in this. I took a breath and reminded myself that I had to be fair and just. That was hard when Sin had been the victim.

I exhaled. "I am going to advocate for his banishment. I don't think there will be much pushback on that, though. I have a feeling it's what my father would decide on anyway."

"So Gregory will have to leave the North Pole?"

I nodded. "And will be unable to return. It's a punishment reserved for only the severest of crimes."

Ezreal finally spoke up. "This is certainly one of those."

Sin thought about that. "Wouldn't it be worse if he had to stay here and live with what he's done?"

"Maybe. But I could never trust him again."

"Doesn't the NP have a jail?"

"We don't. Crime isn't really a thing here."

Sin nodded. "Well, I'm not saying let him keep his job. But being forced from the only home you've known…"

"He would have killed you."

"Maybe." Sin paused. "Or I might have killed him."

Ezreal glanced in the rearview mirror. "Can you, I mean, are you capable of that?"

Sin met his gaze. "Apparently, I am. What I did to his hand I could have done to his entire body if he hadn't stopped me with those ice restraints."

Ezreal's brows bent. "Will that blackness fade? Or heal?"

"No," Sin said. "And if it isn't dealt with, it will spread. He's going to lose his hand."

"He's marked for life, then." Ezreal shot me a look. "You could let him stay. He'd never be able to hide. Losing his hand would be a constant reminder of what he's done and the acts he's committed against the crown. His betrayal will always be evident."

"I hadn't considered that. He'd have to be under house arrest, obviously." I turned in my seat to look out at the night. "I still don't know. All I can think about right now is how much I want him gone."

The palace was as brightly lit and fully awake as I had ever seen it at such a late hour. The windows glowed and the grounds were in full illumination. I wasn't sure the palace had ever looked more beautiful. Maybe that was because of what we'd just been through.

Or maybe it was just because we were being beckoned home.

Bittersweet happiness filled me from the sight of it and the feelings that welled up within me, but I knew beyond all question that I could leave this place behind for Sin.

My world had no color without him. No warmth, no happiness. No magic. I needed him beside me. Wanted him to be the one I grew old with. And when he told me, as he certainly would, that he couldn't make this place his home, I'd understand and tell him that wasn't a problem.

I had made my decision just like he'd made his. I would abdicate, and we would return to Nocturne Falls once and for all. It *was* a great place to live.

That had to be what he wanted. Why else would he ask that Gregory not be banished? Sin didn't want Gregory free in the human world, because that's where we'd be living.

Made sense. Keep the man who'd tried to kill him in a distant kingdom where he could be monitored. No chance of Gregory getting another crack at taking Sin out that way.

Although, when I abdicated, Gregory would get what he wanted. No non-winter elf would sit atop the Winter Throne.

I frowned. In a way, that meant Gregory still won.

I couldn't think of it that way, though. I had to focus on what was best for Sin and me. What would keep us going.

Ezreal drove the crawler around to the south entrance and under the portico. Valets swarmed the vehicle, eager to help. One took off inside, no doubt to let my father know we'd returned.

By now, I was sure the message we'd left with the housekeeper we'd run into at the service entrance had been delivered to my family.

Ezreal opened his door while a valet opened mine and another opened the back door for Sin.

I got out and went to work. "Get medical down here immediately for Mr. Crowe. Get security here for Steward Gregory and call the constable as well."

Lots of nodding and "Yes, Your Highness" answered me.

"Please confirm that someone went to tell my father?"

"I'm here."

At my father's voice, I glanced toward the palace doors. He stood there, back-framed by the light, looking very much the Winter King. Ice vapor swirled around him, showing his mood as he strode down the steps toward us.

"Dad." I couldn't keep my voice from cracking. I cleared my throat and pulled myself together. "Gregory almost killed Sinclair."

He pulled me into his arms. "Are you okay? Is Sinclair?"

"Yes." Sin was still in the crawler, but the rear doors were open on both sides. "Thanks to Ezreal."

My father kissed my brow before releasing me. He peered into the back seat where Sin was. "You all right, son?"

"I am. Your daughter and your office manager are very brave people."

My father smiled. "So are you. I know how many times you've put yourself on the line for Jayne."

Then he straightened and looked at me again. "Did you leave Gregory out there?"

I snorted. "No, but I'm sure he wishes that." I walked around to the cargo hold, my father following, and unlocked the hatch.

It lifted, revealing a snarly, cranky steward who looked more like a trussed Christmas goose than the elf in charge of the winter palace.

Muscles tightened and twitched in my father's jaw. He glared at Gregory.

Gregory held the eye contact for only a moment before he looked away, going pale.

My father put his hand on the hatch and continued to stare for what felt like an eternity. Then he just shook his head and walked back around to the front of the vehicle where Ezreal was standing.

He put his hand on Ezreal's shoulder. "There aren't words for how thankful I am for what you've done."

Ezreal bowed his head. "I just did my job."

"You did more than that." My father took a breath. "Klara and I owe you. The kingdom owes you. Thank you."

"You're welcome, Your Majesty. I was happy to help." Ezreal glanced at the rear of the crawler. "Never a huge Gregory fan anyway."

My father laughed. "We'll talk some more about your role in this soon. But first, Gregory needs to be dealt with, Sinclair needs—"

A team of medics came running through the palace doors.

My father nodded at me. "I see you already took care of that."

"I also sent for security and the constable."

Right on cue, security arrived next. My mother was behind them with Sarha, her lady's maid. "Jayne, are you all right, honey? Where's Sinclair? What happened?"

She tackle-hugged me as she joined the group, and I could tell she'd been crying. "We're all okay, Mom. Sinclair's a little cold but going to be fine."

She pulled out of the embrace to look around. "Where is he? I want to see him."

Sin stuck a hand through the open crawler door. "Back here, Lady Frost."

She went straight to him, feeling his forehead. "You poor thing. What happened? Are you warm enough? Jayne said you were cold." Before he could answer either question, she stood up and directed her next words to the medics. "Why has no one given this man a blanket? Get this man inside immediately. He needs warm blankets, fluids and rest. Sahra, go tell the cooks to get some soup going."

"Yes, m'lady." With a curtsey, Sahra disappeared back into the house.

My father's mouth thinned in the way it does

when he's trying not to laugh, and in a soft voice, he said, "Well, Nurse Klara's on the job."

My mother whipped around to look at him. "I heard that, Jack. Stop standing around and do something. Help Jayne inside. Is Ezreal all right?"

"Yes, honey. He's fine. We're waiting on the constable." My father widened his eyes at me as they lit with amusement. "You heard your mother." Then he looked at Ezreal. "You are fine, aren't you?"

"I am." Ezreal had a bit of a smirk going too. "Thank you for asking."

I shook my head. My mother had a tendency to go overboard in crisis situations. "Mom, we have to talk to the constable. Then we'll come in."

She seemed to consider that for a moment. "All right."

Apparently, that was deemed a worthy task.

"Thanks," my dad whispered.

"You're welcome."

Ezreal was watching the medics. "Princess, I can speak to the constable with your father if you like. Then you can go with Mr. Crowe now. I think they're getting ready to take him inside."

I looked toward the crawler. The medics were helping Sin onto a wheeled stretcher. "That's a good idea. Mostly to make sure Mom doesn't send him to the urgent care ward at NP General. Thank you, Ezreal. Let the constable know I can speak with her in the morning. And make sure Gregory gets medical care for that hand."

"I will, Princess."

My father kissed my head again. "So glad you're both safe."

"Me too." I smiled up at him. "We'll talk about Gregory in the morning, okay?"

"Yes."

I smiled at Ezreal, then impulsively hugged him. "Thanks again."

"My honor, Princess."

"See you both in the morning." I jogged toward Sin. The medics were pushing the stretcher into the palace now.

As I joined them, my mom put her arm around me. "What happened? Just the short version is fine. I know you probably don't want to rehash the whole thing tonight."

"Gregory didn't want a non-winter elf on the throne, so when his plan to discredit Sin and break us up didn't work, he kidnapped Sin and decided to remove him from the equation altogether."

She looked stricken. "Gregory? I can't believe it."

"I know. Me either."

"A betrayal like that cuts deep." She put her hand to her throat. "I'm sick to think he's been living in this house all these years and harboring such feelings."

"Well, it's over now."

"Yes. Good." A questioning look crossed her face. "Do you mean he's…dead?"

"No, just captured. He was in the crawler's cargo hold."

"Oh. I didn't even look." She exhaled. "I wouldn't have been unhappy if you'd have said yes."

"Mom."

"I'm not a very forgiving woman when it comes to harm against my family." She shook herself. "Sinclair will be fine, I'm sure."

"I'm sure too." I nudged her. "He left quite a mark on Gregory."

My mother's brows lifted slightly. "Did he?"

I nodded. "The former steward is never going to be the same."

"Nor should he be." Then she smiled and stared ahead at the stretcher. "That's my boy."

The night went by in a blur. We were all exhausted, but wound up, so the doctor gave both Sin and me something to help us sleep.

I awoke with the sensation of not knowing where I was or what had happened. That only lasted for a second, then it all came flooding back.

I put my hand over my eyes as a sudden weight compressed my chest.

"Mama, wake up."

I moved my hand enough to see out one eye. "Hi, baby."

He pawed my face. "Mama sick?"

"No, not sick. Just..." How did I explain what had happened last night to my cat? And did anyone else ever have to work out a problem like that? "Tired. Last night was very busy."

"Mama okay?"

"Yes."

"Sinclair okay?"

He must have heard all the noise across the hall. Maybe caught a few snippets of conversation. We'd kept him and Sugar here overnight so Sin could sleep undisturbed. "Yep, he's fine too."

A lighter presence joined us. Sugar settled in at the foot of the bed, daintily licking one paw.

"Morning, Sugar."

She put the paw down. "Lady, food."

"Ah yes, the ever-empty cat stomach." I pushed the covers and Spider back and climbed out of bed.

They followed me to the kitchen, waiting almost patiently as I got their breakfast ready.

Then I stumbled into a hot shower that went on for a blissfully long amount of time. When I was done, I put on some yoga pants, a big sweatshirt, and some fuzzy socks. I also brushed my teeth in the name of common decency.

I was going to see my soon to be fiancé, after all.

I opened my door to find a security guard at Sin's door. I stiffened. Had something else happened? "Is there a problem?"

"No, Your Highness. The king wanted watch kept at your doors."

"Oh. That was nice of him. Good morning."

"Good morning, Princess Jayne."

I padded across the hall and into Sin's apartment, using the key I'd taken with me last night. I made a note to make sure the guard outside got coffee, then went to see Sin.

I didn't have to go far. He was in the kitchen, getting himself some of that very same beverage. "Hey. How are you feeling? I can't believe you're up and moving around."

He smiled at me. "Can't keep a good man down."

"That's for sure. But really, how are you feeling?"

"A little beaten up. And oddly, still chilled. But otherwise, great. Especially now that you're here."

"Maybe I can help warm you up." I smiled back and went straight into his arms. "I was so worried about you. I'm so sorry about everything that happened."

He put his coffee down. "I'm not."

I pulled back. "You're not? You want to explain that?"

He shrugged. "Wouldn't you rather have this issue with Gregory come to light now rather than have to deal with it when we're living here?"

There was a lot to unpack in that question. I started with the easy part first. "Yes, but you didn't think he should be banished, so he'd still be here."

"Right, but like I said, he's much easier to keep an eye on here than he is who knows where in the human world."

"I can see your point on that. But let's back up. You want to live here? After everything that's happened?"

He took my face in his hands and pressed his mouth to mine for one too-short moment. "Yes, I do. All of this has shown me what a great place this is. How willing people are to help. How kindhearted and good-natured and wonderful. I'm not going to let one person ruin the rest of my life. Our life."

"But Gregory would have killed you."

"But he didn't. And really, it's a lot harder to kill a necromancer than most people realize."

"Don't joke."

"I'm not. I'm really hard to kill."

A little lump was forming in my throat. "You truly want to live here? Knowing everything you know about this life?"

"I do. It's crazy, but I'll get used to it, and the people more than make up for all the pomp and protocol."

I was not going to cry, I was not going to cry, I was not going to cry. "I was ready to abdicate."

He smiled. "I know. And you know I don't want that. You have earned your place as queen."

"I love you."

"I love you too."

I took a breath. I was dizzy with emotions. Joy, love, relief, happiness, pleasure, bliss, contentment. You name it, I was overflowing with the good ones. "Yes."

He stared at me a second. "Yes what?"

"Yes, I will marry you."

A stunned expression kept his face from moving for the briefest of moments, then a huge smile curved his mouth. He picked me up and kissed me, twirling me around in the kitchen.

I laughed, breaking the kiss. "You're making me dizzy."

He put me down. "Good. I want to make you dizzy for the rest of your life."

"If anyone can, it's you."

His expression turned serious. "You realize this means you can actually put that ring on."

"I will. Just as soon as we get home."

"Why not now?"

I looked at him. "Did you bring it?"

He nodded.

I laughed, giddy with life. "Pretty sure of yourself, weren't you?"

He winked at me. "One of us had to be."

"Yeah, yeah." I stuck my hand out. "I am ready to be the future Mrs. Crowe. Except that due to royal regulations, I'll still be a Frost. But you know what I mean."

"I do know what you mean. And..." He went into the bedroom and came back with the ring box. "I'm ready for that too." He slipped the ring on my finger, and I sucked in a breath.

I'd forgotten just how beautiful the ring was. The sapphires on either side of the center diamond were the most striking shade of blue. And the whole thing sparkled like fresh snow in the morning sun. I stared at it, even though I'd probably be staring at it a lot in the next few days.

"We should probably tell your parents it's official."

I nodded. "We should. You want to go to breakfast?"

"That would be great. I'll get dressed."

"Me too. My mother won't love yoga pants in the dining room."

"Really? Even after what we went through last night?"

I shrugged. "Hey, you're the one who wanted to live here."

"True. You know what else I want?"

I leaned against him, flattening my hands on his chest so I could still see him *and* the ring. "What's that?"

"To move here right away. I want to start our life here as soon as we can. I want to learn everything about the North Pole. All about the people and the jobs they do and the history of this place. All of it. And I want to become a citizen. I mean, properly. Can I do that?"

"You can. That would really make you popular. I mean, the people would love that."

"Good."

"But what about your shop?"

His eyes crinkled as he smiled. "I'll sell it. Besides, the North Pole needs doughnuts just as much as Nocturne Falls does."

Epilogue

Pretty much as suspected, my mother cried when she heard our news.

Actually, over the next several days, she cried a lot. When we first told her our engagement was official. When she saw the ring on my hand. When she saw us randomly together throughout the day. When the *Post* printed the royal notice and our official engagement portrait. When my father made a toast at dinner.

You get the idea. She was happy. So was I. We all were.

Archie asked for early retirement and the ability to have first crack at meeting Sin's asking price for the shop. Sin didn't even make it public, just worked out the details with Archie, who was clearly cut out to be the next in line for the doughnut throne.

My father and I, along with my uncle, had a long talk about Gregory. We ultimately decided that Sin's idea was a good one. Gregory would remain in the North Pole where he could be kept on permanent house arrest under a watchful eye. But even with one hand, Gregory could still be dangerous, so my father ruled the former steward's powers be stripped through the same intense saltwater treatment program that had been used on Lark.

Additionally, the constable's budget was increased to allow for a few more deputies to be put on permanent Gregory duty. None of us were taking any chances.

Dora, Stanley, and Terrance were all proclaimed winners of the tourney and their toys put into production. Stanley asked if he could substitute his translation pet collar, when the prototype was ready. My uncle allowed it.

Mamie and August started going steady, a move that surprised everyone but Sin and me.

Juniper and Buttercup were made comanagers of the toy store and charged with hiring another employee to take up the slack my absence would create.

Sinclair was granted a royal dispensation, allowing him to host a series of classes on the art of the doughnut. The classes filled so quickly, several more were added.

And Ezreal was promoted to steward. For his bravery and selflessness, he was also awarded the

North Star, the most prestigious honor in the kingdom. The ceremony was small and formal and lovely.

When my father pinned the star on Ezreal, my mother cried then too.

Spider and Sugar had a dish of Chicken Party.

Some things never changed.

Want to be up to date on new books, audiobooks & other fun stuff from Kristen Painter? Sign-up for my newsletter on my website at www.kristenpainter.com. No spam, just news (sales, freebies, releases, you know, all that jazz).

If you loved the book and want to help the series grow, tell a friend about the book and take time to leave a review!

Other Books by Kristen Painter

COZY MYSTERY

Jayne Frost series

Miss Frost Solves a Cold Case: A Nocturne Falls Mystery

Miss Frost Ices the Imp: A Nocturne Falls Mystery

Miss Frost Saves the Sandman: A Nocturne Falls Mystery

Miss Frost Cracks a Caper: A Nocturne Falls Mystery

When Birdie Babysat Spider: A Jayne Frost Short

Miss Frost Braves the Blizzard: A Nocturne Falls Mystery

Miss Frost Chills the Cheater: A Nocturne Falls Mystery

Happily Everlasting series
Witchful Thinking

PARANORMAL ROMANCE

Nocturne Falls series

The Vampire's Mail Order Bride

The Werewolf Meets His Match

The Gargoyle Gets His Girl

The Professor Woos The Witch

The Witch's Halloween Hero – short story

The Werewolf's Christmas Wish – short story

The Vampire's Fake Fiancée

The Vampire's Valentine Surprise – short story

The Shifter Romances the Writer

The Vampire's True Love Trials – short story

The Vampire's Accidental Wife

The Reaper Rescues the Genie

The Detective Wins the Witch

Sin City Collectors series

Queen of Hearts

Dead Man's Hand

Double or Nothing

STAND-ALONE PARANORMAL ROMANCE

Dark Kiss of the Reaper

Heart of Fire

Recipe for Magic

Miss Bramble and the Leviathan

URBAN FANTASY

The House of Comarré series:

Forbidden Blood

Blood Rights

Flesh and Blood

Bad Blood

Out For Blood

Last Blood

Crescent City series:

House of the Rising Sun

City of Eternal Night

Garden of Dreams and Desires

Nothing is completed without an amazing team.

Many thanks to:

Cover design: Keri Knutson
Interior formatting: Author E.M.S.
Editor: Joyce Lamb
Copyedits/proofs: Lisa Bateman/Marlene Engel

About the Author

USA Today Best Selling Author **Kristen Painter** is a little obsessed with cats, books, chocolate, and shoes. It's a healthy mix. She loves to entertain her readers with interesting twists and unforgettable characters. She currently writes the best-selling paranormal romance series, Nocturne Falls, and the spin off mystery series, Jayne Frost. The former college English teacher can often be found all over social media where she loves to interact with readers.

www.kristenpainter.com

Made in the USA
Coppell, TX
25 August 2020

34498498R00203